Findol

Adventures
In The
Big Blue

David G. Satchell

Ghostly
Publishing

First published in Great Britain in 2012

Ghostly Publishing, 34 Bakers Close, Plymouth, PL7 2GH

The moral right of the author has been asserted

Published in Great Britain by Ghostly Publishing –

Visit www.ghostlypublishing.co.uk for more information

Connect with the author at
www.ghostlypublishing.co.uk/davidgsatchell/

Text Copyright © 2012 David G. Satchell
Cover Art Copyright © 2012 Neil Trigger
All rights reserved.
ISBN-10: 0-9572434-5-6
ISBN-13: 978-0-9572434-5-3

To Debbie and the Boys

To all my family for their continued love and support, especially Cora and Despina (you know who you are!)

A huge thank you to Ghostly Publishing and Neil Trigger who helped steer me onto the right path and gave me this wonderful opportunity.

Prologue — Into the Blue

'CREAAW! CREAAW!'

Beaks shrieked, loud and raucous. The stench of Guano Rock was still thick at the back of their throats. Their yellow heads, stained and soiled, desperately scanned through the sky, driven by hunger. The leader, Tegan, flew high above, while the other four gannets squabbled amongst themselves over a morsel of fish that one of them had found. They stole it in turn from each other. Finally one of them gorged himself on the piece, throwing his head back and swallowing it whole with a triumphant smirk. The other two kept on bickering and mobbing him until their antics were suddenly stopped by the appearance of a large, black, glistening fin cutting the surface between the waves, far below.

Their attention was taken by the sight of the massive, black and white bulk emerging from the water. A misty trail of water droplets peppered the air as a large mouth opened, displaying a dazzling set of razor-sharp teeth. They glinted menacingly in the light, as an intense squeaking eerily escaped from deep within the creature, claiming their attention.

Cora, the mighty killer-whale, took a large gulp of air and dived once more. Her tail thrashed with all its might, smacking the surface with a loud *thwack!* A trail of bubbles raced to the surface behind her as she slid back into the darkness below.

'What's she doing out 'ere?' snapped Grissel.

The bird continued to search for fish, but it was useless. There seemed to be an uncanny number of pods of dolphins and whales congregating in the seas below, seemingly monopolising any existing fish. The gannet colony was depending on the hopeful news of new feeding grounds and would not be happy on their return with little news for desperate appetites.

The breeze was becoming stronger. It buffeted the swooping birds, testing their aerial skills, as hungry bellies creaked at having to wait a little longer to be filled. They were becoming agitated as the wind-speed continued to grow with each passing minute. It made flying even more demanding. Below, the sea's surface was churning and it was getting harder to see beyond the froth.

The sky, too, was becoming darker. Even the most stupid of the group was starting to recognise that this was unnatural for midday.

'Tegan, what was you saying about this being the day for the ultimate catch? It's gerrin' darker than a festering guillemot's gizzard,' croaked Nostrul.

'Guillemot's gizzard! Guillemot's gizzard!' squawked the twins, Bile and Flem, in unison. They could take the definition of irritating to a whole new level.

Tegan swooped around the birds with his feathers distinctly ruffled. The bad weather was becoming a major concern. Choosing comfort over hunger, Tegan reluctantly decided it was best to abandon the hunt and return to Guano Rock. They would just have to face the wrath of a colony desperate for news of food.

'First time out as our leader, and what has 'e got to show fer it?' snorted Nostrul.

Tegan was about to reply, but at that unfortunate moment he inhaled a large mosquito called Kevin. Tegan entered into a violent bout of coughing and retching whilst doing his very best to try and maintain a carefree, nonchalant manner and fly at the same time. It wasn't easy. The others mistook his actions for cowardice, jeering and heckling as he fought for breath, his wings intermittently snapping at his throat. Finally he coughed, sending a spittle-covered Kevin flying from his gullet.

'You know what's worse than a gannet who doesn't realise that he's stupid and ignorant?' Tegan croaked, as he watched Kevin bounce off Bile's beak only to land *splat* upon Nostrul's rump.

The three of them looked at each other blankly; their minds chewing over Tegan's words. At this point Kevin unruffled his damp, sticky wings and flew off muttering to himself.

'Wot?'

'Exactly my point,' Tegan smirked.

Bile looked at Tegan and locked onto him with a menacing squint, but plainly had no idea what Tegan was on about.

Inwardly, Tegan breathed a sigh of relief. He couldn't let them get the upper wing and present the excuse they needed to challenge his leadership; that was shaky enough already. He was coming up to twenty years of age and getting too old for all that fighting stuff. His joints were stiff and feathers tattered. His aerial manoeuvring was still awry from an encounter with an angry Albatross. At least, it would be until the missing tail feathers had grown back, and it had done nothing to improve his opinion of albatrosses.

'Stupid birds! Like bloomin' ostriches divin' in puddles,' Tegan muttered to himself.

More importantly he was just tired of it all.

Far above him a curious thing was happening. The sun was actually disappearing behind the moon, which was rudely pushing its way over the golden disc. An eclipse was something the birds had never encountered or could even comprehend. Its progress continued to stir panic and promote utter confusion. The sea's choppy surface had darkened to a deep inky blue with white spray blooming in large florets wherever a wave broke, before disappearing just as quickly. An eerie cloak of darkness was quickly being drawn over the world. It was only midday and yet the Big Blue appeared to be going back to sleep.

An old blue whale lazing on the surface some distance away, awoke, slowly turned a lazy eye upward and thought,

My oh my (humphh!), the days really are getting shorter!

He rolled over and dived down, retiring beneath the waves to discuss the matter with his partner, Eenid. It seemed to be an issue worthy of much discussion.

Seemingly from nowhere a group of dolphins suddenly broke the surface, intent on catching the leader, who was dragging a long trailing ribbon of kelp beside him. There were five or six chasers, but it was hard to tell actual numbers, such was the speed of their jumping and weaving in and out of the water. The kelp strand writhed like a hyperactive sea-snake as it glanced on the surface. They each tried to nip it, but the leader was way too quick. He dived suddenly causing the kelp to tear, leaving a strip to remain floating on the surface. He was quickly followed by the others, racing to rejoin the party that was now taking place far below.

Cora, the giant killer whale, was now sheltering the pregnant dolphin, Despina, from the boisterous play going on all around them. There were adults and offspring everywhere, representing pods from right across the world's oceans, as well as those that had travelled far from their natural habitats. All of them had ventured at great inconvenience to themselves.

There was Bella Laball the Beluga and Manny Tymes the Manatee; both elderly Cetaceans who had laboured over great distances to bear witness to the forthcoming event. To many present they were merely onlooking strangers, but in fact they were invaluable stores of Cetacean history and were engaged in loud animated conversations with each other and forgotten friends of old. They discussed slowly, rambling on at great length as only old minds can. Meanwhile the youngsters just couldn't keep still and chased each other around and between their elders, causing much noise and distraction.

'For goodness sake!' Cora shouted. 'Will you please do something useful and offer the beads around!'

The wattling beads were the oceans hidden secret; tiny bubble-like growths on the underside of kelp; oxygen rich and, when popped regularly, allowed indefinite time to be spent below the surface. Cora glared at the youths and gestured them away to the kelp, but it was already too late. A Shellting Flagon of Vintage Clampayne was knocked clean out of the fins of Albie-Nopaler, another Manatee who had also travelled some distance to get there. He was not in the least amused. Thankfully it didn't break.

'Oi, you lot! Just calm down or I will get Norris to sort you out!'

Since Norris was a narwhal with a particularly short temper and spectacularly long, sharp tusk, the youngsters seemed to get the 'point'. Especially as he made a show of rubbing the tusk's pointy end on a rock to sharpen it. A wicked glint flashed in his eyes as he watched them, but it was betrayed by the hint of a snigger that sneaked from his mouth when he spotted a youngster crying.

Cora quietly cursed and tutted at the misbehaving youngsters, who merely flashed cheeky grins back, before returning her attention to Despina.

'My dear Despina, I really do wonder if you have any idea of the true importance of this occasion,' she gushed excitedly. 'I had always hoped for and dreamed that I should live to witness this moment, but was never sure when or where, but now ... Well just look! The *Darkening* at this very time can mean only one thing — our Cetacean history and the seers of old were truly correct when they decreed that this event would happen "at some time" and it is happening now, right NOW ... Can you believe it, my child? You really are part of the future hope for us all; mother to the saviour for all things in our world; a challenger to match the might of Grampus and all who dare to follow him. Our greatest desire for the future can now be within our reach. Now our pr ... '

But the dolphin interrupted.

'Dear Cora, please! Please! You frighten me with these words. For goodness sake!' Despina sighed with exhaustion. 'You know I have always listened to your wisdom, to your advice, and I have the very greatest respect for all that you stand for. But you and the historical tomes that you quote from are putting so much pressure on me! Can you really be so sure and rest so much hope on what could be ... just a ... mere coincidence, maybe?'

'A MERE COINCIDENCE!' Cora boomed as she surged unexpectedly forward, swelling menacingly, and sending Despina shrinking back with fear. 'Do you hear your words, young one?' she said, moving right up close to the anxious dolphin. 'Trust me in this, Despina — your time is almost here. I feel it. Do not be scared. Do not doubt, and trust in me that this is *not* a mere coincidence.

There is nothing here that is a product of chance, I guarantee it!'

The large dolphin, dwarfed by the massive bulk of Cora, rose to the surface. She was concerned that she had almost overstepped the mark by interrupting and questioning the majesty of Cora's extensive knowledge. She passed excited onlookers, youngsters among them, all watching and listening to all that was being said between Cora and Despina. They hung on every word. As they popped wattling beads, the young pups giggled and pointed fins at Despina, exchanging amusing nonsense between them. Cora turned her attention to the expectant faces and scolded:

'NOW, give our sister some privacy and some space please! Remember this is *not* some theatrical show for your cheap amusement. You are here as witnesses to a special moment in our history!'

There were some polite cheers and fin-clapping from the nodding faces before she continued. 'This is a matter for just the two of us and the little heir right now. There will be plenty of time for celebration later. Now, come on … move back, please. You will all get your chance to share!'

An heir? How can she be so sure? Despina thought.

As the last of the sun's light drained away, the large, dark face of the moon became ringed with sparkling beads of light followed by a glowing, ragged rim of fire. At that moment, Despina felt movement within her and she was compelled into giving one strong push.

'My darling little one,' she gasped as the tiny, glistening bundle emerged. Slowly it twisted and turned in its white sheath. It seemed to glow luminous in the darkness that had descended.

Cora's eyes burned, wide with excitement, as she animatedly circled around Despina.

'Look! LOOK! See? See? Yes! There is now no doubt … the CAUL! Just as predicted, the caul he has been born with!' she said. She then proceeded to chatter on excitedly as only she could in the strange language of old Lantica. She performed a triumphant pirouette beside Despina that impressed everyone nearby.

Cora was doing what she did best and that was being the wise old sage, playing to her audience. All eyes were upon her. Her voice echoed loudly around the sea so all could hear:

'He will be born when day is night
Enveloped in a skin so bright.
His path so long, a life course set.
No fear within for the Man Fisher's net.
Grampus will shake and fall at his name
The order of life will be the child's aim … '

'… and so it is said from the Tome of Pax … '

She took a large, deep breath, whilst around her there was a sense that this was going to be a rather long and boring speech.

Despina broke the silence for she was tired and fearful of Cora's expectations. 'Oh Cora! Please. No more. Not now. I … I cannot take this all in. It's really all too much!' She was, after all, exhausted and very anxious to attend to her little one. 'I have never heard these words spoken before. Who could write such a thing about my child? How would they know?'

'Well, actually, young Despina, for your information, my Great, Great Grandmother, Paxodidimus in her book *Thoughts and Premonitions in an Ocean of Pain.*'

Despina gasped. She wasn't quite sure what to expect and was even less sure as to whether she should laugh or cry. 'Oh! I see. It just sounds so … well …' She sighed heavily. '… severe. Tell me — is it really as grim as it sounds?'

Cora — now sidetracked — was on a roll, her mind gushing forth as she excitedly prattled on.

'I am afraid, yes, young one. She used to have many of these wondrous premonitions and thoughts that were scribed into her special book, usually when she was depressed, or just looking within herself, but the strange and wondrous thing is that most of them came true, especially those prompted by mystical events! For example, do you remember the story of the Worm-infested Sea Troll of Crokus? It was banished by Ichabod the Unsure after running riot in Lantica Deep and destroying most of the wattling harvest. And that was after three seasons' careful nurturing in the Caves of Negyxo.'

'Erm. Yes, I think so.' gasped Despina in awe. 'But that was such a long time ago, wasn't it? I mean, I never thought … well, to be honest … I never thought that it was even true. So it really *was* actually her then? That foretold it coming, I mean?'

Cora paused and whispered quietly. 'Well, yes and no. Maybe *that* was a bad example. You see, she did actually miss that one … but on the whole, yes, she mapped out twenty-three generations of plagues, disasters and spooky coincidences.'

Despina began firing off boring historical facts, long buried in her memory from Podling school.

'Okay, what about the Wars of the Proses with the Poetry-wielding Mincing Monkfish of Rime, or the Flatulent Flounder of Flanders?'

'Well, err … sadly, no. No, my child … but trust me, she did see THIS day coming!' Cora was getting agitated and more than a little flustered, but she took a moment to compose herself.

Despina, however, was beginning to wonder just how accurate this famed book was. 'By the way, Cora — how did she actually write it, because I don't suppose Flaytus was around then?'

(Flaytus Gurning was a large hermit crab who currently enjoyed the honourable position of the person to whom anyone with a story worthy of documenting went).

'No, child. She had the best that was available at the time; a "ghost-crab writer" named Caractacus Shellting, I think it was. Well, anyway it's scribed somewhere on the spine. It was produced long before Kriblington City came into being, so was achieved without their touch of quality. Sadly though, it has not weathered well. The salt plays havoc with the scribing despite the very best of Lantic enchantments. The words are more illegible than indelible now. Still … that's all in the past, isn't it? I must show you the book some time, though. It is important that you see it and believe for yourself!'

'Yes, certainly. I would love to,' Despina politely lied.

Around them, the crowds had grouped into little family pods and cliques. Everyone had by now become slightly bored with the anti-climax and the gloomy history lessons. Meanwhile the newborn pup had snuggled up tightly, patiently waiting beside his mum. He let out a sudden gentle sneeze, spraying a cloud of microbubbles into her face.

'Bless! Oh my goodness, I have got completely sidetracked. Where were we, Cora …? Oh juggling cuttlefish! I cannot believe it. You have completely taken over my thoughts; for all this time I have ignored my beloved Fin … '

'FINDOL, I believe,' Cora interrupted. 'Relax, Despina. He is perfectly fine!'

'How did you possibly know that I would call him … his name? It was my secret. How?'

'Later, child, later — see first to your son. He has, after all, a very special mother to meet!' Cora barely whispered this as she gracefully retreated, wriggling backwards into a gap in a large group of rowdy porpoises that reluctantly opened up to accommodate her rather large bulk. She watched, proud and beaming as mother and pup were finally allowed the time and space to share in each other. She smiled, looking around approvingly at all the onlookers, and chose that moment to slip away from the proceedings, leaving Despina to coo over her newborn.

'Oh my beloved darling Findol! My precious little one, I have so much to tell you, to show you! Your father would have been so very proud of you, if only he could have been here. It was his greatest wish to see his own pup born to us, to touch you, to snuggle you …' Despina fought with her emotions, her tears blending with the ocean around her.

Findol's perfect face looked at her and blinked. He opened his tiny, beautiful mouth and blew a thin trickle of bubbles that ran under his mother's nose, tickling as they chased each other away to the surface. His eyes sparkled. They actually *sparkled* with an inner fire; something deep, burning bright as if with a generation of impishness. She watched, amazed, as he took to the water, already swimming, rubbing his smooth little body against his mother's side. He nibbled at her fins, chased around her, twisted and span in circles as if he had already spent hours, weeks, months mastering the skills of his aquabatics.

Despina could only stare and gasp with a mother's pride and joy at her wonderful little Findol revelling in himself and his new world. She smiled, as only a mother can, as she watched her little creation and felt a glow of pride course through her body. It warmed her heart and rekindled feelings of Findol's missing father, Kai-Galant.

Time itself felt like it had paused, yet what appeared to have been an age in passing, had in fact been minutes and now the blanket of darkness was already scurrying away as fast as it had arrived. Rays of light from the emerging sun began bleeding out over the moon's rim. Beneath the sea's surface, the wondrous display was gradually revealed as the beams penetrated the depths and illuminated the squinting, blinking gathering as they readjusted to the light.

For the first time, Despina suddenly became aware of size of the congregation as hundreds of pairs of eyes twinkled back at her and dark shadows gave way to form in the returning light. All of them would have been watching her every action and listening her each and every word. She thought to herself that they would surely remember all that had happened for all time, probably passing the story down right through the generations.

It was only then that reality arrived like a lightning bolt out of the sky and suddenly she realised that if Cora's wisdom was truly right (which was pretty often after all — except for maybe the book) then she was going to have her work really cut out with her dear little Findol, both now and certainly in the future; for it had been obvious from that very moment he was born (and now in her eyes it was confirmed) that here was somebody very special. He seemed so mature for a newborn pup; his eyes seemed alive with a fully-charged and burning life force, as of an adult harbouring a lifetime of mischief, of adventure, of learning — even of learning the hard way! Already he seemed to have mastered the rudiments of complex swimming. She watched as he swam to the surface, gasped some air, flipped over and dived again, before weaving a spiral path around her, finally returning tight up to her side.

He nuzzled up close to her face and smiled a beautiful smile, eyes sparkling. Slowly, he opened his mouth and spoke his very first words: 'Mum, please can I stay for the party ... *please?*'

Despina gulped with speechless surprise. Somewhere, far away in the distance, Cora paused briefly as if listening, a knowing smile on her wise face, before continuing on her way. Presently, she surfaced and inhaled a large breath of fresh, crisp air. Above her, a group of four white birds bickered noisily as they headed for a rocky island far away on the horizon.

Chapter 1
A Special Birthday

Findol was slowly waking up. His weary eyes struggled to open. It felt like he had been dreaming all night long. His dream had started with the very day, four years ago, when he had been born. It felt rather weird, because neither his friends or brothers and sisters could remember anywhere near that far back. Yet to him it felt like only yesterday; that very moment when he had first looked into his mother's eyes. Images had swirled around in his head in no particular order as his dream skipped through key moments in the last four years.

He recalled long, warm days spent playing and exploring, finding special treasures on the sea bed with his friend, Sterbol. Each day he would travel a little further from his home. He remembered his rare meetings with Cora when she would take the opportunity to explain about key moments in Cetacean history and the very fall of Lantica itself. She would talk to him like he was an adult, which was a bit uncomfortable given the serious context of what she said. Much was made about his own importance, his need to prepare physically and mentally and the threats that lay ahead for him. It is fair to say they were not the most lightweight and fun chats a youngster could have had.

Findol soon developed a certain numbness and denial of all that Cora told him. After all, he just wanted to have fun and he made sure he achieved that — big time! He invented the game "Finball" with his friends, and played it to death so that eventually he was less inclined to participate whenever a game struck up, being more concerned with exploring.

Only a few years back, whilst he was out on one of his adventures, he had saved his sister, Lotus, from a boat's fishing net. Foolishly ignoring the huge thing dragging beneath the vessel, she blindly chased a little fish straight into it. The fish was not for food; she was just fascinated with its colour and it had looked "soooo cute and cuddly", he had recalled her saying.

Findol had been in the right place at the right time. He had immediately called Talos — a sawfish friend of his who was nearby — with his powerful whistle that seemed so much stronger than his Podling -school friends' (much to their annoyance). Talos wasted no time in freeing Lotus as well as an awful lot of frightened, gasping, claustrophobic fish, who all thanked him excitedly. One was heard to exclaim, 'I thought it was all over, Wilf. I felt I was one fish that had "had his chips". I saw the light getting ever nearer, like it was calling me!' — although it was just the light on the underside of the ship he had seen.

It was only weeks after that incident that Findol had helped a diver trapped on the sea bed with his foot caught between two rocks. It had been easy enough to rattle one rock loose with his echo, dislodging the weary man, and then slowly raised him to the surface.

Yes, Findol had certainly had an action packed four years and today felt like it was the turning point. This was when many his age could leave home in search of their own partners and form new pods. That fact made him feel strangely different and suddenly very grown up. In a way he felt a little frustrated. Having to leave his childhood behind and own up to responsibility was not an opportunity he relished. After all, where was the fun in that? He knew his future path was going to be something of a challenge, for he had certainly been told enough times, to the point of it becoming tedious. Anyway, he was happy where he was right now, as official alpha male in the family pod in the absence of his father. Like a badge of attainment, it made him feel good inside.

He finally opened his eyes, blinked a couple of times and was ready for the new day; his special day. He was lying on his sleeping shelf close to his stash of wattling beads. Each member of the family pod had identical sleeping areas, high up around the perimeter of the huge Podling room. The room was a large, beautifully smooth, white-walled cave, carefully hewn from the rock over many years and now a legacy of the workers of Old Lantis from long ago. He popped a bead, felt it fizz, then twisted and flipped around to work out the stiffness in his muscles. To please his mum, he nuzzled the kelp mat back into place. She liked all of them to keep the place clean and tidy!

'Cleanliness is next to codliness whereas untidiness is haddock-forming!' It was something she would often mutter, not that Findol knew quite what it meant!

Are Haddock particularly untidy? he thought. He'd seen a shoal only the other day on their way somewhere, twisting and shimmering in perfect synchronicity like a single living entity, looking rather smart and well organised.

Now that he was awake, he was ready for anything and everything, especially today — his birthday!

Me, a young adult! Finally leaving behind Podling status and being treated seriously, he thought to himself, proudly.

Birthdays are great … PRESENTS! And lots of attention!

But then he did have to remind himself that most days of his life had been like that anyway. Ever since his birth he had always seemed to be the centre of attention with much fin-pointing and gossip wherever he chose to go and he had started to feel a little tired of it. There were often times when he wanted everyone to just forget about Cora's silly prophecies and plans for his future, and let him just be the young dolphin that he was. It hadn't stopped him having fun and doing what he wanted, but it was always there at the back of his mind, niggling and gnawing away. Increasingly, his thoughts were drawn to his future and exactly what was to be expected of him

He was reminded of something strange that had happened when he had last seen Cora. He had told her about his previous night, when — in a dream — he had felt a strange unseen presence chasing him. It seemed to have been through some sort of darkness. Weed. Lots and lots of large, dark, clinging weed. The pursuer was always so close, yet just out of sight. It meandered this way and that through the thick fibrous columns of kelp. Then, as if by magic, there had suddenly appeared a giant ring of light that was burning like fire in front of him. It wobbled and pulsed, almost beckoning him into it. Cora had stiffened and looked awkward. She appeared both fascinated and concerned as she listened intently before brushing it off.

'Do not speak or worry of such things at this time,' she said 'It is nothing to be concerned with for now.'

Like that's supposed to make me feel better, he had thought, angry that she had deemed it unworthy of explanation. Today, however, the attention was justified and he swam down below to revel in it. He expected breakfast wouldn't be anything too special. Fish always featured heavily on the menu, but it was what his mother could do with it that made all the difference. Findol was just happy he wasn't a vegetarian like Whitloe Spook.

Whitloe was a very strange and curious solitary dolphin who had arrived in Old Lantica about five years earlier at about the same time as Flaytus Gurning, but the difference was that Whitloe had arrived in a state of complete and utter bewilderment. It had all been very strange, so he was told, because Whitloe had insisted she was not a dolphin, but something called a "herbifor" named Daisy, and couldn't remember how, when, or why she was there.

Some unkind individuals had made rather cruel assumptions at the time suggesting an unhealthy association on her part with too many bottles of Clampayne. At the time of her appearance she had needed urgent help, since she seemed totally unaware of the vitally important wattling beads. It was as if she had no idea of how to survive underwater. This was a cause for great concern for all around. After five years keeping mostly to herself she was a rather sad-looking character. She spent most of the day moping around on the seabed looking for sea-grass that she would munch on in a "chewing the cud" sort of way. Her mind seemed a million miles away. Try as they might, they could not persuade her to have a go at eating fish, let alone join a pod.

'I can't eat anything with eyes!' she would drone on slowly … 'I even draws the line at potatoes!'

As if with perfect timing, the thin, pale figure of Whitloe glided up towards the giant cave, on her daily forage for the green stuff.

'Mooooorning, Findol. 'appy birthday!'

As she slunk up to the entrance she caught his eye and looked lazily up at him. He swam over to her.

'Here's a little gift,' she muttered, pushing a small package in Findol's direction with her bony fin. 'Wish

someone would remember my birthday sometimes! Wouldn't hurt occasionally.'

Now this was all very well, but where Whitloe was concerned, choosing an original present was nigh-on impossible. She was so fussy, since it had to be green and edible. Sea-grass was just about the only thing that seemed to fit the bill and it was such a pain to wrap. Besides, nobody knew her age or birthday anyway — not even Whitloe herself.

But she wasn't stopping; already she sulkily snaked across the sea-bed away from him.

'Thanks, Whitloe,' Findol shouted after her, examining the parcel of sea-kelp pastilles. They were produced over in Kriblington City and had been stamped with the official Kribling seal of approval. The seal in question was called Leesa and why she stood for quality was not entirely clear at the time. Findol shouted after the rapidly receding form of Whitloe as she disappeared in the distance,

'Er lovely. Just like last years! Thanks, I … I will save them for a rainy day!'

Whitloe paused, looked back with a puzzled expression, ruminated quickly over the words, then winked back at him as a distant memory stirred in her mind, before she slowly moved on.

Findol's mum looked at him, puzzled. It wouldn't have been the first time that Findol's strange sayings had left friends and family floundering in their own confusion, although Whitloe did seem to understand his strange sayings more than most. It was only Cora that could truly see what was happening, because he had often seemed to spurt out words and sayings that neither he nor those around him understood. She would say it was all tied into his Cetacean history and latent human empathy, which made no sense to any of them.

'Morning, Mum,' Findol cheerfully shouted as he swam back into the Podling room. The room served as the main area of the giant sea cave they inhabited in Lantica Down and bore the kelp-lined walls which looked particularly pleasant this morning. The neat rows of glow-light sea-urchins cast their eerie greenish-yellow light into the scattered shadows around the large sea cave. Down below, taking centre stage on the floor, lay the giant communal dining clam where the pod always met to eat and was the one place where the pod could all come together and socialise over a meal.

Findol positioned himself on one of the pedestals to survey the clam's delights. Above him on the ceiling there was a layer of petrified kelp rafters, each adorned with twinkling shells, glittering brightly as they slowly breathed in and out. Their colour reflected the mood in the cave and today there was a very definite purple hue. It was like having a living, pulsing, tapestry of light and colour that swirled all around in a gently hypnotic fashion. Anyone watching would easily gauge the mood of the room before even entering. Visitors were often taken by surprise as if they had never seen anything quite like it, but then Findol's family had been blessed with possibly the best accommodation in uptown Lantica.

Dominating the centre of the cave on the floor was the giant dining clam's massive shell and pearly white interior. It was currently full of delicious treats of small fish and squid that Findol was eyeing up. Hung around its rim were delicate strings of thin cochineal grass and aquamarine reedlings, bound together in coloured, decorative bunting plaits. There were smaller clams carefully placed around it that were filled with special birthday breakfast treats. Sea-sponge fingers sat in Angelfish Delight and bowls of Jellyfish Jelly sat beside a clam stuffed with Garibaldi fish-biscuits. Findol's mum was just putting the finishing touches to the spread. She playfully tapped Findol's head, as he sneakily pinched a morsel before she was ready.

Right on cue, little pink Scavits emerged from their hideaway beneath the clam and were already spacing themselves strategically around the base of the shell, each jostling for position, salivating at the mere sight and prospect of the delicacies waiting above. Their small mouthparts frantically twitched with expectation. They secured as much room as possible with keratin elbows pushed out to their limits, in order to exaggerate their size and monopolise space. Their sole purpose was to catch and dispose of the food scraps and bits dropped by the over-enthusiastic younger members of the pod as they fed. Each of the ten Scavits was ready for a serious scrimmage over the awaiting treats as soon as the first droppings arrived. As the family above settled down around the clam ready for their meal, the Scavits would be a constant distraction below. They would squeal at each other, pinching and biting, elbowing and kicking for their share of the meal. When there were special occasions giving rise to such rich pickings it was guaranteed to be even noisier. Findol's mum had often threatened to get a vacuum-cleaner wrasse. They were supposed to be a lot less bother and certainly quieter.

'So where is everybody? Pipsqueak! Lotus!' Findol shouted, as best he could with a mouthful of food he shouldn't have been eating.

'Quiet, Findol! They are not here yet! They left early to fetch your Aunt and Uncle Winslow. They will be here soon enough, though. Wippit and Splinter are still asleep so don't wake them! At least not yet, okay? I know you're excited, but try to be patient. And STOP picking, eh?'

'Okaaay,' he reluctantly answered, as loud as he could, trying not to sound too put out. He looked up at their shelves and saw their shapes hidden under the kelp covers with barely a hint of movement, annoyingly suggesting deep sleep. They were still far from waking up yet, the only noise coming from them being the tiny trails of micro-bubbles escaping from their blowholes as they slowly breathed.

Every now and then he could just hear the gentle pop and fizz of a wattling bead someone popped without even stirring. He was so tempted to sneak up there, when his mum was not looking and give each of them a gentle, "accidental" nudge. Or push a bead into their ear.

That will wake them, he thought with a snigger.

'I can see where you are looking and I know what you are thinking, young Findol. So forget it, please?'

He looked over at her and couldn't help a mischievous grin sneaking across his face. 'Come on, Mum, they've had long enough. They're wasting valuable time.'

Despina had to laugh to herself. 'Your "valuable" time, you mean!?'

It was certainly true what Cora had said about her Findol. From the day he was born until now, he had progressed and matured at an incredible rate. His thirst for knowledge was insatiable and his desire to explore and question was never-ending and ultimately exhausting for those around him. It was as if there was never enough time in the day for Findol to complete his personal agenda and fulfil his appetite for experience. As for his energy — well, others could only watch in amazement. It was difficult to pin him down to staying in any one place for long. School-time was always difficult too, because he seemed to find it all so easy, which always irritated the others. Whereas they would ponder and struggle over homework, he would whip through it and be out playing before you knew it. Professor Sturgeon at Lantica Low-School for Dolphins had nothing but praise for him.

Mealtimes were about the only occasions you could guarantee him lying still in one place for longer than twenty minutes. Even then he would be up and off, exploring and often returning hours later to show them some bizarre artefact from one of the many shipwrecks over near Kriblington Down. Some of his friends lived there. He would then store it away in his own cave. There was never any point in telling him what he could and couldn't do.

Findol had always been a typical youngster, good and honest, mischievous with a wicked sense of humour. He was also driven by an inner purpose that meant he just had to explore and push everything to the limit — even if it sometimes clashed with his mother's wishes. It was as if tolerating his impatience went with the "maternal job". For all his self-centred attitude, however, she loved him dearly. She knew how he always cared greatly and looked out for all the others. He loved being part of such a big family pod — his brothers, Wippit and Splinter; and sisters, Pipsqueak and Lotus.

Cora and her books of prophecies have a lot to answer for! she often thought.

She would just smile to herself, thinking back to the words of wisdom spoken to her all those years ago. Cora had warned her that Findol's time lay many years ahead. It was important for him to grow up as normally as possible, both for his own protection and for that of his family and friends.

She laughed, thinking how it was such an impossible task to try and allow him to be treated normally, when he constantly carried the burden and weight of an uncertain future. Now, thinking about it, she realised just how long it had been since she had last seen Cora and heard her calm, reassuring words.

Barely months after Findol's birth, Cora visited late one winter's night. A bitterly cold current was passing through the ocean at that time, chilling everything it touched and she had quickly beckoned Cora inside. Once she had managed to squeeze through the entrance and settled in the Podling room with its warmth, Cora had filled Despina's heart with dread. It seemed that whilst there had been so much rejoicing and happiness during Findol's birth, a sinister event had been taking place elsewhere; far, far away, under the wastes of the Frozen North. It was something which nothing of pure heart, living in the Big Blue wanted to hear. It was the realisation of all nightmares. It appeared that the dreaded Grampus had returned, for he had been spotted! Cetacean history told of the Portals that once existed for transference into human form on land and back again. But these were long gone ancient things of the past.

Cora explained that the facts were not *entirely* true and hidden Portals could still be found if you knew where to look. Sadly, nine months before Findol's birth, his brave father, Kai-Galant, had fearlessly pursued Grampus, the evil grey whale. He followed him into Kelpathia and through the kelp forest to the secret Portal hidden there. Thrashing through the dense kelp, they had come across the Portal, and both passed through and vanished.

Grampus must have known about the Portal, but poor Kai-Galant never got the chance to see his son. The son he had so desperately wanted, but he never even knew that Despina was pregnant. He had sacrificed that precious future without a thought for himself. At the time, Despina was astonished to learn the true nature of Kai-Galant's disappearance. Now, however, a further nightmare had happened. The eclipse that presided over Findol's birth had somehow allowed the passage of Grampus back into the Big Blue. Once again he was free to develop and nurture his malicious evil in some twisted need for power and revenge. The very nature of his cold, black heart would normally have prevented his return through a Portal's enchantments; however the *Darkening* had somehow changed that.

Whatever had happened, the protection from the pure-white magic of old that was bestowed from their mother, Lunassis, of the moon above, had failed in one of the few remaining Portals and Grampus had somehow been ready to move and find his way back through at that very moment. Not even Cora had been certain of the existence or location of remaining Portals, yet Grampus had somehow found this one in the Frozen North. Magnus, the Sentient Lantica Jellyfish — a wise being from the times of old — had sensed the awesome presence of Grampus the moment he had returned through the Portal. He immediately alerted Cora as best he could with all the energy he was able to muster, but at terrible cost to himself. Sadly the exertion had proved too much for him and he had passed peacefully away. He had been unable to identify the exact location of Grampus.

Despina had stared and listened, motionless and wide eyed to hear this news. Cora had needed all her skills in reasoning to reassure Despina that there would be nothing to fear for some time.

'His actual powers are so weak, my dear Despina. Your beloved Kai stripped him of much of that. His followers are scattered far and wide. Only his intent is strong at the moment. He will be long in restoring himself and we will be ready for him when the time comes. For your Findol is, and will be, our greatest hope. His head and heart beats with generations of inherited experience, both in and out of the Big Blue. You know this. He might not really know or feel it yet, but his time will come and when he is ready, he will burn with a brilliance that we can barely imagine!'

'I do hope you are right, Cora! I am so very fearful of these prophecies and for his life! To me, he is still but a pup with his whole life ahead of him. Yet you talk of confrontation with the very beast we all dread!'

'I think it is time you knew more,' Cora said, ushering Despina closer.

It was then that Cora explained about the whole history of the Portals, including the details excluded from Podling School. She told how the Spatial Gateways existed for the passage from a living form in the Big Blue to that of a human on land. There were once thousands scattered around the ocean and on land that allowed the morphing of beings from one medium to another — land to sea and vice-versa.

Whatever the environment, it was the individual's own sub-conscious that drew them to the Portal. An ability Mankind had all-but lost, through time. The Portals had existed for thousands of years from the dawn of creation itself. It was said that Mother Lunassis had decreed all living creatures in the Blue should be able to experience life on land as well, so as to fully understand the elements

29

that drive the spirit in both environments. Equally, Humans could escape the stresses and demands of a harsh, demanding life on land to a wholly different lifestyle in the Big Blue, where there existed an order of peace and spiritual harmony. Each living creature knew and understood its part in the cycle of life. There would be only truth and honesty, kindness and consideration for others — a perfect society, free from the disease of evil, selfishness, cruelty and desire.

These ideals had become sadly corrupted over the years as populations and expectations on land grew. Mankind grew complacent and contented with his lot. A trend started to grow that split opinions. A few wise Humans made conscious decisions to stay permanently within the Big Blue. They had just spent so much time there that memories of land faded and the will to return to the reality of an altogether more demanding life became less attractive. Thoughts became confused, values changed, priorities re-evaluated. They evolved into a group of "Cetacean Lingerons" becoming the "Cerebros" or "Wise-Ones" who eventually formed the ruling council that presided in Old Lantis. They oversaw the safety and care of the ecosystem of the Big Blue, adopting the motto: *'the balance of life cannot be tipped in any one direction — stability rules! Harmony lives on!'*

The power of Old Lantis was great. More than that; it was massive, for all the existing Portals drew their power from the 'Oldlantica Pool'. Mother Lunassis had invested much of herself in them and was pleased with the result.

For many years all was well until an altogether different element managed to sneak through into the finely balanced system that was working so perfectly. Until that moment, life in the Big Blue was serene and beautiful, but then everything changed. An evil presence arrived, that manifested itself as Grampus the Great Grey Whale. His greed and cunning was only matched by his desire for power and his love of chaos. He was responsible for many of the wars and atrocities committed on land and had now turned his attention to seeking new territories and challenges.

Grampus had a cruel and dark agenda. He viewed intelligence as a threat and so his plan was to eradicate the "Cetacean Disease" (as he called it) of the dolphins and porpoises, and sow the seas with his evil brood. He would swell the numbers of whales, sharks and barracuda, Conger and Moray eels, giant stinging octopuses and "Berserker" Barnacled Kamikaze Goliath Crabs. All would bend to his will by persuasive promises and intoxicating dreams that filled their small minds. His hope was to take his newly-formed armies back through the Portals and wreak havoc continuing his reign of terror on the land he originated from.

Grampus's influence quickly spread like a fungus, finding easy prey and willing followers in weak-minded individuals. Here he found a new world where he could extend his black cloak. Many of the sharks and barracuda turned to his favour with ease; Hamrag the giant humpback whale and Kreegan the giant conger eel. The most dangerous and evil became leaders themselves; keen to serve their master and achieve dominion themselves. There were many others, all ready to fight and kill in Grampus's name. Each had a hidden agenda that usually included their own desires for territory and destruction of particular victims, but always with the lure of a controlling interest on land.

The ruling council of Old Lantis became desperate and fought long battles of words with each other, recognising that all that was bad about Mankind had found its way into their once perfect world. In doubt as to how best to tackle the problem quickly, to limit the damage done, and after long and bitter discussion, it ultimately came down to the one possible solution. Each member sadly knew it was the only way. The Portals had to be closed to prevent the further pollution of the Big Blue by the plague of evil, and to allow for the council to regain some control to restore order. The oldest and wisest of the ruling council was called Karn. He reminded the other seven members of their "special commitment" to keep at least one Portal open, since it was essential for the integrity of all the "Other Worlds" that existed and was responsible for the binding of each to one another like a sensory network. It would also be vital for unexpected emergencies of unforeseen events. It was agreed for it to be hidden and so he chose the one residing in the kelp forest of Kelpathia. He decided to enchant it with the "Golden Vortex" that would allow all through, but further prevent those of impure heart and mind from returning through it. The theory being that the Evil would be effectively flushed away.

Karn's wisdom was quickly agreed and acted upon, but the price to pay for closing all the other Portals was high. The cost of removing the power that supported all of them and their ultimate closure was massive and meant that Old Lantis itself would be destroyed in the very process to prevent future attempts to procure its special powers. The greatest folly in the plan turned out to be in thinking that Grampus would not somehow find a way to return back into the Blue.

So it was that, as Findol was born, the stain of Grampus returned to the Blue to seek revenge on the Lantica pods and all who shared their hopes and dreams. The way in which he had returned was still a mystery. Were there truly Portals still hidden out there? Had they really not all been destroyed? It was a tantalising riddle that not even Cora could answer for certain.

'Enchantments and magic are sadly not impervious to error, young Despina,' she had said.

Cora had made it obvious that there was even more to the history, but she stopped herself, saying, 'Enough is enough for now and I'm tired. There will be time in the future for more talk.'

But that had been some years ago and Despina found herself thinking about Cora and Findol more and more as each day passed. She started dwelling on the thought that day by day, Grampus was increasing in strength. For some time now she had harboured a strange feeling in her belly, not unlike the feeling of a sudden change in weather or an impending storm on the horizon.

The hidden threat of Grampus was constantly there and the complete absence of any news concerning his current whereabouts or actions only made it worse. Not knowing just what he was up to made it all the more scary. Yes, the Big Blue was going to blow, she was sure. Somehow she felt this day, her Findol's birthday just might somehow be the start of it!

Meanwhile, Findol had eventually got his way; Wippit and Splinter were soon reluctantly awake. They yawned, and before he knew it, Pipsqueak, Lotus and his Uncle and Aunt Winslow were there. They all squeezed around the dining clam, rejoicing in the delicious treats his mother had prepared and toasting his health with clamberry juice. He smiled politely, but Findol's mind was a million miles away. Within him, a strange sense of urgency was growing that he couldn't explain. He thanked his mother as he hastily finished his breakfast, food dropping in all directions — creating more battles below as the Scavits fought between themselves. He gratefully accepted his presents and showed his appreciation with one of his more amusing, cryptic rhymes. As usual, it left everybody looking quizzical, yet supplying amused and polite smiles as he finished. He apologised for not opening the presents straight away, but promised to look at them later. His argument was that he wanted to devote time to them. Right now, however, he had something very important to do. Despina was going to reprimand him for being a little rude, but sometimes she sensed how he was feeling and something inside her said to let him go.

He didn't know quite what it was, but he had a strange sensation (or was it just a thought) which bothered him. It tugged at his mind and demanded his attention. He could hear a voice within himself. He was sure it was female and strangely hypnotic. The words and music seemed woven together. It was as if the Big Blue was calling him, like a haunting song playing eerily in his head — a soundtrack to his very existence. Eerily, he found himself breathing in time to the haunting sound. Suddenly, Findol was hit by a wave of strange claustrophobia, he just had to get outside. The song pulled and tugged at his heart, now racing, his body aching to be out there and all the time it was calling him … *Come, come, come and play!*

Findol couldn't get out quick enough. He raced forward, through the cave entrance. 'Bye, everyone! See you later! Sorry I've got to rush off, and thanks again for everything!'

The call of the Blue had never been so strong and its power had taken his breath away. Perhaps he had also been thinking: *Yippeee! Time to play!*

Yes, perhaps even that. But today, however, tides were slowly turning and there would be no play involved.

Chapter 2
Kriblington Down

Findol burst out of the cave entrance as fast as he could, with an explosion of bubbles escorting him. Strands of loose kelp danced in his wake. He liked to surprise any unsuspecting individual that passed by, minding his or her own business. Unfortunately, today it was the unlucky shape of Flaytus Gurning that was innocently wandering along on his way home.

The shockwave caused by Findol's explosive emergence sent Flaytus reeling sideways with a yell of surprise. His belongings scattered in all directions as his thin arms desperately fought to contain them. Deep within his shell Flaytus felt a flagon of pickleberry juice break and splash its contents over his rear end. Staggering and swaying with his large shell precariously wavering behind him in the current, Flaytus hurriedly gathered up his belongings from the seabed. Being a somewhat large hermit crab was all very well, but came with its own problems. It meant he had to find a large, empty shell to accommodate himself and his possessions, so it necessitated the use of a Herculean Conch that was big, heavy and not easily manoeuvrable. It also was not particularly attractive to look at since barnacles enjoyed making their homes upon it, but it did have the big advantage of being a nice shade of green.

'Erm, sorry, Mr Gurning,' Findol shouted back, whilst struggling to contain something that was between a snigger and a chuckle.

Despina heard the fuss and poked her head through the cave entrance to look outside. 'FINDOL! Will you PLEASE be more careful next time!' she called after him. And then: 'I'm so sorry, Flaytus.'

'I should be t'inking so too, so you should! Dat son of yours, Mrs Lantica — bejaybers he's nothing but trouble to be sure!'

Flaytus was red-faced and extremely angry. It was a new flagon of juice that had been wasted. A particularly good year of manufacture to boot!

'Now tell me something I don't know, Flaytus,' said Despina, shaking her head. 'It really isn't my fault though, is it? I mean, after all, what with all your research, you must know our history better than most now. In fact, even some of the elders do not know as much, so I guess if anyone should have a good idea of just what he is like, then you should!'

'It was deliberate I'm telling you', Flaytus moaned, as Despina began helping him collect the last few scribing quills together.

'Sadly, you are probably right, Flaytus' Despina sighed. 'He is at fault and I will try to talk to him. I can't apologise enough. I really am very sorry. It's his excitable, impulsive nature, isn't it? At least, that's what I am forever being told and led to believe. You've seen how headstrong and blinkered he can be when he sets himself a task. He doesn't always see the consequences of his actions!

Dear Flaytus, believe me when I say that I promise to have a really long talk with him, whenever he chooses to return! I know he is a terror for scaring people as he races outside and it isn't right, really. Would you like one of my squidling patties to take on your way, for your lunch maybe as a small token gesture?'

Flaytus accepted her apologies with a gentle nod and the stern look disappeared to be replaced by a friendlier smile.

'Erm, no thanks very much. I have a bit of the old tummy trouble, if you know what I mean.' A small stream of bubbles appeared from his rear end as if to confirm this. 'Oops, sorry!'

'Okay, never mind, but they are rather nice, even if I say so myself. Are you really sure I can't tempt you? You don't know what you're missing!'

'Oooh … I think I does.' A creaking emerged from somewhere within him, echoing ominously in the mighty shell, and he gripped his abdomen in earnest.

'Fine. Maybe some other day, then, eh? Anyway, what are you working on at this moment then, Flaytus? One of your *Detective Halibut* crime stories? Or are you scribing something for someone else maybe?' Showing interest in his work always guaranteed in mellowing him.

'Ah-ha, well now, dat's a question and a half, isn't it?'

'If you would rather not say … if it has to be a secret, then that's fine.'

'Fer goodness sake, it's okay, Mrs Lantica. I'm not trying to be secretive at all. It's just that my current project is a little bit sensitive if you know what I mean. It's a big, big subject and will remain unfinished for some time, I'm thinking!'

'Don't tell me it's another one of the *Edgar Allan Roe — Tails of the Undetected* series?

'No, no, no … yer swimming completely up the wrong current there, I'm afraid. It's something new and rather special fer me!'

Despina was now intrigued. 'Oh, okay, now I am curious. You are simply going to have to tell me, Flaytus!

Come on, what's it all about then? Please. Put me out of my misery!'

Flaytus shuffled awkwardly, avoiding making eye contact as he idly dragged three of his feet in the sand, marking out the shape of a curious four-and-a-half leaf clover (not that he realised what he was doing).

'Ah well, now! We're getting to the conch, so we are. Look, I'm not supposed to be saying! I'm under strictest instructions, so I am, but then it's churning me up something rotten. You see, it's actually about yer son, Findol. There being so much interest in him and all dat. He really is an ideal subject and that's no doubt. I'm thinking there will be many interesting chapters! There … dat's it. The catfish is out of the bag!'

He looked very relieved. 'So … waddaya think?'

Despina had been rather taken aback as she listened to him and she took a moment to collect her thoughts. 'Well, now, what do I think? I don't know what to say. I mean, I'm not really sure how to react to that. Should I be flattered or apprehensive? How can you know all the facts or how it is going to end, or why or who is going to feature in it or … '

'Calm down, calm down, Mrs Lantica. I take yer point and understand yer fears, but to be fair it were not my decision to choose yer son, now. I think you need to be addressing yer concerns to someone of greater importance than myself.'

Despina stared at him fixedly.

'Well? Just who then?'

'Look … if yer really must know, then I can tell yer that Cora contacted me not so long ago. Urgent, it was. She said she had a sudden desire for me to document the entire story of yer son fer the benefit of future generations to learn from and to start as soon as possible. She said it was very important that I did not drag me shell on this! She wants it to be a tome to go wid that Grandorca Pax's one.'

Despina mouthed the name, 'Cora'. Cora had asked for this, but why? What was the need? She would always have and know the information to pass on to whoever would take her place. That was the way of things, surely? Unless she was planning on leaving …

It just proved the truth in all that had been said if she really wanted a book written about Findol.

'Well, Flaytus … I honestly don't know what to feel about all this … or just what to say on the matter. Though I think Cora should have warned me.'

There was what seemed like a long pause and Flaytus thought he should be on his way. He felt movement within his bowel as gas shifted around.

Despina spoke slowly, still deep in thought. 'Well okay then, Flaytus. You must be busy. I will not hold you up any longer.'

'Thank you, but listen: yer must be understanding that this will all be working out well and fer de better in the long run. It is, after all, about the lad's destiny.'

'Destiny? Destiny! DESTINY! If I hear *that* word one more time I think I will scream. Everything with Findol is about his des … I'm sorry! … I really am so fed up with the worry … the strain … You know I sometimes really wish I had just a normal little pup!'

'Now come on, Mrs Lantica. I wager yer not meaning this in yer heart. The lad is a one-off. He has been blessed by the mighty Cora. He holds her spark in his eye. I've seen it, I'm sure. You can only feel great pride for him and yer late husband. May his soul rest in peace.' He drew his pincers across his chest and looked mournfully down.

'Now hold on just a minute there, Flaytus,' said Despina. 'There is nothing to say or show that I will not see my beloved Kai-Galant again. In my heart of hearts I know I will see him, I am sure of it! There is absolutely no proof that any harm has befallen him!'

Flaytus knew when he had overstepped the mark and said too much. 'Yes, yes. Yer right of course. I am sorry, I wasn't thinking ... and goodness me I've not been watching the time. I really must be scuttling along. Take care, Mrs Lantica. I will be seeing you!'

He hurried away toward his home carrying his precarious load, muttering and tutting to himself, and clutching at his stomach.

Despina watched him go, dragging his large shell behind him. It sent up clouds of silt wherever it bounced on the seabed, and a disgruntled, purple sea anemone that had located itself unwisely at the rear of the shell close to where a trail of bubbles sporadically erupted made good use of the cover as it evicted itself and floated away on the current.

***

Findol, meanwhile, was in a world of his own, racing along the seabed, meandering in and out of spectacular, colourful coral fans of all shapes and sizes, edging closer and closer to rocky outcrops before swerving around them. His passage raised a cloudy path of silt behind him and caused sea-grass to squirm and writhe in his wake. He chased small fish in and out of caves and tunnels before letting them escape, but not before flashing them a cheeky grin.

As Findol skimmed over the sandy bed, shocked sea anemones quickly withdrew their tentacles and small fish hid unsure as to whether the dolphin was hungry or merely playful.

Two panicking crabs skirted a large clump of purple kelp in avoidance of him, and collided with each other, tiny starfish suddenly dancing before their eyes. They tutted before brushing the starfish out of the way and continuing to make their escape.

A pipefish named Clayton poked his head out of an empty sea-urchin, spied Findol, sighed and muttered, 'Oh it's him again!' before resuming his foraging.

Findol suddenly changed direction and climbed upwards, launching himself towards the surface, leaping out of the water to greet the warm, fresh air. He took a long, deep breath, filling his lungs. Wattling beads were all very well, but you couldn't beat a good lungful of fresh air. He winced at the bright bursts of sunlight reflecting off the water and returned below the sea's surface where the light was diffuse, familiar and comfortable on the eyes.

Scanning below with his echolocation, he couldn't help but smile as he thought about the day so far. Yes, it was his birthday and he felt great! The sun, high above in a clear sky, shone brilliantly; its rays bringing out all the colours and textures of the sea-life down below. He watched, fascinated by the way the light gave a whole new radiance to everything it touched. When he felt as good as this, it was as if he was a king of this undersea world. He drank in all of its beauty and dined on a platter of wondrous sights, sounds and experiences. He felt like he had nothing in the world to fear. Even as a youngster, Findol had known that, apart from predators, Man was the only other creature that could really spoil his idyllic world. They had big boats that spewed the "black stuff" into the water, the chemicals and worse, dumped in The Blue. They cast nets that trapped fish and, all too often, others of his kind, leaving them to die agonising deaths, starved of precious oxygen. He thought how lucky Lotus had been to have had him nearby.

He looked up at the shimmering sunlight. It was both fierce and beautiful; its path broken into delicate shafts by large floating masses of kelp whose long, green blades reached down into the depths. He avoided the delicate stinging strands of a small group of jellyfish as he dived lower. The light flickered in stroboscopic delight as filaments of the kelp floated on the surface, passing quickly across the light's path. There was no denying it, this was the best place to live, he thought, as he nibbled off some wattling beads from a nearby strand.

Suddenly and without warning a strange feeling passed over him like a fast moving cloud in a storm obscuring the sun. In a flutter of panic his acute senses kicked in; something was sneakily following him, of that he was sure. He immediately hid behind a large rock, nestled tightly into the side — and waited. His breathing quickened. His anxiety increased. He heard and saw nothing, apart from the silt from his passage slowly settling again. Pressed close to the rock, he remained as still as possible. To his right, on a small ledge a mere foot away, Pinkerton Gallop, a tiny sea-horse, blinked back at him in a nervous, but excited manner. 'Hiya, Findol,' he said in his high voice.

'Oh, hi Pinky,' whispered Findol. 'Erm … this really is rather a bad time!'

'Yeh, sorry, but I've got some really exciting news to tell you, though. I'm in training for the Sea-Pony Express! Remember, I said I was applying?'

'Wow! That's great, Pinky,' said Findol, anxiously. 'Look can we talk about it some other time maybe?'

'Yes, okay! And guess what? Old Mister Cantor reckons if I can do the Lantica Run in less than a day, then I am in the team!'

'That really is great. Now please, Pinky, this is not the time. I'll catch you later, okay?' Findol whispered.

'Sorry, what did you say, Findol? Can you speak up?'

Findol shook his head. 'It doesn't matter, Pinky. Just forget it!' He turned to move off around the rock and came face to face with Wippit.

'*Waaaah*! What in the Blue are you doing here, Wippit!? You fool! You scared the life out of me!'

'Following you, of course — Big Brother!'

'Are you mad? Haven't you thought about the danger you could have put yourself in, out here alone?'

'Yes, of course I have, but I am not alone, am I? You are here and you didn't even hear me swim right up on you!'

'That's not the point, is it? You know as well as I do about all the things that we have to be aware of, being so far from home. There's plenty of scary stuff out here that even I couldn't save you from. After all, you know who lives out here; that wretched pain-in-the-blowhole, Scaybeez, who makes a career out of being trouble. Worse still, what would have happened if Grampus or Kreegan was here and spied you, eh? Or maybe Hamrag and Obi-Sness might have just been wandering along and saw you as a bit of fun!'

'Yes, well that's all rot because Mum says they haven't been seen around our parts for simply years and the latest rumour is that they may even be dead.'

At that, they both heard a faint, stifled snigger from some way ahead of them. Findol gently pushed Wippit to one side and concentrated his eyes, focussing his senses.

'Don't you believe it, Wippit. But even that were true, it makes no difference.' As he talked he silently manoeuvred himself toward and around a large coral-encrusted rock mound that jutted from behind a large bloom of kelp. 'There are still dangers out here that I cannot even imagine, and none more so than … Scaybeez! Hah! Just as I thought!'

Findol pinned the helpless individual beneath his tail. What an ugly specimen he was, a large box-shaped fish with bug-eyes and the external appearance of having survived a particularly nasty beating which, given his odious personality, was not altogether an impossibility! Scales hung off his body in decaying threads and the skin underneath was an angry blistered red. He blamed his unfortunate appearance on his nerves. He was constantly itching, which meant he was forever found close to anything abrasive to rub his putrid body against. It didn't really help the itching and only served to make his appearance even more hideous as he was left with strips of skin and scales hanging pathetically off him. Disgusted, Findol lifted his tail off his captive, and wiped it on some kelp.

'So Scaybeez, what are you doing around here and what is so funny?'

Scaybeez moved out and pressed against a rock.

'*Haargh*, you fools. You'll see! *(Ooh, ooh that's better)* You can believe what ya wanna believe. Did mummy tell you the world's a safe place, diddums?'

Findol stiffened and was about to retaliate, but checked himself.

'Go right ahead,' Scaybeez went on, 'see if I care, but I know diff — *(Ooh there! Just under the dorsal. Aah, that's better)* — erent!'

It was hard to have a conversation with Scaybeez, whilst he was constantly writhing and contorting himself over any available coral or rough rock surface.

'Look just tell us, will you?' said Findol, as flakes of detritus and scales wafted in his direction. 'Get to the point … and keep still, stop scratching!'

'Yeh, well can ya take the point, eh? The point is *(hold on … Oooh, that's the spot!)* Grampus is alive and well — *hah!* That's made yer listen, ain't it? Good old Hamrag too; he's running a large scavenger party of barracuda and sharks up in the Whiteland Wastes. Kreegan's running the business side if ya know what I … *(Oooh! Aaargh!)* … mean. But he is always looking for "certain individuals", shall we say?'

He aimed a well-chosen glance at Findol.

Suddenly Findol didn't feel quite so clever and all his good feelings started to drain all too quickly away, but he wasn't about to show it. He pushed Scaybeez roughly to the side.

'So what? If they know what's good for them they will stay away!' He couldn't think of an emptier threat. He knew Grampus was big and mean, despite his old age, whilst Kreegan was all teeth and evil intent, with the speed and ruthlessness of his younger years. When Findol compared himself to either of them he felt like a very little fish in a big, big, sea. He really didn't think they would consider him a serious problem, despite the prophecy, which brought his self-confidence down with a bang.

Scaybeez seized the opportunity and disappeared in a cloud of dust and scales.

'See? Let that be a lesson to you, Wippit! The danger is definitely real and we are both lucky they are all so far away. You, however, have got to go home. I could probably outswim them by myself, but you would not have a chance!'

Reluctantly Wippit agreed. 'All right, Findol, you are right as usual, but I just wanted to be like you, to share in your fun, that's all! You always get to go out on your adventures on your own!'

'I know and you will too, soon enough, but for now let's get you safely home. Listen, you must not breathe a word of this to anyone, least of all Mum. I'll tell her when I get back later. I don't want her to worry unnecessarily!'

Findol did enjoy being the big brother. He realised he was maybe taking on the role his father would have played and it made him feel good to think that, but it also reminded him how much he missed the father he had never met. He hurriedly escorted Wippit back to within sight of Lantica's cave mouth.

'Remember, not a word — okay?' And with that, he was off again. Now he could resume his course for Kriblington Down — a place where there was always something new to explore and find with his friend, Sterbol. It was difficult, however, to put the news he had received to the back of his mind and it forced him to think about things.

Maybe this is where it all starts?

He flitted this way and that, meandering along the seabed, snacking on unsuspecting flounders until he at last came to the far Lantica Rim — a wall of rock that rose up from the seabed to within twenty feet of the surface before dropping sharply and deeply on the other side. It was all that remained of the edge of Old Lantis — The Enchanted Kingdom.

He swam over and looked below to Kriblington Down — a massive area of treacherous rock pinnacles that in some cases reached up almost to the sea's surface. It was little wonder that careless navigators of Man's ships were regular victims to the perilous seas and the hidden dangers below the surface, often resulting in abundant wrecks that littered the eerie seascape nearby.

Grabbing another breath of fresh air, Findol plunged down into the depths. He travelled down the length of the largest rock wall until he arrived at the hollowed-out base, where there was situated the spectacular complex that was Kriblington City.

Construction had begun many years before and over the course of time the city had spilled from deep inside the cave to the outside. It was maybe a little grand to call it a city, but then the Kriblings always had big plans and big ideas — mostly about themselves. They were a highly industrious race, constantly renovating and improving their dwellings and maintaining the area around the city entrance, which they kept impeccably clean and free from the usual mess like seaweed, detritus, shipwrecks and such like. Building a city in such a dangerous area of the sea was after all not without its hazards. The risk of accident was always there, despite the rarity of any incident.

However, it had been only two years ago when Archibald Nuckles and Krustee Claws (who were outside playing with a pet dogfish) had been flattened by an oil drum that had been thrown off-deck when a ship above hit the rocks. They had only just moved into the Old Pincers Home on the far side of the Down. It was a terrible shock and a timely reminder to all, to look left, right and UP when crossing the Down.

Kriblington City was without doubt the most important post-Lantis development, since it had rapidly become the main manufacturing centre for many of the things that were now taken for granted in the Big Blue, like Flaytus's Albinokelp parchment and quills, Nautilean Discs for Finball, shellsuits for wearing on those "special occasions", all manner of jewellery, ropes and bindings of every description, tools for just about any purpose … the list grew and grew with each passing day. It was often the case that an individual suggested something that might be useful and, if it could be made, it would be produced, usually with great haste.

The industrious Kriblings proved the point that waste, often too quickly discarded and abandoned in the Blue, could serve other, more useful purposes and did not have to be needlessly thrown out. Whether it was decor for housing — flying fish hanging plaques being very popular for rather plain cave walls — all manner of illumination or scribing materials (which Flaytus employed to the full), they had a motto for their sales pitch:

If there's anything needed for work or just fun
Give us the nod and consider it done!

If they were able to make it, then it was constructed, simple as that! Most of the materials for their creations had either been discarded into the sea or came from the many shipwrecks, providing a huge and surprisingly varied collection of materials. But much could be made too from the natural refuse of the Blue itself, shells being great favourites. You could say, in a way, it was a form of natural re-sea-cycling.

Now the Kriblings were in actual fact small red lobsters, but together as a collective they had a unique talent. Their success story was down to an amazing bit of luck and a little assistance from Mother Nature herself. It had been many years ago, when during another confrontation with Sloth the lazy conger, a number of them decided, quite spontaneously, that enough was enough, and so instead of retreating in a cloud of silt, as they usually did, they would make a stand! For an invertebrate to show such backbone was unheard of, but thanks to the motivational speeches of Billwallis, one of the older and stronger Kriblings, they found the courage to stand up for themselves. And by forming a group huddle they also found that an abundance of claws and pincers was actually an extremely useful deterrent against slow-moving foes. From that day to this, the Kriblings were no longer easy pickings and, for his part, Billwallis was forever remembered as "Braveclaw".

Over the years that followed, the Kriblings trained and honed this ability so that they could quickly link up, one behind the other to form a mighty excavator, fighting machine, or … just for partying (especially when dancing the "conger"). It was not unusual to have as many as twenty individuals making up the collective at any one time, making them a formidable deterrent to any would-be predator. This was confirmed by many of their success stories, citing how their collective ability had saved them from certain digestion.

At parties and celebratory occasions, the older Kriblings would often laugh, animatedly slapping each other on the carapace whilst recounting tales of their bravery, such as the story of Borax, the fearsome stinging octopus, who had turned ashen with fright after chasing and trapping a single Kribble (a young Kribling), anticipating a quick and easy tasty snack — or so he thought — only to turn a corner and come face to face with the multi-clawed and pincered Kribling Juggernaut.

Borax wisely saw the error of his ways and being full of remorse quickly became a good friend, often helping and assisting them with the moving of awkward objects, or jobs that involved the employing of many strong arms at once. He had realised the sense and wisdom in having them as friends rather than enemies.

So it was from then that the Kriblings quickly became excellent excavators and builders, which accounted for the spectacular entrance hall to Kriblington City. It was as if the concept of working together had resonated with them and fuelled their ambition. They developed an interest in all things creative and pursued the art of dexterity and manipulation, soon finding an inner natural ability to create and manufacture almost anything from the simplest of materials. Kriblington City had started out as a huge cave with many small entrances to the living areas within, but they quickly had almost all of the walls and tunnels adorned with small pieces of artefacts and had created many wonderful pieces of furniture from whatever they could find.

With the help of Borax, some huge items had been skilfully manoeuvred within, like the giant Imagico Wall that greeted guests in the huge entrance hall and was in fact a complete circle of enormous silver dinner plates secured side by side to the walls with barnacle gum and razor shells. This mighty mirrored interior was constantly being polished and cleaned by Scrublings (Kriblings with brush-like appendages instead of pincers). Its perimeter was encrusted with Jou-Jou barnacles that pulsed and twinkled with a myriad of different colours, generated as they ate the microscopic organisms filtering through their digestive systems.

Hanging clam illuminants lit up the large ceiling over the entrance hall, powered by the magical albedo grains of the Luminus Weed (*Lunaris Illuminatus*). Nurselings (Kriblings with a caring attitude) kept the clams constantly supplied with the precious grains that they harvested from the weed that thrived in the rich waters around the wrecks. The Luminas Weed abounded wherever a host of opportunist organisms had taken foothold on the stricken vessels.

The City's grand entrance also housed a large goliath clam filled with wattling beads for visitors; well actually just one visitor — Findol — since he was the only Cetacean that actually bothered with them enough to want to know them as individuals and not just as "the shellfish who could manufacture goods".

So it was that the formation of the collective was the start of a journey of self-discovery that resulted in uncovering the hidden talents of each individual and giving them high status as leaders in the development and manufacturing of most things useful in the Big Blue. The *"Another quality Kriblington product"* stamp on all products was the ultimate seal of approval. Originally this was achieved with a special Embossington clam with the design etched into the surface courtesy of Lanky Wicks, the highly respected artist. Soon after, an additional design incorporating Leesa the Seal was used as a further mark of quality. Leesa had acquired this great accolade by saving the life of many foraging Kriblings when they were trapped under a panel of decking that had given way and pinned them down. She had shown her strength of body and mind and they rewarded her as such.

There was always a Guardling (Kribling with attitude) at the entrance to the city — wary of any predators or undesirables that would try to gain access. Findol was used to seeing Rubble or Granit standing guard, but today it was first watch for Kwaartz.

'Hiya Findol. How's things with you?'

'Oh fine, thanks, Kwaartz. I've actually come for Sterbol. Is he around?'

'I expect so! I will send Shale up for him. He's new at the job and likes to feel important, bless him!'

While Findol waited he looked at the guard and thought about when the Squibblets had tried to gain access in a hopeless attempt at overthrowing the city and so gaining an industrial takeover. The Squibblets were a large band of Icelandic squids that had seized on the Kribling concept of working together, thinking they too could do the same. They called themselves the BERG collective. Seemingly acting as one, they were in reality a bunch of arrogant, conceited, greedy individuals who had everything — and yet nothing — in common.

On the day they had sneaked in through the gate into the entrance hall, the guard was actually dozing, but one of the Squibblets had a panic attack when turning and being confronted by his own reflection in the Imagico Wall sending them all into a tangled frenzy. The resultant BERG mass was a knot of intertwined tentacles and embarrassed faces. Having alerted the Guardlings they had to suffer the indignity of seeing the Kriblings rolling about, some on their backs in hysterics, pincers snapping in delight, and shouting things like 'Suckers!', whilst one of Lanky Wicks protégés, a Madame Holly Fairbear, sketched the amusing sight on her specially created "Can-Can-Canvas".

As if lessons hadn't been learned, it was only a few months after that when the UltraSquibblets, a very real menace, had attacked the city with their ally Quillton Pringle, a malevolent lion fish who charged the gate, and succeeded in maiming two Guardlings before tackling two Scrublings who were just returning with cockling baskets full of illuminant grains.

Luckily for them they had thrown the grains into his face and managed to blind him partially in both eyes before he had made a desperate escape. The UltraSquibblets had backed down at the sight of Quillton retreating. There were minor attacks by small congers and sharks over the years, but on the whole most marine life left them alone.

Well, except for the time the dreaded Worm-infested Sea Troll attacked many years before — but that was another story, as was the Itching Snufflefish of Katarr! Both are well-documented in Flaytus's famous tome of unusual creatures, *Stranger than Strange*.

Finally, Sterbol arrived, leaping out of his tunnel in dramatic fashion. The scallop shell door snapped shut behind him.

'Tarrrah!' he shouted as if expecting applause, pincers outstretched, bending down on one thin knee. He had been delayed because he had been giving his pincers and claws a well deserved manicure. Earlier that day he had trod in some discarded barnacle gum and it was sheer murder to remove the stuff.

I'm just glad I didn't get any on my mandibles, he had thought. 'Well, Findol, what do you think?'

Findol looked in horror at the spectacle. Sterbol had some Pilkington periwinkles hanging from each side of his head somewhere near where his ears would have been had he any. The shell's multi-faceted surfaces flickered pulses of light in all directions. Each of his feelers was braided with sequinned catfish gut, and around his neck he wore a large Bilious Sharkskin Velcro Bandana — ideal for attaching a plethora of other fashion accessories.

'Sterbol, what do you look like? Just what do you think we are doing today? We are hardly going to the Manta-Ray Midsummer Fishball. Why are you dressed like that comical grouper, Dandini Beano?'

'Well you know, Findol, I just thought I would have a change. Sometimes I feel I do not make the best of my assets. I am trying to make a fashion statement, you know. Trying to discover the real me!'

'Come on, we are going exploring, not to a fashion parade. You will be asking to shop at Far-Sarchies or Goochy-Goos next, and I dread to think of the strange looks you'll get from going out looking like — well, like you!'

'All right! All right! You've made your point,' and he hopped onto Findol's back and started putting some of the offending articles in his mermaids purse, frowning as he did so. He was unexpectedly thrown back as Findol surged forward without warning, his powerful tail thrusting them along.

'I think we should make for the far side of the wrecking zone today, eh? We haven't been over there for absolutely ages! What do you think, Sterbol?'

'Er, I don't know … it's dangerous over there! Mum has always said so. She says the congers and the morays like to hide there. Besides, there're lots of scary caves and tunnels, and there's rumours of large groups of barracuda roaming around!'

'For goodness sake, Sterbol, where's your spirit of adventure? I know all that, but we can be careful. You stay close to me, and nothing will catch us as long as you hold on tight!'

'Why does that not fill me with confidence?'

Findol couldn't help but keep looking back at the ridiculous sight of Sterbol, thinking to himself: *just because he has blue-blood ... thinks he's royalty or something!*

'Look ... Sterbol — I really think now is the time to lose all of the headgear!'

Sterbol stashed the bandanna and the purse back in his pack, and sulked the rest of the journey. They skimmed over the rough terrain beneath them. Ragged rock formations jutted out between patches of sea-grass and clusters of coral, that in some cases crept right up to within feet of the surface. Many of these "Ocean Claws" had been broken near the surface where they had made their mark on Man's ships. Large fractured pieces of rock lay on the seabed with broken skeletons of rotting hulls and lost artefacts smashed and left decaying in the water. Occasionally something exciting would be seen and they would endeavour to retrieve it. Often, though, the object would be too far degraded to be of use or too heavy to move by themselves.

'Sterbol, over there,' Findol said excitedly. 'Look!'

There, plain to see, far beyond an old whaling ship, there was the distant outline of an almost complete trawler — its keel bearing the deep gaping scars of damage from the cruel rocky talons, but everything else seemed intact. Judging by its appearance it had not gone down that long ago. The splintered wood still looked fresh and the ragged ends were sharp as needles as it rested, eerily listing upwards on the seabed.

'These are the very boats Man uses to farm our Blue and our food, Sterbol! Worse still, many of my kind have been lost in their nets. Do you remember me telling you about Lotus?'

Sterbol swallowed hard and nodded. It was after all something that happened all too often with many of the seas inhabitants, and especially his kin. To think of it upset him greatly. The broken trawler had been sunk only months before, but seaweed, corals and huge numbers of barnacles were already firmly established. Small shoals of fish were swimming inside and reappearing out of some other entrance in the boat's cabin. A large net, barely secured, hung splayed out and lifeless, floating eerily just above the wheelhouse with its bindings frayed and rotting. Ragged lengths of rope danced around lazily, doing the slow-mo twist and shimmy in the gentle current as orange buoys bobbed at their topmost ends.

'Sterbol, you can cut through this. Come on, then we'll get through into the wheelhouse easier!'

The lobster craned a non-ear. 'The what?'

'It's what they call the place that steers the boat, I believe.'

'How do you know?'

'I don't know, Sterbol — I just … do.'

Sterbol shrugged and dutifully complied with Findol's wishes, his pincers making easy work of the rope. As he cut through the last piece, the torn net slowly and gracefully pulled away and floated up to the surface, the buoys almost appearing triumphant, finally achieving something. The rising net captured clumps of seaweed in it and a few limpets attached to the weed opened their eyes wide in excitement. 'Yippee, we're on the move!' they cried, collectively.

Findol, meanwhile, looked distracted, his head cocked to one side. 'Hold on a minute, Sterbol. I will be right back.' He disappeared up to the surface and was back almost as quick.

'It's okay. I heard something up top, but it's just some birds diving for food. Come on,' he said with relish. 'Let's explore!'

Above the sea, a large group of gannets were having great fun in the strong gusts of wind that had whipped up. In-between swooping, stalling and bickering with each other, they dived spectacularly into the water — each trying to impress and outdo the others with the biggest catch and most dramatic entry. They were plainly delighted to be feasting on a particularly large shoal of fish and would enjoy adulation returning to their colony with the news of its location. One bird had been so intent on attracting the attention of the others that he forgot to draw in his wings at the right moment and belly-flopped on the surface with a loud slap, wings wildly splaying out across the water.

High above the frenzied action, another individual was lazily gliding around, riding on the wind's thermal cushion, almost oblivious to everything below. He was older than the others and distinctly uninterested in peer pressure and showing off. His eyesight was not what it used to be and he now had a permanent squint which meant that most objects in the sea were decidedly blurred, turning hunting and feeding into very much hit-and-miss affairs.

Suddenly, the bright sunlight caught something interesting down below, flashing enticingly just beneath the surface, and he decided to take his chances. He felt he could and would still show the youngsters a thing or two about strength, skill and timing, and more importantly, *style*.

Tegan dropped like a stone, eyes watering and straining to focus on the target, his wings pulled tight to his sides and his head tucked down. He hit the water hard and ploughed down, way below, to his prospective meal, mouth opening and ready to feast. However, there was no fish — just a strange bandana decorated with Mother of Pearl Blinkleton scales; worse still, he was trapped by some kind of a creature that seemed to be gripping him tightly, clasping his wings, pressing them against him.

The more he struggled, the more the net clung to him. He was only a couple of feet below the surface, but those two feet from the precious air might as well have been two leagues. Panic arrived rapidly in abundance, his desperate thrashing quickly draining him of vital oxygen and energy. He had two fleeting, simultaneous thoughts:

I wish I had tidied the nest this morning — all those damned herring bones!

Do lobsters have ears?

His lungs were ready to burst. Unconsciousness was knocking at his door. His feathered soul was packing its bags and almost ready to wave goodbye, and amid all of this he was barely aware of something being forced into his beak (he nearly gagged); something which fizzed in his mouth, and suddenly there was air. Not much, just a gulp, but it was enough. Blurry images — a flash of silver grey and pink; a smiling face close to his; claws; pincers; being gently elevated to the surface. It was all happening so quick, yet he watched as if in slow motion. At the surface he burped loudly and spent a good few minutes coughing, spluttering, gasping for breath and regaining his composure.

His lungs and chest ached with many of his feathers looking even more tattered and he felt distinctly foolish, but he was alive! Slowly, his head cleared and he became aware of the jibing and taunts sounding far above him from the unruly mob wheeling around in the air. The twins had even more of their family with them, which was pretty unbearable. He did his best to ignore them and allow himself to calm down. At last, feeling a little more composed he became aware of his saviours. He saw a smiling dolphin with a lobster perched on the back of his head which was kind of odd and he thought: *I guess I didn't make it after all! This is a strange Heaven and no mistake!'*

'Hi, I'm Findol and this is the Mighty Sterbol — King of the Kriblings. I feel I may be slightly responsible for your accident, so please accept my sincere apologies, sir!'

Tegan was at first taken aback. 'Ha, forget it, young Findol — I am just glad to still be here. I don't think I have ever been that close to … well, anyway, I am Tegan — retired Commanding Officer Cod Squadron 2.'

'Well sir, I am very pleased to meet you — the circumstances could have been better, but at least you are safe now — though not from the ridicule of your friends above, I notice!'

'Pay no heed to them and please call me Tegan!' Suddenly something flashed in his mind at the sound of the dolphin's name as a distant memory unravelled. He continued. 'It could be that you have saved me a lot of wasted time. It could also be argued that maybe fate has worked in mysterious ways here. You say you are Findol — a name I remember from many years ago — the time of the *Darkening*, I believe. There was a great deal of excitement that day. I think Cora was there too, was she not, and a lot of talk of great things to be done, prophecies to be realised — all associated with your good self.'

'Well, yes, sir. I mean Tegan, it's true. I have tried to put all that to the back of my mind as much as possible to protect those around me and myself too, for I do not know what lies ahead.'

'Well Findol, I fear that you cannot go ahead in life without accepting what you know or have been told. You must be brave, for I fear indeed that a black tide is turning. There are dark times on the horizon and I don't mean rain-clouds.

'Many months ago I flew far up north where the white-lands are and the water is icy cold. I must admit that these days I try to keep myself to myself so that I rarely bother with other animals. It cuts down on potential animosity, if you see what I mean. However this day I spied a bird in distress, alone in the cold sea. It, or rather he, was an arctic tern named Glycol who was being attacked and held onto from below by something that was gripping hard and fast to his tail. Maybe I should not have intervened or I was a little too rash … I don't know, but anyway I swooped down, dived in and hit the attacker, which turned out to be a huge barracuda. It let go of his tail and let me tell you I almost let go of my heart, I was that scared. It was the last thing I expected to see in such cold waters.

'Anyway we escaped and landed on a nearby 'berg. Glycol thanked me and explained that he had recently been a reluctant spy for Hamrag the Humpback Whale who was searching for his master Grampus the Grey. Glycol and was under strict instructions to bring word of any sightings of a particular dolphin called Findol that Hamrag had plans for.

'Seemingly, Glycol had heard about you, but more importantly, he had heard about the good you have done — the tern you saved from some fishing line last year was a good friend of Glycol's. He decided he would not give up the news so readily to Hamrag, but in doing so he nearly paid the ultimate price for that silence, when a "slip of the beak" gave him away to the barracuda, allied to the evil one. So you see, one good turn deserves another or in this case an arctic one.'

Tegan chuckled at his own joke before continuing. 'But the real worry here is the news that Hamrag is helping to put together an army of sharks, barracudas, congers and other sea creatures and they will all be bent to his and Grampus's wishes, fed by his lies and promises of power and corruption. He is desperately looking for his master, so intent is he on sucking up to him. Glycol told me to try and find you and warn of Hamrag's intention to move his army south when he finds Grampus and when they are ready to put their plan into action.

'So you see, today, fate dealt you a very good fin and you can benefit greatly from this news by being one fathom ahead of them.'

Findol swallowed hard.

Tegan winced and stretched his wings. 'I need to go now, Findol, but I will not stray too far from this location. My nest is on Guano Rock should you need to contact me urgently. Row 24, Aisle 6. Just to the right of the large guano stain on the broken periwinkle. GR24 IL6 for short. Take care!'

Tegan launched himself upwards with great effort, struggling to lift his damaged and sodden wings, but soon he was soon gone, leaving Findol reeling with the ill news and feeling decidedly sick.

Sterbol had sat quietly, taking it all in, not knowing quite what to say. Today had definitely taken a "tern" for the worse for his friend.

Findol felt nauseous and had lost all interest in exploring for artefacts, or even in light conversation, and he decided to take Sterbol back to Kriblington City as quickly as possible before making a hasty return to Lantica Deep. On the way, Findol hardly spoke and Sterbol knew then that Findol was really worried. He felt pretty helpless, and tried hard to think of things his large family might do to help.

Findol knew that, no matter what, today was a very real turning point. Cora words — in his mother's voice, for they had come to him from her — were beginning to take shape and become reality. The drumming in of historical premonitions and prophecies were spinning giddily in his mind. He didn't like it. It was not fair. Why should it be him anyway? There was, however, no point in dwelling on "ifs" and "buts", he knew that! It was quickly turning into the time for action and maybe now it was his place to come up with the answers to everybody's hopes and wishes — if he only knew what they were!

Chapter 3
Findol's Cave

Resting on his sleeping ledge, Findol opened his eyes and looked lazily around. Troubled, he nibbled at a wattling bead, rolling it around his mouth, feeling it pop and fizz. After the previous day's events his thoughts were jousting with all manner of terrible demons, and his impulse was to swim away and hide, passing his fears onto someone else for them get on with his destiny for him.

Wippit swam over to him and was about to say hello, but judging by the look on Findol's face and the almost complete absence of colour in the cave, he realised that it was probably unwise to do so. He felt that whatever it was that was troubling his brother, it was best left to be sorted out in its own way.

A piece of kelp floated towards Findol and he blew it away, gazing at its ragged form, flipping and twisting in the current. He allowed himself to be mesmerised by its hypnotic motion and briefly enjoyed the distraction. With its thin blades hanging down, it almost looked like a strange green cuttlefish. He made it jerk upwards again, and managed a wafer-thin smile before he got bored and let it float down past him to the floor below.

His mum had already called him for breakfast, but he really didn't feel hungry. In fact he wasn't even sure if he could be bothered to eat or even venture out. He couldn't break free from his depression for long because Scaybeez had really unsettled him with the news of Hamrag and Grampus, made all the worse by Tegan's confirmation. It now seemed his whole world was falling apart and was twisting in a new direction against the tide of reason and security. It was a path he was so reluctant to consider taking. In the space of a day everything he held as safe, cosy and normal now looked fragile and vulnerable. He saw the freedom that he and the others enjoyed, dwindling away. There was a feeling, deep in the pit of his stomach; a tight knot of agitation and dread that was welling up within him, threatening to get out of hand and take control of him. Normally he could sense how his immediate future would work out — his mum called it *dolphintuition*. Cora had said it was rare, but he had it in abundance. Now his inner vision and echo powers were decidedly numb, and clouded by all the darkness swirling around in his head. His stomach ached, not due to hunger so much as the griping it was performing for the benefit of his agitation.

He lay there in silence, thinking and then as he did so, the anxiety he was feeling started to draw something out of him, something tucked away deep within his very soul. He found that the darkness of his feelings had a sobering effect.

Hearing a commotion, he looked down and spotted the Scavits bickering over a large piece of food that Splinter had dropped. Everything connected with his domestic life seemed so trivial compared to the scenario he had been imagining. Hamrag and Kreegan, controlled by Grampus, was not a pleasant thought. Both were cold, ruthless killers, devoid of mercy or compassion. Grampus however, was altogether a different adversary. He was too wise and cunning to be considered a mere psychopathic killer. His evil operated on many different levels in many different worlds. History had shown that he always had a secret agenda hidden within his scheming, that made him all the more dangerous if he were not taken very seriously. It meant that the reasoning behind his actions were often unclear until it was too late. When the dolphins covered Cetacean History at school, the names of these foes had cropped up all too often, so Findol was well aware of all their capabilities.

In spite of his efforts to outwardly appear as strong and carefree as usual, Findol was certainly feeling sorry for himself. He looked and felt like a dolphin carrying the entire ocean on his dorsal, for he knew that his problems would not go away and would ultimately become everyone else's too. For the first time in his life he really wished Cora was there to offer advice. After all, she knew the answers to most questions.

He felt (and recalled) a thought … a fragment of something buried deep, from long ago. Just after he had been born, Cora had whispered a message into his tiny ear, pressing the importance of it to him: 'Do not fear, child. For you will know when the time is right. Trust and love are two of your greatest assets. Courage, young one!'

But no matter hard he tried, he could not recall the rest of it. All he knew was that at this moment he really needed some reassurance and guidance. He couldn't talk to his mother, despite desperately wanting to. It wouldn't be fair.

He turned towards the wall in frustration and slapped it with a flipper. As he did so, the glistening white rock seemed to shudder and vibrate. A small area of its surface *changed* and took on an opaque hue. The rock became fluid-like, softening, swelling and undulating gently, and then reformed into the aged face of Cora.

The visage smiled at him out of the rock. Findol squeaked in shock and delight, clapping his fins together, but then regained control of his surprise so as not to draw attention from the others below. He quickly glanced down and around to see if any of his family were looking, but all were too involved in the usual morning routine to notice.

'Come on, Findol, your breakfast is getting warm!' his mother shouted up to him.

'Erm, yeah, okay Mum. I'll be down in a minute!' he replied. The image in the wall was alternately blurring then re-focussing back into Cora likeness, gently smiling back at him all the time. This lifted Findol's spirit and warmed his heart.

(Soon, dear Findol, soon. Have no fear! Be strong, my little soldier; my warrior of the Blue!)

It was a soft, hushed voice that seemed to echo in his mind. He wasn't even sure if he had really heard it or whether the sound was a subconscious wish inside his head. Either way, it warmed him, and lifted his mood. He had so many questions ready and waiting to ask her that his heart was pounding, and he struggled to get his thoughts in order.

What should I ask first?

Where is she right now?

When will she come here and visit?

Then suddenly the image dissolved and faded away, as quickly as it had arrived.

No. No, wait ... Cora! Please, not yet! Wait!

But she was gone, and he was left with his heart pounding. He lay there, shaking his head, stunned; not sure if he had imagined the vision or not. He was frustrated that he had had no time to talk to her and yet he still felt an inner contentment as if he was covered by an invisible blanket of warmth and relief. The very thought of Cora was like a quilt for the soul.

Findol allowed a smile onto his face and looked down below, his attention finally arriving back in the real world.

Lotus and Pipsqueak had left early to take Aunt and Uncle Winslow back home to their cave near the Eastern Lantica Rim a short distance away. They had stayed overnight in the guest cave that adjoined the main one. Findol felt a little guilty that he had not given his aunt and uncle more of his time, since they had actually taken the trouble to come over for his birthday. When he had arrived home he had been in no mood for talking and had gone straight to bed, much to everybody's surprise. It was unusual because he always liked telling everyone about his adventures, so his silence was worrying for his mother.

Wippit and Splinter were down below playing Finball with an empty sea-urchin. Despina was shouting at them.

'You two! Stop playing with that in the cave! For goodness sake there is plenty of room outside. Besides, you haven't even finished your breakfast or asked to leave the clam yet, have you?'

Findol heard a reluctant 'Sorry, Mum' as they returned to the clam to continue eating. Most of the Special Kray had escaped and had to be rounded up and herded back inside the scallops they used to contain them.

Findol swam down to his mother and brushed up to her. 'I love you, Mum,' he whispered in her ear as he nuzzled in close. The others weren't looking. He didn't want to appear too soft in front of them.

'I love you too, Findol. What's this for then?' she said, slightly taken aback and looking at him suspiciously, searching his face for clues. 'Are you scheming for something?'

At that moment Findol was very tempted to tell her everything that had happened the day before, but he chose not to. He knew that her concern would end up getting him upset and he didn't want that. He also rightly guessed that she would curb his exploring and long days out if there was even a hint that he might get into any sort of serious trouble.

'No, I'm not scheming. Honest! I just didn't want you to think that you were being taken for granted, Mum.'

'That's really sweet, darling, but it wouldn't matter anyway — it's my job, isn't it? It's called unconditional love.' She smiled and gave him a big hug with her fin, nuzzling her snout against his chin.

Findol decided that he would sit with his family and have some breakfast — much to the delight of the Scavits (the more children at the clam, the greater the chance of food for them). Findol was quite reserved at the table though, and didn't rise to the normal bickering and cajoling from his siblings. One of the younger Scavits cheekily nipped Splinter's tail fin, hoping Wippit would get the blame and incite a food fight, but instead all it got was a cuff from its mother.

'Shame on you, Brintul, have you no pride?' she said.

Findol was just finishing his scallop of Fin-lice Krispies when his mother settled beside him.

'Are you all right, Findol? Only you were not your usual chirpy self last night, were you?'

'Oh … yes, I'm fine, Mum. I just had a bit of a headache, that's all.' He didn't dare look up with his guilty face.

'Okay, just as long as there's nothing worrying you. Are you going out today?' She saw his anxious expression.

'Well, I wasn't going to, but maybe I will, now you mention it.'

'Okay, well take care. Remember not to be too late because we're going out tonight.'

'Yes, I won't forget! How could I?' Findol eagerly sped away, relieved finally to escape the tension. 'See ya everyone — bye!' he called behind him.

'See you later, galley-hater,' Wippit shouted after him.

'Swim a mile in single file,' Findol replied.

'What does he mean?' asked Splinter, though he had an idea that nobody would really know.

Findol decided to go over to his own cave, a place he often went to when he needed time and space to himself for thinking things through. His brothers and sisters knew of it, but none would dare to go there unless he invited them. It was one of the rare occasions when they actually respected his wishes.

Over the years, Findol had decorated it with many of the artefacts collected together from his travels and he was rather proud of it. It was a small cave situated at the base of a large underwater rock formation not far from his Lantica home and on the way to Kriblington City. Nobody else, except his family, knew about his secret cave. Its entrance was cunningly hidden behind a large naturally growing pad of yellow-green kelp that kelp tasted disgusting which is how it earned its name: *vomit kelp*. Besides tasting bad, vomit kelp was also free of wattling beads so most people tended to avoid it. Those that didn't paid a terrible price for their mistake.

Still, the putrid weed had one redeeming factor; it ensured that no creature came near the cave's entrance and that was just how Findol liked it. After all, with such a large family and their constant visitors he needed space to himself. He liked being able to lie on his own sometimes and quietly think about things. Best of all though, it meant he could decorate it as he wished.

Findol checked for onlookers before he swam through the kelp curtain and entered his little sanctuary. As he passed through the entrance he stroked an illuminant sea-urchin that immediately bathed the cave in yellowish light, creating a warm, homely feeling to Findol's den. All manner of ships' ropes hung down in loops from stalactites in the cave's ceiling. There were thick ones, thin ones, and some threaded with cork rings that made them look like mariners' giant Christmas garlands. Barnacles and coloured shells adorned the walls. The ends of the thickest ropes were encrusted with sparkleton jewels. As Findol moved about his cave, they snaked lazily in his wash like glittering sea-serpents.

On the floor, and covered with a thick Kriblington Kelp mat, was the inverted wooden lid of a large old sea-chest. Findol down upon his bed and rested, ruminating on his thoughts whilst nuzzling open a storage clam full of wattling beads, nipping one in the process. He looked around his little kingdom, and admired the way he had personalised it with so many of the treasures he had found over the years.

On one wall was a display of faded ceramic plates, attached by sea-cucumber juice and barnacle gum. Some of the plates had not stuck too well and had fallen to the silty cave floor. Usually they didn't break and Findol was able to put them aside for reattaching at a later date. Just in front of these, Findol kept a few drawings of members of his pod. They were drawn by a lamprey named Lanky, who had drawn them as a thankyou to Findol for saving him from the jaws of Jinja Vitus, a toothless barracuda who had lost most of his teeth, but still had a deadly suck.

Another wall showcased Findol's own creative talents; a collage pattern fashioned from hundreds of pieces of rusty, misshaped cutlery. Each was covered in a delicate layer of flora that greatly enhanced the beauty of the finished display. He was rather proud of it, since it had taken a long time to complete. The attaching of all the pieces had been a mammoth task, and with that thought he spotted Wichita Grub slowly making his way over toward him.

Wichita was a pretty depressing individual even by sea-cucumber standards. He was in a bad way when Findol first found him, and Findol had taken pity on the wretched creature and had taken him in, telling Wichita to stick with him — Wichita had taken those words to literal levels, meeting Findol's every adhesive need by helping attach all his decor and anything else that needed fixing. He stopped inching across the cave floor and gazed up at Findol.

'Do you need me today or what? Only, I'd like to go out foraging. It's been a long time. I need to get out more you know. Can't dwell on the past forever, can I?'

'I guess not. And I'm glad to hear it!' said Findol, slightly taken aback. 'Look, you go and enjoy yourself, Wichita, but take care out there!'

The little creature made his way out leaving Findol alone in his cave. Jou-Jou jewels and sparkleton beads were studded everywhere and anywhere that was not already occupied by something or other that had fallen off a wreck or been dumped overboard by uncaring seafarers. Findol lay there thinking, and a niggling thought inevitably came to mind: just how safe was his little world now?

Findol's mother had sometimes mentioned the enchantment that had been bestowed on their Lantica domain from the days of old when much of it was known as "Old Lantis" (Atlantis in the tongue of Man). She only knew patchy details about it, but it seemed that magic was far more commonplace and accepted back then. Carrying the Lantica name gave Despina a level of protection from dark powers. To Findol, though, magic seemed a difficult thing to believe in. Sure, there were rumours that Flaytus could pull a few tricks, but that was as much as he knew of the supernatural. Enchantments and spells, morphing and dream-dancing in the times of old, all seemed to be nothing more than whispers and rumours and as far removed from *their* life as they could possibly be. He really didn't hold much faith in any charm keeping a purposeful battalion of berserker barracuda or savaging sharks away from them. He knew there were always individuals with issues to pursue.

Only a few months back, a pipefish called Mia Shawm and a bundle of accomplices had decided to punish poor old Flaytus over something he had scribed in *The Big Fishoo*. He had dared to question the role of pipefish in the ecological circle of life, suggesting they had evolved from marine toothpicks used by the largest of whales for detritus removal. After attacking him, they had scurried away, muttering between themselves about him being a big shell of wind, which was a point few could disagree with.

Findol began to doubt the wisdom of not telling his mother about the previous day's events. Just how wise was it to keep those he loved the most in the dark? But he knew that once she found out it would change everything. However, he began to see the bigger picture spread out before him. The rest of his family wouldn't be safe either. Wippit, Splinter, Pipsqueak and Lotus may all be stepbrothers and stepsisters, but he loved them all dearly, no less than if they shared his blood. He remembered how their parents had been captured in Man's fishing nets only a few years before, to a fate he didn't want to think about. Despina had adopted them immediately; feeling both pity for the children's loss of their parents, but also a more selfish need for healing her own grief caused by the absence of Kai-Galant.

Findol's head hurt with the growing pressure of realising just how many vulnerable individuals there were close to him. He hadn't even considered all of his friends and could barely count the numbers involved, but then he reminded himself that if — when — things kicked off, it would affect *everyone*. But it was the not knowing *when* that was worse. He thought and thought until an idea began to form in his head that seemed to make sense. He decided he would have to make it his job to somehow form a chain of communication and information that would allow him to be alerted as soon as possible of any suspicious or mysterious movements of predatory hordes, suggestive of Grampus and his cohorts.

He knew many of his friends would be only too keen to help, since it would ultimately be in their interest too. He decided that he would call it his Secret Communication Highway and refer to it as the Hint-at Net, since he would use it to draw in any information that would help. Hopefully it would buy him valuable time if and when he needed it. That way he would only have to act when he knew the time was right and events were really taking place.

It was scary taking on such a role, but he felt within his heart that it was sensible, and it was what Cora would wish. Maybe, for now though, he could try to enjoy his life in as normal a way as possible, whilst it was still safe. Whilst there were no untoward signs to threaten otherwise.

His thoughts now closer to home, he remembered his mother's words from earlier in the day. They were all going out that night and not just anywhere but to Sea-Czar's

Palace — a really special treat as a late birthday present. It was *the* place to go — and the original entertainment centre of Old Lantis where all the best Cetaceans (and some of the worst) went to experience the greatest music and dance available.

The burying of Old Lantis and the withdrawing of its magic had not lessened the appeal or quality of service provided in the Palace. Findol lay back and let his mind race with the prospect of the forthcoming night's treats in store. It was, after all, a place he had often heard referred to, but seldom seen. He had only glanced at the outside when he passed by and it only opened at night, when, until recently, he would have been tucked up on his sleeping shelf. But tonight would be different! It was, after all, tradition for those leaving Podling status to go there, marking their passage into adulthood.

Findol was deep in thought when suddenly he was startled by movement at the cave's entrance.

'Hi Findol — can I come in?' It was Stradi Boran, the fiddler crab.

'Yeah, sure you can. Hi Stradi. You all right?'

'Fine thanks,' said Stradi, twitching with nervous energy. 'I had to come over. Sorry! I know you don't like to risk drawing attention to the entrance. I've finished a new piece of music and there wasn't a better place for it to be heard than here, if it's okay with you?'

'By all means, I am all ears,' said Findol, adopting a look of great concentration

Stradi tapped his fiddling claw on a timpani shell for effect and launched into a sweet, delicate solo, swaying this way and that, his face contorted into a look of anguish and pain, conveying the powerful emotions within the music. Eyes pressed tightly shut, he smiled and grimaced in the highs and lows of the piece, and all the while his fiddling claw flicked back and forth across his catfish-gut fiddle. Then he tripped on a rock cluster ornament and somersaulted without missing a note (not that Findol would have noticed). Bringing his performance to a crescendo, Stradi punctuated his composition with frantic drumming on his back shell with a hind leg whilst hopping on the others, which looked a little bizarre.

When it was finally over, Findol cheered, greatly impressed by the gymnastic display as well as the music. He clapped his fins together loudly, his enthusiastic applause blowing tympanic shells off nearby shelves and sending them clattering to the floor.

'That was marvellous, Stradi — so powerful and emotional — almost had me crying and I don't even know why!'

'I am glad you like it. Because, in a way, it is for you. You see, I have called it "Findol's Cave."' Stradi's cheeks actually blushed a little. Then he looked down, swaying left and right in an awkward manner, scraping patterns in the sand with one of his feet.

'Stradi! Thanks! That's really kind. It was beautiful. It sounds like a real classic.'

Stradi, as fiddler crabs go, was a bit of a shy loner. Instead of playing Sea Jigs like the others, he liked to play music that had powerful and emotional depth to it. When he studied the violin he resigned himself to composition only, with an occasional impromptu performance for small select audiences. It seemed to be the better option.

Somewhere along the line he discovered he could record his music using "Retaining Conches Shells"; shells that were able to contain sound within their interiors. Millions of fibres inside the shells mapped, copied and stored the music they recorded. The problem was in getting them to release it. This was achieved by stroking them gently, allowing an echo of the particular piece of music to be regurgitated. This wasn't always as easy as it sounded. In the old days they were used mainly for sending secret messages, since the intended recipient would be the only one knowing the correct pattern of stroking for the arriving conch. Back then, it was known as "interconchinental communication" and was popular for only a short while. After all, those that required a secret service were not very popular with the Sea-Pony Express, who had to carry the cumbersome things back and forth between conversing parties.

One famous case in particular revolved around Sheik Speer who had recorded a twenty-minute monologue from his play Anchovy and Lee of Petra, which, when played backwards, was supposed to give secret codes and locations of some historical enemy or other, but actually sounded more like the Jelly Turbots (a group that young starfish liked to watch).

Stradi was, however, extremely popular in Kriblington City where many of his recordings were bought and sold. The constant hive of activity was always such that his music became the perfect antidote to the stress and pressure that the Kriblings lived and worked with. Although he rarely made live performances, due to his shyness, he occasional made an exception for them and performed concerts in their large entrance hall on the condition it was done behind a kelp screen. He felt it was the least he could do for his fans.

And of course, he trusted Findol, and didn't mind performing in front of him, especially when he wanted to try out his new material.

Right then, Stradi remembered he had a gig planned. He said goodbye and tottered off, leaving Findol to return, once more, to his thoughts about his friends and family, the threat of Grampus, and the Hint-at Net that would trawl in any news and information of his movements.

Findol decided there was no time to waste and he wanted to "start the Finball rolling". He proceeded to leave his cave, stroking the illuminant urchin on his way out, its light gradually fading like a marine dimmer switch. As he left the cave, head full of his thoughts, he unexpectedly came face to face with Flaytus who was frantically scribing in shortclaw on some Kriblington Bond parchment.

'Hi Mr Gurning, what are you doing here?'

'Ah, bejaybers! Call me Flaytus, would yer? You know, I was jus' thinkin' I must write a shopping list. I've got … err … relations comin' fer tea. Would yer believe it? I don't know … jus' when the old pantry's empty at that!'

He flashed a cheesy grin that made him look uncomfortably manic and more than a little mad.

'Well, I have to say you are a bit of a dark seahorse,' said Findol. 'I didn't think you had any family or friends. I was told you just sort of appeared around here one day with no memory of anybody else!'

'And that's very true so it is. Yeh would be right in saying that. But memories do return and there is somethin' I forgot to mention … Yeh see, I was adapted. That's right. Adapted.'

'I think you mean adopted,' interrupted Findol.

'That's what I said … please don't be interruptin' now. This is hard fer me to say.'

'It's not easy for me to understand either,' Findol added cockily.

'Yer see, there were this pair of hermit crabs who had never had any of the blessed Criblets fer their own. So yeh see, they became me beloved ma and pa — in a matter o' speaking.'

Flaytus was obviously floundering, but Findol couldn't think why. It just seemed a rather odd conversation to be having.

'Oh, right. Ok, well, sorry Flaytus! I really didn't know and obviously I am very pleased for you. Have a nice evening; I guess you are preparing some food for them then?'

'Oi most certainly am. A traditional meal. At least I'm thinkin' it is … Eye-rich Stew. It's made from de … '

'It's okay, Flaytus. Whitloe has already mentioned it to me in passing and I am not sure I want to know the details. You enjoy your evening. Bye.'

If it was possible to sweat in water, then that's just what Flaytus did.

Bejaybers! I don't know how much longer I can be lyin' like this, all fer the sake of a book that the young'un cannot be knowing about! thought Flaytus. *Still, an inspired bit of fiction on my part, I think. Just hope he didn't see the old crossing-the-pincers-behind-me-back trick.*

Findol continued on his way, but at the back of his mind he couldn't help but think: *I thought Flaytus said he was once a lepreecorn, or something like that! What was all that about being adopted? It doesn't make any sense!*

He spent the afternoon flitting here, there and everywhere around the Lantica Rim to various pod groups and individuals telling them all the same story about Grampus, Kreegan and his Hint-at Net and asking them not to mention anything to his family just yet. Spangul and Blint were all for it. They found it quite exciting until

Findol reminded them of the danger and the reality of the situation. Pascal and Filbut felt that he should inform his pod immediately, but Findol reminded them that maybe nothing would happen for ages and he could be grounded all that time for nothing if his family knew. He promised to inform them the minute anything suspicious was noted. Felspar and Krystul swam off almost immediately to carry the word far and wide.

During the afternoon, everyone Findol met was very keen to help. After all, it was in all their interests too. Grampus might have his sights and plans directed at Findol, but Kreegan, Hamrag and whoever else would certainly have their own plans too. Bladda Rak the giant octopus; Conen the Cob, the hammerhead shark; and Poison Ivy the Man o' War jellyfish were just three evil individuals from past encounters that drew fear from all concerned.

It was agreed that the Sea-Pony Express was the obvious choice for speedy passage of any vitally important information. Findol spoke with Lippizana Stirrups, Pinkerton Gallup and Piebald Fetlock and all three agreed to pass the word around to their colleagues and particularly those stationed along the Lantica Rim and beyond. He arranged to meet up with them in a week's time to see how things were progressing. Eventually, late that afternoon, Findol wearily reached his home.

'Hi all,' he said as he passed through the entrance. His mother had been busy making some squidling patties, using some little squids rolled in mulligatawny weed leaves. They were delicious, hot and spicy. His brothers and sisters were busy playing "tag-tail" with a ring of bound kelp, the object of the game being to place the ring over another's tail fin. There was much frantic activity with shouting and occasionally things would get knocked over, at which point their mother would intervene:

'For goodness sake, can't you play outside instead of making all this noise and disturbance in here? Now look what's happened! Someone's crushed a Scavit! Who did it? Come on? Fine! Well, if no one can answer, the ring goes away!'

Despina swam over, snatched the ring, and placed it where she was working.

'Don't mind our Clark, will you?' snapped one of the Scavits who was busily dragging the victim safely back under the dining clam.

'Out now, all of you. Go on! No, no, not you, Findol. You have hardly done anything wrong, have you?'

Other than be economical with the truth, Findol thought to himself, guiltily.

'Had a good day, love?' his mother said to him as Findol nuzzled up close against her.

'Yes thanks, Mum. Fine. I bumped into Flaytus again today. You know, he always seems to be around wherever I am, these days. It's a bit weird isn't it? I thought he was supposed to be busy working on some epic story or something!'

'Oh, I don't know about such things!' she nervously chuckled. 'He is a funny one, though, isn't he?' She looked a little flustered. Changing the subject she added, 'He never seems comfortable with that big shell of his, does he? It's like a real burden that doesn't belong to him. What with his muttering complaints and wittering on about strange things we have never heard of. I mean, what exactly is a four-and-a-half-leaf clover?'

'I don't know! Sounds like something Whitloe would be keen to eat, though!' Findol added helpfully. 'He did say it was something guaranteed to bring him luck. I guess we could all use one, eh Mum?'

'Yes, we certainly could. And as for his pots of gold hidden under trees! I mean just what is *that* all about?'

'I really have no idea, Mum'.

There was a long pause before Findol continued.

'So anyway, why is Flaytus so secretive about his latest book? He was really weird today. Even more than usual. Going on about shopping lists. But surely he wouldn't use his expensive Kriblington Bond parchment for it, would he?'

'Yes, that is odd. I have seen how fussy he is about wasting the stuff,' she added hurriedly. 'Anyway, come on. Findol, can you help sort out the mess and get everyone back in? We've got to get our tea under our fins so we can get ready for tonight. Your special night, darling!'

He beamed back at her and then he went outside.

Findol munched through his tea, deep in thought. He was thinking about the coming evening's trip out to Sea-Czar's Palace. Wow! He had passed by the entrance a hundred times or more, though not in the evening when the place really came alive, and he was certainly never allowed *inside*. His tummy squeaked with excitement at the thought. The reputation of the finest food, drinks and entertainment swam dreamily in his mind, and thoughts of Grampus and the others had faded for the moment into the distance. Tonight was going to be his special night and nothing was going to spoil that!

***

Many thousands of miles away, somewhere in the northern oceans, a huge pack of barracuda were nudging a shaking individual forward.

The captive dared not raise his head to look directly at the hideous face before him. Cowering, he spoke of what he knew. The monster replied slowly with malevolence etched on every word.

'So ... you are *sure* it was the bird known to this dolphin? ... And you know of this ... Guano Rock?'

The monster paused.

'TAKE ME THERE!' he hissed.

Chapter 4
Sea-Czar's Palace

Findol and his family approached the grand entrance of Sea-Czar's Palace feeling somewhat dwarfed by its size and reputation. Findol gazed at the spectacular columns hewn thousands of years ago from the old rock-base that would have formed part of the magical kingdom of Old Lantis. He had passed it by many times before and never really given it much of a thought. This time, though, he marvelled at the intricate detail and expertise that had gone into its creation. It had been constructed by the ancient Cetacean builders, using skills easily matching those of the Kriblings.

They all looked closely at the huge doorway with its images of mythological creatures of the Blue. The carvings were just stunning and looked so fresh and new, with vivid attention to detail. The Worm-infested Sea Troll looked as if its skin was actually *writhing*, while Osti (the bone-crushing octopus) had tentacles that projected menacingly outwards from the rock. On the carving of the Flatulent Flounder a little rock plug could be pushed to produce a black puff from the fish's rear.

There wasn't a hint of weed or algae anywhere on the whole structure since it had only recently received its regular makeover. It was looked after and maintained by the Kriblings, who carefully worked to keep the design looking as fresh as if it had just been carved. Special Masonlings would make regular trips to the palace and spend many weeks working hard on both the carvings (and their rather peculiar handshakes). It had only been a few days prior, when the last annual service had been completed by two of the finest Kribling Masonlings, and the Palace exterior simply gleamed.

Findol and his family paused at the front entrance. Lights of different colours blinked and pulsed enticingly, bleeding from between cracks in the doorway, and muffled music could be heard, teasing their senses in the distance. Suddenly, the huge doors were thrown open. Music and bright light came blaring out in equal measure. The pod quickly moved to one side as a large grouper turfed out a group of small fish that were mouthing off at him in a barrage of shocking insults.

'You lot are barred and that's final! If you don't like it, I suggest you take it up with Mr Garibaldi.'

Findol and his family regarded the commotion in alarm, sharing anxious sideways glances.

'It's okay,' Findol piped up in a loud whisper. 'I've heard about this happening when it's a Friday night. There are always a few idiots around ... School's over for another weekend and that's when the troublemakers are out,' then hurriedly, he added: 'We-e-e-ll ... so I'm told anyway. Spotjaw Blenny and his gang are well known for doing just that!'

'How do you know all this?' Despina asked, looking quizzingly back at him.

'Aw, come on, you know me. I pick up on all the news, Mum! Besides, I did have a bit of a run-in with Spotjaw a few months ago. He'd captured a small group of flatfish and was trying to make a Skateboard out of them. I didn't think it was fair, so I persuaded him to let them go. Food is one thing, but playing with it is an entirely different kettle of fish. He wasn't happy about it, mind. He might think he's sharp, but he isn't so clever. He surrounds himself with so-called mates, but they are just sucker-fish if you ask me; he's never going to win MY respect.'

Spotjaw recognised Findol as he passed by, and hissed at him. Findol immediately jerked forward threateningly and in doing so, Spotjaw instinctively backed up, straight into a sleeping octopus. The startled cephalopod reacted by attaching itself in defence around Spotjaw's head, its tentacles hanging down like slimy dreadlocks and an inky cloud darkening the fish's looks.

'Nice Bob Marlin impression, Spotty!' said Findol, laughing out loud.

Spotjaw turned purple with rage. His eyes watered from both the stinging ink and his hurt pride as Despina beckoned Findol towards her.

'That will do,' she quietly whispered. 'Come on. Stop causing trouble. I really don't know what it is going on between you two, but let it go for now. Don't spoil the night, okay? Now … let's go in!'

'Sorry, Mum,' Findol said as they moved forward, but he still couldn't help smirking as he looked back at Spotjaw.

Above the Palace entrance he saw a painting of a group of dancing crabs with arms and legs jutting out in angular poses that spelled out the word WELCOME. Passing through the doorway, he found himself in a corridor just before the reception area. The walls were adorned with lots of sketches by Lanky Wicks, portraying a great many likenesses of previous artists that had performed there. Findol recognised some of them, as he loved his music and kept up with all the latest artistes. He spotted Salmon Dave and Flatfish Sam, and Marlinion (with their enigmatic lead singer, Hagarth). In the row above he saw Hake That with Gary Barnacle in the front — although the view was mostly obscured by a small group of girl groupies who were clamouring hysterically around the picture making wet smooching noises. Findol sniggered as they passed them.

As he reached the foyer, his heart beat faster with anticipation, though he relaxed a little when he spotted Lippizana, Pinkerton and Piebald "working" at the door.

'Oh. Hi Findol! Hello Mrs Lantica!'

Despina she smiled politely back.

Findol, meanwhile, sidled up to them. 'Hi Lippie! Err … what are you doing here?' he whispered. 'What were we talking about earlier? Remember? The … Hint-at Net!'

The sea-horse looked blankly at him, then smiled in a wave of realisation. 'Don't worry! It's all taken care of, honest! Obbi-Oss, Trigga, Shadowtax and some of their stable mates are doing a sweeping circuit of the Rim. It should only take them a couple of days, although more likely it will take weeks at the rate they move. Apparently Trigga's wife wasn't too happy about him going though. He was supposed to be staying at home looking after the brood and there were a couple of hundred of the nippers at the last count. I guess he's not in too much of a hurry to get back!' The others giggled as they listened in.

'Don't worry though, they will soon change gear and will certainly hurry if they have to … no problem. We will start doing our bit in a few days and meet up with you as arranged, okay?'

'All right, that's great. Thanks. Just don't forget the importance of all this, okay? So … why are you here working on the door?'

'Well isn't it obvious? We have all got to earn a crust as my Uncle Ovis would say.'

By now the rest of Findol's family felt they had waited for long enough and were now growing impatient.

'Come on, Findol! We want to get in before we miss anything!'

'Sorry guys, just one more minute!' He looked back at Lippizana. 'Okay then, Lippie. Just don't forget our plans! Look, I've gotta go in, all right? See you later!'

Findol rejoined his family, who, he noticed, all wore the same impatient expression. He flashed them a smile. 'Oh, come on. Lighten up. It's party time!'

Despina swam up to the pay-desk — a small hatchway into a little cave where a rather miserable-looking fish called Remora was working. She was bent over, de-scaling her tail with a fin-file and applying some lip gloss to her already-garish features. Despina coughed politely as she offered her fin, clutching some Lantica Credits, tiny Mother of Pearl discs used as currency in the Big Blue.

'Oh! I am sorry … It's Mrs Lantica and family isn't it? Good Evening! Mr Garibaldi sends his kindest regards and wishes for it to be known that your evening is "on the house" as we say.' She stamped some leather kelp tickets with an Embossington clam that sighed with boredom, and handed them over.

Despina was totally taken aback and rather confused. 'Free entrance. Why? Please, *erm*, yes please thank Mr Garibaldi most sincerely for me, would you?'

'I can, but I am sure you will find him inside and be able to thank him yourself!'

'Okay, well then… thank you,'

Despina ushered them all forward, slightly embarrassed and wondering just who this Mr Garibaldi was and why they were getting in for free. They pushed through the Carapace doors into the brightly lit hallway and realised that the light and sound had even managed to penetrate this extra corridor as well. The walls were studded with spectacular sparkleton jewels, arranged in coloured patterns that spelled out:

Sea-Czar's Palace:

THE plaice for sole music!

Jou-Jou jewels and giant illuminant clams were attached to the ceiling, creating dazzling, swirling bands of colour. The light swept around the narrow passageway floored with red-dyed kelp matting that further increased the appearance of lavish wealth.

And this is before we even get inside, thought Findol.

As they approached the main theatre doors, Findol took a wattling bead from one of the many mermaid's purses hanging from the wall. He took a deep breath as the doors opened.

Smiling John Dories gushed compliments and pleasantries at everyone that entered. 'You are looking stunning tonight, madam, please have a wonderful evening. Ah, young sir is quite the "Head of the Pod", isn't he?'

Findol wasn't particularly sure that he liked their forced smile and polite yet condescending manner, but he supposed they were just doing their job. As the family passed beyond the doors and into the cavernous theatre, there was an immediate and spectacular assault on their senses. The corridors and foyer had been impressive enough, but this was simply incredible. None of them could have imagined that so much light could have been created to fill such a huge theatre.

Above the massive arena, and running its entire perimeter, was a ledge from which extended many large stumpy tubes supported on giant periwinkle plinths. Strategically placed at regular intervals along the ledge, each of these *Super Grouper Illuminants* projected a swollen column of light onto the stage. They were controlled by rather bored-looking Giant Spider Crabs, who busily adjusted the roll, pitch and yaw of the illuminants and occasionally changed the coloured "pastelweed" cells at appropriate moments.

In-between controlling the lighting the crabs were forever pointing out members of the audience to each other. They shared rude remarks by the use of complicated sign language and gestures involving gyrating spare limbs and unusual twitches of their rear ends. Findol thought he would have loved to have known what they were saying and laughing about. One of them, as he was cackling, lost control of his tube, which spun around and cracked his neighbour on the head. There was a brief argument between the two before they resumed their work.

Findol's attention was soon absorbed with everything else going on around him, filling his senses. He could tell that the rest of his family felt the same way.

Splinter and Wippit were gawping in all directions, open mouthed. 'Mum … it's simply wonderful! It's like a dream!'

Despina could barely hear them above the music, but then she didn't need to. The joy in their faces was easy to read and she just knew what they were thinking and saying.

She spotted a large and very fat bloater making its way over to them. He was dressed in a black "Silks of Mayfly" Tuxedo with a red-dyed spongiform cummerbund wrapped tightly around his rather ample middle. Thick black bristles above his top lip were twisted together on either side and curled at the tips. A trace of sea-garlic emerged as he opened his large mouth,

'Misseeeezz Larntica! Eet is indeed a pleasure to be in the presence of one so bee-oot-iful! I wonder … might I be so bold?'

He kissed her fin delicately, an aroma of expensive Calvin Slime surrounding him. Findol and the others stared, exchanged amused glances, and tried hard not to snigger. They scrunched up their noses at the smell; the garlic had been bad enough.

'I am Hercules Garibaldi. You are my very welcome guests.' He pressed his face up close to Despina's. 'I am indebted to your late husband so please eat and drink all that you can! You are all most gracefully received and very welcome!'

'Thank you, Mr Garibaldi! You are too kind!' Despina said as she pulled back from him a little.

'Tish! Tish! It is myself zat is honoured by your very presence 'ere! I will be looking after you and making sure your evening is perrrrrfect!'

Despina was more than a little embarrassed again as her cheeks flushed at the attention he was giving them with his loud booming voice. She could see that all around heads were turning, and the music suddenly seemed to disappear in the background. Finally, their host continued on his way and was soon lost in the crowd, his cheesy grin and overwhelming aroma a slightly disturbing memory!

A large Damselfish usherette appeared nearby and escorted them all to suitable seats with a waiting dining-clam, complete with a large, brightly-coloured lattice-weed parasol. They felt like royalty! Clamberry Draughts were regularly placed on their table whenever one was emptied. Findol and the others found it fun to keep drinking them to see how quick an empty clam would be replaced. They soon got fed up though when they had to keep going to the toilet. Besides, their mum had told them to stop being silly and Findol didn't want to appear childish. Splinter was also looking a little green and feeling decidedly sick.

Findol embraced his love of music. He had Stradi to thank for that, but he had never been to any sort of theatre to hear some really up close and "live". He sat, rooted to the spot, listening to the group that were playing their hearts out on the main stage. It was Celia Canth and the Rock Lobsters and they were currently in the middle of their set. They had a really good groove going and the audience were either swaying or slapping fins to the beat. Wellard Steelclaw, a large soldier crab, sat at far side of the theatre, cracking his claws so vigorously on his table that it collapsed and landed on the tentacles of an unfortunate octopus lying underneath. She squealed in pain and was swiftly attended to by a pair of young nurse sharks.

Findol recognised the kettlefish drums and the harmonious trumpetfish, but many of the band's other instruments he had neither seen nor heard of before. Deepbass conchaphones belched out sounds so deep and low they rattled his insides, tickling his tummy. Then there were the "Lurchin' Urchin" maracas and the cuttlefish bells. But above all, Findol's favourite instruments had to be the Kribgut-stringed guitars. They produced the loud rhythmic sounds that he loved. Findol had repeatedly begged his mum for a guitar. She had said he could have one when he was older and able to stay in one place long enough to learn how to play it.

Meanwhile, back on stage, Celia was coming to the end of her set. Findol started joining in, smiling to himself as he thought about Spotjaw outside.

'I wonder if he's removed his octopus wig!' he smiled to himself.

Swaying excitedly to the music, Findol admired all the fantastic details on the stage. He could see that it was inlaid with Mother of Pearl, so that its overall appearance was of a large, white, glistening deck, swathed in curtains of light from the various illuminants trained upon it. The illuminants sent spectacular flashes of colours washing onto the stunning floor as their crab controllers hurriedly swapped and changed the coloured cells.

The edge of the stage was decorated with hundreds of Textile Cones and Zebra Winkles that gave it a stunning border. Bleached Kriblington Kelp Calico Curtains hung down each side in dramatic fashion like giant columns. Narrow lines of glinting sequin-adorned starfish moved up and down each them on both sides, and each curtain opened with intricate patterns every time they were drawn. Two thick golden sea-snakes waited nearby on "tie-back" duty. They both smirked to each other whenever they got a bit of attention from a stray beam of light.

As the band wound down, Findol's stomach started to rumble, roused no doubt by the aroma of all manner of exotic dishes being prepared in the palace kitchens. Concealed doors suddenly swung open and large whiting waiters carried the food orders to the tables. The rich smells wafted over to him and he suddenly felt very hungry indeed. Findol noticed the small Box Crabs known as Wotlin Wollas dragging shells laden with wattling beads for those that needed them.

They think of everything here, he thought, then he realised that they would probably have to if they wanted everyone to stay put. *Catering for the customer's every need*, he thought.

Suddenly the main lights dimmed and the audience fell silent (apart from the hushed hubbub of whispered chit-chat). Findol heard two of the Wotlin Wollas muttering about corns on their claws and chafed knee joints, and something about "working conditions". Then the illuminant groupers powered up their tubes, the curtains opened, and the applause returned.

Findol looked and saw that the host of the show, Barnacle Groans, had shuffled back on stage. He was a giant grouper who looked so incredibly miserable that he made other groupers look positively radiant and glowing with personality. But of course it was just part of his act and he soon launched into his well-rehearsed routine.

Findol started to get a little bored with the adult humour. He decided to while away time by counting the fin-lice crawling over the back of a large and rather old female dolphin just in front. He watched, fascinated, as a couple of them fell off into a clamberry tart her husband was just starting to eat. Findol tried hard not to laugh and draw attention to himself. He virtually exploded when the old dolphin remarked to his wife how nice the tarts were, especially the "crunchy topping"!

Barnacle finished his routine and introduced the next act with a smug "humble-me" expression on his face. From there, the evening progressed nicely with Barnacle fairly bouncing on stage between acts to joke with the audience before welcoming the next act onto the stage.

Findol was looking around taking everything in, when he spotted Flaytus Gurning arrive over at the entrance. Flaytus had burst through the doorway loudly humming one of his traditional Irish tunes to himself. His arms and legs moved erratically in an attempt at rhythm, and his large shell scraped through the doorway and rattled along on the tiled floor.

'Ooops! Sorry feh the intrusion! Bejaybers! T'is loud in here t'be sure!'

Now Flaytus was a nervous individual at the best of times, but it only took a few stern faces and vitriolic curses to put him totally off his stride. He always blamed it on his past, saying, 'Can yer be blaming me now? One minute I'm thinking about de best compost fer me shamrocks and me prize Flatulentis Horribilis,' (the Cursed Trump Weed) 'and the next I is suddenly gasping fer breath and dragging this thing round wi'me', he gestured behind him at the offending shell. 'T'is no wonder I'm needing therapy or something!'

As he entered the cave, everything happened that shouldn't have. He stood on a Screaming Clam that someone with a wicked sense of humour had left in just the right place for an unsuspecting victim. It did exactly what its name suggested. Despite its tiny size, it produced a horrendous, conch-piercing screech. All faces turned as one in Flaytus's direction whilst anyone nearby covered their ears with their fins. A few small Grumpulfish that were nearest, moaned about permanently damaged lateral lines and threatened him with legal action.

However, the upshot of all the fuss led to the music droning to a halt. The current act stopped singing in mid-verse and stared with affectation, fins folded across his chest, whilst all eyes and attention were focussed on the culprit. Even a blushing bryde anemone was outshone as Flaytus's poor cheeks burned a deep crimson red. Angry faces further increased the heat within him. To make matters worse, Barnacle Groans leapt on stage and started to hurl abuse.

'Oi Flotsam! Sling your shell will you? Never in me entire career (which is considerable) have I had the misfortune of addressing a clumsier "shell dragger" this side of the Rim than you! You big carapace-crunching carbuncle of Karn.' The audience loved it.

'Ooh, he has such a way with words!' gushed one of his aged fans, whilst poor Flaytus desperately wanted to hide in his shell. It suddenly felt rather small, but he knew there was no point in seeking refuge. The singer, meanwhile, had kept quiet and composed throughout it all. He was staring ahead and maintaining a poise with his fins outstretched, pointing upwards. He turned and tapped Barnacle on the shoulder.

'I am sure he meant no harm,' he smouldered, curling his top lip to the side. The crowd (at least all the *females* in the crowd) suddenly went wild with excitement as he swung his rear-end towards them. A bass drum struck once for effect and he returned to his poise, pointing just above the audience.

Flaytus backtracked, firing frantic apologies to all and sundry in his desperate retreat. Unfortunately his claws got tangled in the tall Kelpington Velour blinds that lined the doorway. His ever-present cargo of quills and parchment spilled out of his grasp and went scattering in all directions. Poor Flaytus! Even Neddy Conkins had never had it this bad! Eventually the audience settled down.

'D'y'all want me to start again?' the singer leered as he snaked his body in a rhythmic, thrusting manner that — as earlier — generated hysteria in the female members of the audience. Screams of delight filled the arena as the band, on cue, launched straight back into the song.

Once the attention was off him, Flaytus relaxed a little and quietly started to hum nervously to himself.

'*Blue moon of Killarney … keep on shining …*' he sang, as he went about retrieving his possessions. Poor Flaytus had spent most of the evening so far in semi-darkness, scurrying about, under and between seats. He apologised profusely as his shell battered into everyone nearby, while he gradually collected up his dropped belongings.

'A thousand apologies, sir and madam. Pardon me terrible clumsiness — it's de curse of the wilting shamrock, so it is!'

A cloud of bubbles emerged from his rear, complimenting a drum-roll from the stage. Finally, having retrieved everything, he went about his business, leaving sometime before the finale.

Findol laughed as a wave of screaming females rushed the stage in an effort to get as close to the charismatic performers as possible. The performers themselves quickly finished their act and beat a hasty retreat behind the curtain. Barnacle re-emerged, and stated as dramatically as possible: 'Elmer … has left … the building!'

There were laughs and cheers from the males and tears of frustration from their partners.

Findol was really enjoying the evening, especially as he had not expected to see Hake That. Ali Tosis the juggling octopus was up next. The highlight of his act was juggling twenty-four sea-urchins at the same time. Blindfolded, he whipped them in and out of each tentacle. Part of the act was getting a reluctant volunteer to tie the blindfold, not that blindfold tying was particularly difficult or dangerous. The reluctance was due to them putting themselves in the vicinity of Ali's exceedingly bad breath.

As Ali started juggling, one of the sea-urchins started thinking to itself: *Oh no, here we go again! I hate this motion-sickness!*

As if with perfect timing, the urchin proceeded to empty its stomach, just when it was circling Ali's head. There were a few disgusted gasps from the front row, but most of the audience didn't realise what had happened. They just thought it was a spectacular part of the act and Ali had carried on undeterred like a true professional.

After Ali left the stage, Winnie Bago and Jim Karna, the Stunt Sea-Horses, put on a dazzling display of speed and agility. They raced around the edge of the stage, pulling their Nautilean Shell chariots behind them, just missing each other in a brilliantly-timed display of skill and bravery, whilst Epee and Parry the swordfish twins fought a precision dual in a dazzling show of skilful swordsmanship. The audience gasped and whooped with joy in all the right places and Findol was mesmerised by the whole spectacle.

There was so much more to see and do, so that by the end of the evening, none were more exhausted than Findol. He had protested, though his eyes were drooping, that he wasn't sleepy and didn't want to go. Eventually, Despina had to virtually drag him away, together with the others, with promises that they would go there again some other night. They wearily made their way home, heads full of all the sights and sounds that they had witnessed that evening.

Findol, for a time, was free of all thoughts of his nemesis, Grampus, and the dread that name conveyed.

Chapter 5
The Hint-at Net

The following day, Findol awoke bright and early, feeling refreshed and full of fun. He raced down to the dining clam before his mother had even called breakfast. The night out had been just what he needed to bring him out of his recent moodiness and regain his spark. Still buzzing, he laughed to himself when he thought about some of the evening's amusing incidents. It had certainly been a night never to be forgotten, for all concerned.

Despina, too, had loved the show, and also the late night journey home. She had loved watching Findol with his brothers and sisters trying to remember and sing some of the songs out loud — often getting the lyrics wrong. They had fought with tiredness, but refused to give in to it when there was still time for fun, but finally they dragged themselves wearily to bed when they got through the cave doorway.

After a hurried breakfast, Findol wasted no time in going outside with his siblings. The others were fooling around pretending they were performing on stage. It was whilst they were doing this that Splinter, swimming backwards, hit a pillar with a large Pandora clam placed on top of it. Unfortunately it toppled and fell backwards straight down onto Whitloe Spook's head. The clam opened and two amoeboid appendages shot out and slapped Whitloe about the nose. The tentacles returned into their shell as quickly as they had appeared, before it dramatically snapped shut.

'Well that's typical, that is. That's just the sort of thing I expected to happen today,' Whitloe sighed, her nose smarting and glowing painfully. 'When I woke up this morning, I just knew it was going to be one of them days!'

Findol swam over. 'Sorry, Whitloe,' he said. 'They were just having a bit of fun. They got a bit carried away I think!'

'That's all right, I suppose. After all, I'm used to pain and suffering. It's what my life is all about these days. Pain from my back and my sinuses and my head at the moment. Then there's me teeth and worse … but do you know the hardest thing to bear?'

Findol sighed quietly to himself beginning to wish he was elsewhere, as she continued.

'It's the pain of not being able to run about in a field of long, lush, delicious graaass.'

Findol had heard it all before on numerous occasions and had to stifle a yawn. 'Yes, we know, Whitloe! We are sorry for you, really!'

Whitloe sloped off — grazing, as she muttered to herself. 'You don't really know. You've got no idea. Oh the pain! The pain!'

Findol watched her slowly disappear and then returned to his brothers and sisters where he indulged them, playing Tag-Tail, Finball and Shelly Knocking. The latter involved sneaking up on an unsuspecting crab and tapping it hard on its shell with a pebble. The trick was in swimming away quickly enough from the rather agitated and surprised crustacean without being spotted — or worse, nipped.

At last, worn out after hours of frantic play they slowly swam back home. Along the way they exchanged comical banter and shouted goodbyes to some of their friends from the Lantica Rim who had joined in the fun. Findol paused to snack on a few small squid, but was suddenly aware of movement at the corner of his eye. Something had just disappeared behind a group of rocks on his left, he was sure of it! He cautiously approached and then stopped as a few small streams of bubbles snaked their way in racing ribbons to the surface from behind the rocks. He caught sight of a pair of eyes blinking nervously as he got closer.

I'm sure I recognise …

Then he remembered his friends. 'Hey you lot, wait for me!' he shouted and raced after them.

Flaytus breathed a sigh of relief, gulped and carried on scribbling his notes for the day.

Phwoar! That wuz a close un, he thought.

Near home, Findol caught sight of an old friend — Flash Scaling. Flash was a cleaner wrasse who specialised in giant sea bass.

'They are the best source of edible delights for the discerning detritus muncher,' Flash would say. He had travelled with a large shoal for some time now and Findol had often encountered him during foraging trips, when he was eating out. Flash was rather prized and much admired amongst the bass community. He not only kept their mouths ultra-clean and free from parasites and waste, but he also carried a good tune whilst he cleaned them up!

'Hi Flash, how is it going?' Findol shouted excitedly. He hadn't seen him for ages and this meeting could not have been better timed. The wrasse looked over at him, but carried on swimming.

'Hold on a minute!' Findol shouted after him, and he had to swim at quite a pace just to keep up with the shoal, whose ever-changing direction was a little distracting when one was trying to have a serious conversation. To be fair, Findol's presence had made them all extremely nervous.

'Findol, you rascal, I haven't seen you since our encounter with Brutus Sludge last year. D'ya remember,' sniggered Flash.

Oh! Yes, I'd forgotten. Was it that long ago?' Findol chuckled. 'Even for a moray he was horrible, wasn't he?'

'Yeah … still we got the better of him, didn't we? Or rather YOU did.'

'True. Still let's not worry about that right now, eh? I need to ask you about something. What are you up to at the moment? …WHOAAH!'

Findol narrowly avoided colliding with a large red sponge as the shoal unexpectedly veered to the left and straight under an overhang. The sponge lurched to one side in the swell before resuming its position. Unfortunately it evicted a family of disgruntled whelks in the process.

Flash beamed as followed the shoal this way and that, matching their movements perfectly. 'Findol I'm quite excited! I think we are migrating up north, but I am not entirely sure. You know this lot, they are very fickle. They just go with the plankton flow, as they say. One minute we are on our way to the frozen north, then suddenly it's the warm Med — plays havoc with my metabolism, I can tell you. All this hot and cold water; it's a wonder I don't catch a chill or something.'

'Don't you mean a Krill?' Findol jokingly added.

'Oi … watch it. Do you think I'm a whale or something?' chuckled Flash.

'No … I'm just joking! Look Flash, speaking of whales, I need to ask you a really BIG favour and it is incredibly important. In fact, you could even say it's a matter of life and death and that's really no exaggeration!'

'Oh my gosh! Findol, are you for real? That sounds serious. What is it?'

'Well, look, you know all the times we have talked about Grampus? Remember, we have sort of joked about the what-ifs, if he ever returned.'

'As a bit of fun, yes. Why?'

'Well, if you haven't guessed yet, there is some really bad news … and I mean BAD news. It actually looks like he has returned, full of revenge and hate. I can only guess at a lot of it, but based on what little I know, I am sure he will be looking for Kreegan, Hamrag and goodness only knows who else. He is building an army, I am sure of it.

'Apparently, he was spotted far north a short while ago, but we cannot be sure where he is now. Basically, I really need you to get a message back to me if you get any news or signs or of him. Especially if he's on the move — okay?'

Flash looked very serious as he considered the news. 'Gosh! Yes! Of course! Now that you mention it that does kind of explain things. We haven't seen many, if any, barracuda or sharks around for quite a while now and they're normally never far from us. If he really is getting an army together, then you can bet *they* will be involved. But yes, of course — anything! But why are you involved in all this? He's never really got involved with your kind of Cetaceans before, has he?'

'Oh don't you believe it! He's had his moments with porpoises and the like. Remember the slaughter at the Bay of Shoals from our history lessons? I thought you knew about that, Flash — or have you forgotten already? My father chased him through the Portal in Kelpathia. It now seems that I am somehow implicated in his return. I think his belief is that I'm in the way of his Masterplan or he just has a serious revenge thing going on. Either way I've got to come up with a solution and I tell you something Flash, between you and me … I am scared! You know, *really* scared!

'We all have our bad dreams that we wake up from, shaking with terror, but dreams are really all they are, and we can usually see reason and shake the fear away. My bad dream has been made real and will not go away by itself. I know that I am supposed to be some kind of special hero. Can you believe it? Me? But I sure don't feel like it and I haven't got a clue what I am supposed to do and that's what scares me. Everyone seems to have these great expectations of me. They think I am going to sort it all out. ME! Just think about all the demons and monsters in my mind that are now made real. I'm going to need all the help I can get to outwit them.'

'Sorry, Findol, I feel like a right Blenny now. I didn't realise this was all so serious, or that you had so much on your mind. Look, if it helps, I can promise that if I get the slightest rumour of anything that you need to know, I WILL get word to you. I will not rest for a minute. I will be on constant lookout for any clues or signs, trust me. Better still, I'll take along some Sea-Pony Express friends of mine to get any urgent news quickly back to you.'

Findol told him about his Early Warning Plan with all his friends on alert and said his help would be really appreciated. Flash nodded back.

'Try not to worry, Findol, I will do all I can. Take care and stay lucky!'

'You too, Flash.' Findol watched as the thousands of fish, together with his friend rapidly receded into the distance. A few nervous individuals glanced back at him just to check his movements and reassure themselves he wasn't tempted to take a quick snack.

Findol watched the giant fish-ball lurching this way and that as it weaved its way into the Blue. Much as he liked Flash, he was not sure that he really wanted to get any news from him. After all, it would almost certainly be something he didn't want to know, and would surely spell trouble for him. It was a crazy situation to be in, he thought. At least he felt confident in his plan, now that he had Tegan and Flash up north, and his dolphin friends covering the far eastern and western boundaries beyond the Lantica Rim.

Piebald, Pinkerton and Lippizana were carrying out their own plans in order to help him, and he had sent a message to Leesa the Seal, who he had befriended by chance the previous summer, way down south. She would spread the word to her friends Tusker the Walrus and Adelie the Penguin. They would put their respective colonies on alert and watch his back too, he knew it!

Findol (for the moment at least) appeared to have all areas covered and he now felt a little more content and prepared, thanks to his Hint-at Net. It was as complete as he could hope for and all he could now do was hope it would do its job. With the system safely in place, it was now a matter of waiting and preparing as best he could for the unexpected. All that, whilst trying to live his life as normally as possible. He thought it all through once more until he was completely satisfied.

Just as everything seemed sorted, and Findol was about ready to go home, a sudden overwhelming feeling of a presence came over him. It came from nowhere and literally took his breath away. He span around, looking this way and that, but saw nothing. It was as if he could feel a large flipper brushing on his side and then a gentle voice that could only have been Cora's, whispered quietly in his head.

(That's my little prince … you are nearly ready!)

Findol's throat tingled and itched. He swallowed several times until the feeling went away. Then he slowly made his way home.

Chapter 6
Turns for the Worse

The lazy summer days soon passed into weeks with very little of great matter occurring. The Hint-at Net seemed to be working just fine, and life in the Blue progressed with little incident. Apart from the strange, almost complete absence of predators, everything in the Big Blue seemed normal with everyone getting on with their lives.

Findol met with Lippizana, Piebald and Pinkerton regularly, but the only reports they made were that there was nothing unusual to report. There was no sign of the "big three", and the few whales and sharks that had remained seemed to be keeping to their own. There was, however, a curious development as they started to notice unusually large groups of electric eels passing through. It was blamed on an exceptionally powerful migration instinct; an excuse they used for getting together to discuss any current affairs.

Findol's world turned in its own slow way; each day an adventure (more often than not with Sterbol along for the ride) and that was just how he liked it. His cave continued to fill up with yet more wondrous things — cutlery, crockery and a large reel with a strange metallic cord wrapped tightly around.

Stranger still, was an orange barrel-shaped object that had L I F E R A F T printed on the side in large black letters. Despite scanning it with his echo, Findol couldn't work out its function, which he found frustrating. There was also a toggle dangling enticingly at its base that he really felt warranted exploring further, but something inside told him to leave it well alone! His intuition had often helped in the past and so he trusted it. He put the object in a corner and it remained there to be subjected to further investigation at a later date.

At the far end of the cave there was a lobster basket that Wichita had made into a little den. He had stuck material on the inside to create his own "cave within a cave". There was also a collection of plastic buoys of all colours and sizes that scuttled about as they moved in the current, trapped against the caves ceiling. It had been quite a feat transporting them back to the cave; he lost count of the number of times he had let one slip and was forced to race up after it. Now they were safely located inside, he had attached small illuminant clam clusters to the ropes that dangled from their buoyant orange heads. The strings of lights snaked and bobbed around as the additional weight caused each buoy to dip slowly and then return to the ceiling. It had been tricky to get the number of clams just right to create the desired effect, but, now complete, it looked great. It was his way of reminding himself of his favourite time of year when they would be visited by Sandy Claws. He was the famous enigmatic Red Lobster who brought all good sea-dwelling creatures presents.

For Findol and his friends, life had passed slowly by with little incident apart from occasional mishaps resulting from the usual hazards encountered on a daily basis. Splinter, for example, got stung by a stonefish whilst rooting for clams. Panaseeya had used a Tentacle Poultice to quickly draw out the poison before it took hold. Wippit got a nasty shock from a very large group of electric eels that he had accidentally swum into. Luckily he got away before and serious lasting damage was done.

One day, Findol and Sterbol were returning from one of their last trips into the wrecking zone over on the Lantica Rim. Findol was just resigning himself to a poor day's exploring with nothing of interest, when suddenly he spotted, half-buried in the silt, a shiny brass disc with a glass top. He took hold and carefully pulled it out with his mouth.

As he studied it, he could see curious markings etched into the brass around the glass, and inside the glass was a flat needle that seemed to move slowly around whenever Findol moved the odd thing about. It stirred his curiosity and didn't take him long to figure that the needle inside somehow seemed to point in the same direction all the time, no matter which way Findol pointed the object. It definitely had to be a clue to its purpose. It was quite a weight though, but Findol was certainly taken with the idea that it would prove valuable and was determined to keep it.

When they returned to Kriblington City, Sterbol fetched a strong piece of kelp and attached both ends to the disc with some barnacle gum. Findol was able to put his head through the resulting loop and carry his find comfortably around his neck. Findol said goodbye with a big grin on his face, and started out for home, stopping by at his cave along the way.

Days like these are great, he thought. One *minute it's total disappointment, and then it's pure surprise with just a hint of joy!*

As he neared his cave, he rose sharply up and broke the sea's surface, enjoying the feeling of the spray dragging around his fins and the cool air on his face. It lifted his mood even more as he glanced at the horizon. The sun was sinking, snuggling down into its crimson blanket, its golden rays warming his skin as it began to slip out of view.

Diving back down to his cave, Findol brushed through the kelp curtain and gently deposited his most special of artefacts in a clear space on his sea chest, and then he lay down, staring at it, musing on its function. All of his fears had been put to the back of his mind as the safe routine of each day enticed him away from his concerns. He mistakenly began to forget about any approaching menace with hardly a thought at all for his destiny.

***

The game of the moment was Breaching Finball. Played like the basic game, the difference was that this was played at the sea's surface, specifically in the shallows around an island. Both teams were separated by the Enteric Lantica-Rim Wall (a thin partition of coral that extended up and out of the sea creating a ragged boundary that served as a net. It was perfectly suited to separating the two opposing teams.

Players were divided equally (usually with much bickering) and a small Nautilean Disc was the play-piece. It was actually a Nautilus shell filled with the finest sponge and sealed with gum to give it strength and buoyancy. The players were not allowed to grab and hold the disc for longer than six clicks (about three seconds). They then had to toss it to another player on their side or leap out of the water, hurling it over the Coral Line and into the opponents' playing area. It was very simple to play and very loud, thanks to the enthusiastic shouting and squeaking of the players. It was also very tiring and so called for frequent breaks (where opportunities for arguments often arose). There was, however, also an element of danger from getting too close to the unforgiving surface of the coral. The very nature of the frantic play would cause serious damage to even their tough skins if they made contact. Some of the best and bravest players sported suitable scars as if to prove the point.

Findol had a special move that he liked to use. It involved throwing the disc into the air whilst performing a forward roll and whacking it with his tail. He called it his "Scorpionfish Flick". Most of the others just used their fins, but Findol had perfected this little trick, much to everybody's amusement. When he got it right the others had no chance, since there was no way of anticipating where the disc would go.

The only other hazard was really more of an inconvenience than a danger. Seaweed was regularly swept in by the ever-moving ocean currents, resulting in it getting caught and tangled around the coral. This meant it was easy to get snagged up in it if they did not concentrate on where they were swimming.

They were into the deciding moments of the last of many games, when Findol dramatically flicked the disc high in the air. He performed his trademark double-somersault and with a mighty *thwack!* sent the disc thundering into opponent Virgil Blint, bouncing off his head in the process.

'Hey, watch it! That's not fair. What could I do with that? You are too fast, Findol!'

'Sorry!' he smirked back. He didn't particularly like Virgil. He was one of those individuals who chose *if* and *when* he wanted to be a friend. Both usually depended on what Findol had to offer him, or rather what he, Virgil, was after — and pretty much amounted to the same thing. Findol always said that if somebody couldn't like and accept him for what he was — and not what he could give them — then they weren't worth bothering with. It seemed to be a good philosophy to adopt since he had plenty of real friends that he knew he could rely on, just as they could on him.

The whole series of games had probably taken only a couple of hours, but it seemed to them like it had taken most of the afternoon. All were exhausted and Findol's team were just about to beat the others by twenty-one to seventeen. In fact they had all been so engrossed in the play that a large boat had silently crept up close to them. It had cut its engine's power some way back, gently drifting in toward them. On-board, men and women ran excitedly from side to side with their children, keen to glimpse the proceedings below.

'Winston, look! Look at them! You could almost think they were playing!'

The sulky kid scuffed his feet on the deck and moaned, 'Why Dad? They're just big fish. What's the big deal?'

'For goodness sake, what are they teaching you these days? They are dolphins, Winston! And they are mammals, like us.'

'So what?' skulked Winston. His face betrayed a miserable expression as he looked deliberately above the scene as if to prove his indifference. 'D'you think my new Playstation game's arrived back home yet, Dad?'

Mr Kemp looked despairingly at his son as he shook his head.

'I don't believe you! Just why did you bother coming if that's going to be your attitude? This is better than any blooming game! Why, this is REAL! Nature at its best. Not some series of electronic pixels on a screen. What is the point of you being here, eh?' he said, but the boy had his usual reply ready.

'You made me come. I didn't ask to, did I?'

'D'you know something? Most kids your age would give *anything* to be where you are right now! This is a once-in-a-lifetime moment. Don't you see that?'

'Yeah, well Craig Kowalski says that you can eat them as Sushi!'

'Don't be so bloomin' stupid! What does he know?'

They were distracted by the loud sound of a bird squawking, high up, a dark silhouette against the bright sun. Winston looked up at it muttering, 'Stoo-pid bird!'

It was a very large wandering albatross that had been circling overhead and had now chosen the precise moment to release a large deposit. It landed with a sickening splat on young Winston, catching him square in the eye and trickling down his rather spotty nose. His father gasped, but couldn't stop himself letting out a large chuckle. He thought how fate moved in wonderfully mysterious ways — and some rather amusing ones too!

Natures revenge! he thought.

High above them, the culprit, Sammy Sheckles, screeched, 'Bull's eye!' Then another spasm gripped his belly and made one more deposit that gave Old Man Ricketts a greyish white toupee.

'Oooh! You look just like George Clooney!' his wife cooed.

The bird smiled at the scene below and started to sing:

'Oh ... I wander here ... and I wander there,

Or do I wonder ... or do I care.

That those below ... I splat each day,

See me the culprit ... fly away!'

Sammy was in fine voice, singing loud and proud, totally lost in his glee, eyes shut and revelling in his good fortune. He beat his wings with great exaggerated movements as he circled the gently rocking boat. The large mast of the boat was deceptively tall and impressively unforgiving, and topped by a particularly large and solid light-fitting. The swaying light smacked Sammy cleanly in the face on the side of his bill, scaring the living daylights out of him. He screamed in shock as some of his tail feathers snagged on the fitting as he tried to wheel away, and more than half a dozen were roughly plucked from his posterior. What had started as a moment of joy quickly left his feeling very un-clever (and rather sore) as he gazed through blurry eyes at the feathers that span down towards the deck below.

'That'll teach him!' a few concerned voices remarked, more than a little relieved that he'd missed *them*. Winston ran into the bathroom to sort himself out amidst sobs of embarrassment. A muttering Alf Ricketts wiped his head with a handkerchief which sported a series of multi-coloured stains. It looked disturbingly like a fabric map, recording every spillage that the environment and his body had thrown at him over the last month. Daisy-May, his grand-daughter, watched him, staring at the handkerchief and making a mental note to avoid him wiping her nose again.

There was the urgent whirring sound of tiny buzzing motors as electric cameras flashed and clicked. Frantic scrabbling began amongst bags festooned with zips as hands juggled with lenses and feverishly fiddled with tiny memory cards. A lady sat at the rear of the boat. She had been eating a large chicken mayonnaise roll whilst witnessing the assault on Winston and Alf's heads. She was clutching at her stomach and throat, trying to avoid the inevitable vomit, as the boat bobbed up and down in the swell. To make matters worse for her, the smell of seaweed was particularly strong and was now playing havoc with her delicate innards. She shouted for her husband, 'Peeet … er, HUGHWEEEEE!' as she bent double over the side of the boat, retching and convulsing like a cat with a huge hairball. Her clutch-bag spilled open and a ridiculously large and expensive platinum-tipped pen exited, slipping gracefully into the depths of the ocean below. Her partner cautiously approached from up-wind, offering a tiny tissue at arms length, face turned away to the side.

Back at the bow there was much jockeying for position as each passenger tried to secure the best site for getting the perfect photo. People shuffled impatiently whilst bodies swayed to maintain steadiness as the boat rose and dipped and rolled. Richard Pickins was showing off with his very latest acquisition; his new video camera.

'Oh yes, it's state of the art, this!'

Everyone around him was getting rather bored and looking for excuses to avoid getting engaged in further conversation. They had suffered him for too long.

Chip Skate sheepishly lowered his rather inferior instamatic camera and hid it under his tattered pullover. Next to Richard Pickins stood an agitated man who was obviously fed-up with the way Pickins was carrying on. As he admonished his bragging neighbour, his voice got progressively louder.

'Yes, right mate! Look, excuse me, but if it's all the same t'you I've got to concentrate and I for one hate show-offs, okay?'

Pickins seemed to get the point and he shut up immediately; nervously adjusting every setting he could, as the loud man continued to glare at him. In his desperation to look busy he flipped the battery release catch and the exceptionally expensive battery sprang out, plopped into the water below, and see-sawed down to the seabed. A stifled scream rose up within him as his rising blood pressure turned him scarlet. A few people close by tried hard not to allow giggles to escape.

Twizzul spotted the battery, as it settled in a little cloud of sand.

'Cor, Findol. The things they throw away into the Blue. It's a disgrace!' The dolphins watched the strange and curious Humans above with much amusement.

'They are fascinating creatures, aren't they?' whistled Tewnis as he spun around and flipped over the others.

'Stop showing off, will you? It only encourages them!' they all replied. 'Then they'll never leave us in peace!'

'Oh come on, look at them,' said Findol. 'It's always nice to see them happy, especially the little ones.' He was looking up at a little girl peering through the railings. He swam up and broke the sea's surface, flashing her a big wink as he did so. She stepped back and tugged vigorously at her mother's sleeve. 'Mummy. Mummy did you see that?'

'See what, darling?' her mother asked, not really listening, but more concerned with applying sun-lotion to her daughter's shoulders and adjusting the child's sun hat.

'That dolfing winked his eye at me.'

'Did he now Daisy? Well isn't he clever? You must tell Granddad when he comes back.'

The amused dolphins continued to study the Humans.

'Do you know they're descended from us? They are! Honest!' Flotsam whispered in Findol's ear.

'Err, yes. I did know that actually. Remember, we've all been to school too, but I think it's a bit more complicated than that.'

'Fun to watch though, aren't they?'

'Absolutely. Hey, watch out! Here they come! Doesn't take long, does it?'

'Well I'm not indulging them. I want to finish our game!'

'Oh come on now guys, just humour them!' Findol smiled as he saw the first of the men and women shakily entering the water, but his friends stayed away. Only a few of the people got in — the water was bitterly cold for the pale Humans. After furtive attempts to try and swim with them, the passengers returned to the boat, shivering under sodden towels once they were back on deck.

The captain on-board was watching the proceedings.

'Sorry! I should have packed the wetsuits. Too bloomin' cold! I'm 'fraid they're not too obliging today, they aren't. Mind, they're so bloomin' fast. Guess they're prob'ly in an 'urry or summat. Wanna get back to their homes, I shouldn't wonder! Still, never mind. There's always another day.'

There was a sudden splash from the back of the boat as a figure in a wet-suit leapt in.

'Aha, now that's what I call being prepared that is. Don't you be long, mind,' the captain shouted at the figure in the water.

Many of his friends had decided to give up on the game and had started to leave, but Findol hung on. There was always a special attraction that he felt to Humans, despite the dangers they represented.

'Careful Findol, you don't know what you'll catch!' Kwava shouted back as he raced away after his fleeing friends. 'Be seeing ya!'

'Yes, and we will finish the game another day, I promise! See you Kwava!'

The man was swimming around Findol with a strange box-like object in front of his face. A slight mechanical whirring sound followed by a click emanated from it at infrequent moments. With each click came a sudden flash of light that hurt Findol's eyes. Every now and then the figure would swim to the surface and water would squirt out of a tube that seemed attached to the man's face. Findol could see it was something to do with his breathing. He thought with a chuckle, 'If only they knew about the wattling beads.'

The man was using his underwater camera, capturing Findol every time the dolphin manoeuvred around him. He clicked and flashed away as the minutes passed. Up above on the boat, the captain was getting a little concerned as he realised how close they were getting to the coral rim, and he was having difficulty in keeping the boat away from it. The boat was bobbing and swaying in quite a big swell. As if to testify to the motion of the water, many of the passengers had green-tinged faces and sweaty hands clamped over bulging mouths. There was a danger of real damage being done to the boat if it got too close to the reef, so the captain decided to start up the engines and shouted down to the figure at the surface.

'Let's be having you, Mr Styles, please! It's time to go I'm afraid.'

Then suddenly, everything seemed to happen very quickly. The man — Cody Styles — was so engrossed in snapping away for his new sea-life book that he failed to notice a blanket of kelp that had been stirred up by the boat's propellers and had wrapped itself around his left flipper. He quickly became entangled in it and understood the danger immediately. He began thrashing about as best he could to draw attention to his predicament, and all the while cursing his foolish mistake. At that moment the ship was caught by a large freak wave that sharply pulled the boat around.

The captain engaged hard astern to avoid a head-on collision with the reef. Suddenly the boat was reversing straight back into the path of the struggling man. There was a loud drone of the rotor blades and a ripping sound as they emerged, whirring out of the water. Froth whipped up dramatically in angry sprays, the noise was deafening to Findol's sensitive ears.

Findol saw the man's distress and instinct sent him straight over to help. He immediately set to work nipping and tearing at the rubbery kelp that bound the man's legs. Above, on the deck there were screams of agitation as despairing faces shouted at the captain to steer clear. One of the elderly women screamed: 'The dolphin's eating him! It's horrible!' Parents covered their children's' eyes while they themselves watched on with morbid fascination. One man held out his swanky new camera-phone in an outstretched hand, thinking a valuable YouTube upload was in the pipeline.

Despite his experience, the captain was fumbled at the controls as everyone shouted conflicting instructions at him, serving only to add to his confusion. He accidentally increased the reverse thrust instead of changing to "Forward". A cloud of panic swept over him as he stalled the engine and swore with anguish. Luckily the struggling man, with Findol's help, broke free of his bindings and quickly moved away from the dangerously close rotor blades. The engine restarted with a cough and loud splutter. The boat's exhaust belched out a cloud of oily smoke that bloomed underwater. The surprised man swam away as he pulled free, but accidentally fired the camera's flash, that was just inches away from poor Findol's face.

Temporarily blinded and confused, the poor dolphin didn't see the dangerous propellers advancing on him until it was too late. Findol's eyes cleared, then widened in terror, and without warning there was immediate excruciating pain like he had never felt before, along his back and tail. The boat's propulsion threw him back as he came to rest violently against the rough coral. Its jagged surface scraped cruelly at his skin. Broken pieces quickly mixed with a growing cloud of blood and debris that sunk to the seabed. Driven by sheer shock and fear, Findol immediately dived and swam down as fast as he could. He could feel skin opening where it was cut and the pain was unbearable. His adrenaline kicked in and fuelled his muscles as he swam faster than he had ever done before. Panic and pain produced tears that mixed with the passing water as he raced homeward. Fear gave him one thought and one thought only: *Mother!*

He frantically raced back toward Lantica, swimming for how long he had no idea. The agony drove him on and on, until eventually exhaustion forced him to slow down. He was terrified at what injuries he had sustained as he couldn't turn his head far enough to see. Perhaps that was a good thing, but it didn't stop his imagination from running riot. Too exhausted to carry on much further, he desperately watched and listened for anyone who could help him.

Wippit was first to see him as Findol shakily approached. He looked in horror at his brother's damaged body and the trail of blood in his wake.

'Mum. MUM, come quick. Findol's hurt. Hurry!' Despina dropped what she was doing and raced outside to see Findol weakly swimming towards them. As he struggled over to her, clouds of blood bloomed from his terribly wounded back and tail.

'Oh my baby come here, come here! What has happened to you, my darling?' She gazed in despair at the deep gashes on his tail and back, and the ravaged dorsal fin that was now missing its tip. She ushered him inside and gently rested him on a Silkington Sponge Futon.

'Wippit, you must go and get Panaseeya right now, quick as you can.'

Panaseeya, the nurse shark, was well known for her ability to perform marvellous medical feats when needed. It was said there wasn't a disease or injury she couldn't cure or assist with. Despina gently applied a Frombus Poultice to the damaged skin to stop the bleeding. Then she pulled an Eiderkelp Quillting over Findol and snuggled up to him as he moaned quietly.

'Sorry, Mum. *Owww!* Sorry.'

She understood immediately the nature of his wounds. 'Yes, I know you are sorry! Because let me guess … you have been Man-watching again, haven't you?'

'Sort of but not on — *owwwwch!* — purpose.' He paused, catching his breath. He explained to her about the Finball game and the boat sneaking up on them and the man in the water.

'Well, I know that unselfish action is typical of you, Findol, but you must remember to look out for yourself!' she said frantically. 'You could have been killed!'

'I know Mum, but I couldn't let the human get injured, it would have killed him. Either he would have drowned or he'd have been hit by those whirling machine things.'

'Yes, but just think a minute, Findol. Do they ever come to our help and give us any thought when we are trapped in their nets, just like your brothers' and sisters' parents? Don't forget Wippit last year. Look at how many of us have been hit by their boats and the spinning things that move them! Do they feel bad about that I wonder? What about the terrible things they throw in the Blue. Our Blue? When will you learn, Findol? *When?*'

'I'm sure they are not all bad, Mum! The man I saved. *Owww.* I had a really good feeling about him. He didn't try to hurt me and it seemed like he treated me as if I was special!'

'Well you should be used to that, shouldn't you? Because you are special, my dear!' she smiled gently.

'You know what I mean. He didn't pose any sort of — *ooow* — threat.'

'That's the problem with the Humans, Findol, and it's why we have to be so careful. They don't always mean us harm, but things have a habit sometimes of running out of their control. Fate has a mischievous habit of swimming away from you, given the chance, and when you least expect it! I guess they just need educating somehow ... '

Panaseeya soon arrived and took over managing Findol's wounded body. She worked quickly and gently, bathing the wounds with special floral unctions and packing them with compresses that would speed the healing, always talking gently and reassuringly in her quiet Scottish accent.

'Now now, young scallywag,' she would chirrup in her jolly manner. 'What in the world have you been up to, getting into this mess? Have no fear, Panaseeya's here.'

Through the use of gentle words and thoughts she had been able to perform some wondrous feats. It was because of her special abilities that she was much sought after and rarely in one place at any one time. Findol suddenly remembered something.

'Mum, I'm supposed to meet Piebald, Pinkerton and Lippizana tonight!' he uttered weakly.

'You're not going anywhere, youngster!' interrupted Panaseeya. 'You will need to stay here for some time and not t'be moving your tail or fin. They have to be left to heal for a couple o' weeks, I'm afraid.'

Weeks? WEEKS! thought Findol. His mind turned somersaults at the horrendous thought of being imprisoned for weeks on end, confined to home, trapped and barely able to move. A cloud of despair swiftly arrived and settled above him, raining down depressing thoughts of the frustration that would ensue with each passing day stuck at home.

'Mum, surely … '

But Panaseeya interrupted. 'That's enough, young Findol. I do not want t'be hearing another word on the matter. I do not make threats lightly, so be warned. You must do as I say or you may never swim properly again. I know just how important your abilities are to you, so trust me in this and do not cross me. You have been warned.' Panaseeya glared down at him, the faintest hint of a smile at the corners of her face, for she too, loved him so. 'Mind what I say and you'll soon make a full recovery, young one. Okay?'

'Okay, I hear you,' he drawled, 'and thanks.'

'Helllooooo! Hello, Mrs Lantica … I thought yeh might be grantin' me permission to be coming in to see the little fella.'

'Flaytus! Why am I *not* surprised to see you? Yes. come on in, by all means.'

'I heard about the little one's accident with the boat an' all. I thought it would be fitting to be visiting if that's alright. If yeh take me meaning?'

She beckoned him in, wondering just how quickly bad news spread. 'Yes, yes. Of course, dear Flaytus, come in by all means.'

'Thank yeh kindly!' he said, releasing a small trump as he passed through the entrance. 'Ooops! Still better out than in, as me mother used t'say!'

Definitely! Despina thought as she pushed the Shellting blind across the doorway.

'Now how is the wounded soldier? By the power of the wilting shamrock, I'm wishing yeh a speedy recovery, so I am!'

'And just who is this strange person might I be so bold as too ask?' Panaseeya questioned abruptly. 'Cos if it be all the same to yeh, I would appreciate you removing yeh blasted shell from my throbbing tail!'

'Oh curse me fer stealing a pot of the Goblin King's gold. I am so sorry, O Grand Healing One. I just can't be getting used to the thing.'

'What do yeh mean? Fer goodness sake have you not been using it all your life?'

'Well, it's not been as simple as all that, missus, and that's a fact. And so at this point I think I will be taking my leave of you all, but I will return with a little something fer the invalid so I will.'

And maybe when yeh not here too missus!' he thought. Flaytus dragged himself outside; a large bubble escaping from his rear and splashing upwards on the Lantica home ceiling.

'Och. How disgusting!' said Panaseeya.

The following day saw a constant flurry of activity in and out of Findol's home as family and friends came to visit and make sure he was okay. Secretly they were all rather curious and wanted to know the full story of his encounter with the boat. All Findol could think about between visits was his cancelled meeting and what had happened to Piebald, Pinkerton and Lippizana. He felt that should have got a message to them somehow, at the very least. The fact that they hadn't come to see him to find out why he hadn't met them was niggling him greatly. He knew they had been out delivering messages as part of their jobs (and also as part of his Hint-at Net). If they had heard about his accident though, he knew they would have been constantly there, pestering his mother to see how he was doing. Their absence was worrying and he could only hope the delay was nothing of great concern.

***

Far away in deep dark waters, Grampus was revelling in his own scheming. He smiled at his armies proudly displayed before him. Whales, barracuda and sharks jostled for position to hear his words, each one hoping for recognition and glory in whatever was to come. When finally he spoke his orders, they were few and to the point.

'FOLLOWERS! We are now ready to go. We will seek. We will find. And we will KILLLL!'

The thousands of assembled troops let out a deafening cheer that resonated eerily for miles throughout the darkness.

Chapter 7
Darkness Falls

It had been more than a month since Findol's accident and he was nearly fully recovered. The whole experience had really sapped him of all the positivity he had built up and was a bitter lesson in the very fragility of order in his life. His excitable fun self had gone on vacation and all those that knew him hoped it would soon return. He had found it so annoying and frustrating that the healing process took so long. His wounds had closed and healed over, but he had lost so much strength and his muscles were stiff, making the simplest of tasks difficult and tiring. The long, laborious process of building himself up was not happening quickly enough, despite Panaseeya's efforts. She had given Findol a series of stretching exercises to help wake up dormant muscles and build strength where it was needed. He just thought they were all rather silly and embarrassing, and was terrified of being caught in the act by any of his friends or family, knowing the fun that would be made of him.

Time passed agonisingly slowly and it was the start of the Big Blue winter' where temperatures started to drop sharply. Cold currents brought discomfort into their environment causing problems for the ill-prepared. Thermal coral-fan heaters that radiated heat as they fed were brought into the Lantica home. It was the time when thoughts strayed to anticipation of Sandy Claws and all the fun of the season.

Findol shivered as he ventured out for one of his small swims around the outside perimeter. It annoyed him how quickly the smallest effort exhausted him, and he couldn't risk straying far from home. Very slowly, over the weeks, his body gained in strength, helped by the gradual return of his appetite and the rich nutritious food his mother was giving him. Her special draughts of Red Krill seemed to boost his energy levels dramatically. The frustrated desire within him to get back out and start exploring with his friends further aided his recovery. It helped him to focus and to push himself at his exercises, so that soon, he was nearly restored to his old self.

His mum often made him her Sea-squirt sponge cakes as special treats, barely finishing preparing them before he started tucking in. Any other time he would have got a severe reprimand, but for now she was just glad to see him enjoying his food again. Despite the added inconvenience of having to stay at home for so long, it had been nice spending so much time with his mum. She had been able to show him how she prepared a lot of her delicacies. How she made delicate material from sea-grass and kelp, binding them carefully together. Best of all though, she told him lots of stories; especially the unwritten ones — passed down by word of mouth from generation to generation. They were all about their family history of long ago and also the Way of the Morphing between land and sea, that Cora had imparted to her.

Despina had spoken briefly about Cora, who she said was old beyond measure, for nobody actually knew her true age. There were rumours she had lived as a young Orca for a while at King Neptune's court of old. As a young adult she had devised the plan that led to The Great Wattling Harvest in the Caves of Entonox. It had been successful in ending the great crop failure during the Year of the Wattling Blight. She had been good friends with a fellow Orca, Ichabod the Unsure, and there had been talk of a romance, but it amounted to nothing. It was the one and only time Cora had been associated with a partner.

With so much spare time on his fins, Findol had asked his mum about his father, but Despina could not tell him much more than he already knew. She had looked at him with a gentle smile as memories were stirred and emotions rekindled. Kai-Galant had been a wonderful partner and would have been a marvellous father. Sadly, he had no knowledge before he went away that Despina had been carrying his child. It would have been her greatest surprise and gift to him. It seemed such a short time that she had actually known him. Yet, in that time, she had learned much about the wonderful qualities he had.

They had met by arrangement through Cora, who had said that a friend's son would be the ideal mate for her, and Despina hadn't been disappointed. They had both been very young to make a commitment. However, the minute she first set eyes on him waiting outside Sea-Czar's Palace she just knew that he truly was the one for her. He had clearly echoed her feelings too. They had swum to a nearby small lagoon, where it was fashionable to go when you were young. There you could have fun and hang out with others, and sometimes there would be "open-water" live music there. Back then, the singer Jessie Ray was incredibly popular along with bands Bream Theatre and The Coral.

Despina and Kai had swum together for what seemed like an eternity. Her heart had never stopped racing, unable to take her eyes off him. Deep inside, her blood had felt like electricity running around her body. She blushed as she recalled how she had tingled whenever they had touched, and as they surfaced they had embraced beneath the moon. That moment, they pledged their undying love for each other as they looked up at the bright moon in the sky. It was not long after that time, they had both committed themselves and sworn undying love to each other, taking the name of Lantica as their shared title.

They had moved into Lantica Deep and were making plans for their future together when Kai was called away one night by Cora. He had been gone for many hours and when he returned had seemed strangely shaken; his mind distant, deep in thought and anguish. He would not be drawn on the conversation he'd had with Cora or why his mood had changed. All he had hinted at was the growing concern over Grampus and his plans.

It was less than a week after seeing Cora when he had suddenly said he had to go away for a few days. He had offered no explanation and a terrible sadness had been in his eyes. His mood was unusual and he had embraced her passionately and swore his eternal love before he left. Curiously, that night he had worn a strange pendant around his neck. The purple stone at its centre had glowed with an almost magical brilliance. The image of that pendant had haunted her, for she had never seen it before and had no time to ask him about it, yet there had been a strangeness about it.

It was to be the last time she was ever saw him.

After Kai's disappearance, Despina had quizzed Cora, particularly about the curious stone. Cora had merely dismissed it as nothing to be concerned about. She said it had been a good luck stone that she had given him for safe-keeping, but even Despina had been aware of the magic it seemed to possess within.

Shortly after, Despina found out she was pregnant and expecting someone very special.

'Yes! It was you! My little treasure!' she said, snuggling up to Findol who had been listening, hanging onto every word, wishing he could visualise his father.

'Do you think we will ever see him again, Mum?' Findol asked with a deep yearning in his heart. The more his mum talked about his father, the more he wanted to meet him.

'Findol, I can tell you — flipper on heart — that I am certain he is alive somewhere. My feelings are mixed because I know he has somehow, for some reason, forgotten about us. I am certain that all it will take is something to trigger those memories! Either that or he cannot get back to us for want of trying. I trust the feelings in my heart. Besides, as Cora says, "we will all one day meet at the ledge, and no power on earth can stop that happening!"'

'I hope you're right, Mum! Do you think it's okay if I go out a little further today? I feel really like I am ready for it!!'

'Yes, go on. You must get your old self back I suppose. I know you so well, but listen — take care and don't stay out too late, do you hear?'

'Okay, message received and understood,' Findol chuckled back.

For the first time in ages he could race for the entrance, bursting out just like he used to and it felt so good. No more careful, leisurely rambles; this was time to get back to living again. Despite his muscles complaining at the unexpected demands he made of them, Findol revelled in the feeling of freedom; the Big Blue was like a friendly fin caressing his skin as he raced on and on.

He was so used to the boredom of normality that he had nearly forgotten about his Hint-at Net and was actually wondering whether he had really needed it after all, when suddenly he recalled another of Cora special sayings: "Fools die in complacency!"

He spied Flaytus and Whitloe talking up ahead and decided to use the opportunity to "wake them up" a little by buzzing past them at high speed. As he approached, Findol couldn't help but overhear a snippet of their conversation. It sounded like Flaytus was interviewing Whitloe.

'Errm. So tell me now, Whitloe. When did yeh first think of expressing yerself as a "Cow"?'

'Well (*chew chew*) … what business be it … (*munch-munch*) … of yours, eh? I mean … (*scoff-scoff*) … coming from you … (*burp!*) — pardon me — … of all creatures! That's rich, that is! After all (*chew — munch — chew*) … you think you were a leperreecorn … (*scoff*) … or summat, eh?'

'Now fer the sweet love of me mother, who's doing this blooming interview?'

Whitloe continued on regardless. 'For that matter … (*ooh that were tasty*) … ain't it strange that you and I both arrived here at the same time all them years ago!?'

'Well, now that yeh mention it … I suppose yer right, … but that's not what I was asking yehAARGH! FIINNN-DOLLL!'

Both were sent tumbling by the shock wave as Findol blasted past with a loud 'Hiya doods!' He left them reeling in surprise and headed for his cave. By the time he got there he was quite exhausted. He had really pushed himself for most of the short journey and now he was paying the price. He passed quickly through the concealed entrance, gasping, and flopped onto the chest lid he called his C-Bed. It had been little over a month since his last visit, but it sure felt good to be back in his private den. He lay there munching on some wattling beads, replenishing his oxygen reserves, and rooted out some TripleK (Kriblington Kelp Krunch) to snack on.

Out of the corner of his eye he spied something glinting in the light of the illuminant clams. It was the round metal disc he had found when he was last out with Sterbol. Findol picked it up and spun around with it trying to catch it out, but as ever the pesky needle always settled pointing toward his mirrored wall. He imagined it onboard a ship and tried to guess how men would use it. He confirmed what he thought before; it had something to do with direction. The markings inside, around its edge, were surely the key. He laughed at his own cleverness.

'Glad dumbody's happy,' sniffed Wichita from a corner of the cave. He had been feeling rather sorry for himself. "Gluey Flu" was a most unpleasant ailment for sea-cucumbers and not much fun for those around them either. He was blocked up all the time, congested with "gut-tar" he called it, and occasionally coughed up pellets of gum that were as disgusting as they sounded.

'I'm doh dorry, Findol, but I do feel derribly bunged up. I won't be much use for a while.'

'Forget it, Wichie — I understand — you've got to get yourself sorted. I just hope you get better soon. I know only too well what it's like to be stuck at home, feeling lousy. Medicine is what you need and I know just the answer — Panaseeya's amazing FlemDip, and a rub down with some of her All-Bass Oil. Mum swears by it! It will clear your head and gluesal passages. I will get you some when I get back home. Oh, before I forget, thanks for looking after the place!

'Thanks, Findol. And you're welcome.'

Findol then busied himself pottering around his cave, rearranging a few knick-knacks and ornaments. It was amazing how much mess had accumulated whilst he was away. Cockles and barnacles, anemones and small sea-urchins had all found a home in his cave. He wouldn't have minded so much, but for the fact that they never cleaned up after themselves. He hated living in a cloud of detritus courtesy of uninvited guests. Then it hit him like a Stonefish …

Oh no! What am I doing? Here I am tinkering around as if I haven't a care in the Blue and I haven't given any thought to Pinkerton, Piebald and Lippy!

He still hadn't received any news of them. It had been bad enough when only few weeks had gone by with no word from them. Now, just how long had it actually been since he was supposed to have met up with them? A month? Two? He couldn't remember.

'Wichie — I have got to go out on urgent business. You remember my seahorse posse? I need to find them.'

'But Findol, surely you need to conserve your strength. You are still exhausted.'

'I know, but I can't afford the luxury of waiting around here, can I? You take care of yourself. I hope you feel better when I get back.'

'*If* you get back,' Wichita sniffed.

Findol exited in a flash, not even bothering to conceal his emergence from his cave. He immediately raced towards the Lantica Rim where he hoped to spot one or more of his contacts.

His reactions were still a little slow and he cursed each time he caught himself on jutting spurs of coral and brittle sea-fans. More than once he scraped his flanks on the sides of the bedrock, or found himself getting tangled up in floating curtains of kelp. He soon began to realise it was going to be some time before he got his coordination back properly. There was a pain in his head too; an incessant thudding, which slowly grew as he pushed himself on. And to top it off, that annoying itch in his throat was back.

Findol swam on, stopping frequently to rest and echolocate some beads. After swimming for some time and wrestling with the developing headache, a nagging thought suddenly occurred to him. Apart from the shoals of bass, blennies and other shoaling fish, he had not actually seen nor heard the sound of any of his friends. This was strange, as he always bumped into someone, or at least picked up on distant conversations as he crossed his undersea world. In fact, now that he thought about it, there was very little noise coming from the direction in which he was heading. All that he could detect was a strange sort of suppressed crackling that was coming from somewhere in the distance, but nothing identifiable as speech.

Behind him, he could detect the worried sounds of young fish late for school and rays hurrying along to stinging practice. Somewhere far above him, some basking sharks were taking it easy — humming to themselves, but nothing else. Findol started to feel rather lonely; a feeling he had never had to feel before.

Where were all his friends — the threads of his Hint-at Net?'

The echolocation that he constantly used, like all his Cetacean kind, showed nothing. He seemed to be swimming blind into the unknown and he felt stupid to feel that way. The longer he pushed forward, the more a feeling of foreboding began creeping over him.

He anxiously began to swim upwards, passing over a large rock formation littered with a collection of large rusty drums. Discarded from a ship some time ago, they had wedged themselves in crevices and lay piled on ledges. Some had split open, spilling their poisonous contents into the surrounding waters over weeks and months. Disgusting splashes of slime (and worse) clung to them. Virtually nothing lived in or near the area.

Findol had almost forgotten about the poisoned place and he quickly gave it a wide berth. He could taste the bitterness in the water and was glad he had not been there when the pollution was at its worst. He had nearly reached the top of the formation and was about to pass over the ridge when that terrible feeling of dread hit him again, so strong now, down deep in the middle of his stomach.

Winded, and with his head pounding hard, he stopped sharply. He brought his flippers around his head as if trying to block out the pain. The strange crackling noise was getting louder and he was no longer sure of its direction, let alone its source. It almost seemed to be coming from inside his head.

He tried to calm down as best he could before cautiously swimming from rock to rock until he found shelter under an overhang. Gasping with effort he stared intently ahead, senses fully focussed and nervous with anticipation. Despite the pounding and strange noise in his head, he screwed up his eyes and concentrated on focussing his echo. It took him a while to grasp just what he was seeing and sensing. At first he could not believe his eyes. There, right in front, just above the Lantica Rim, there appeared to be suspended a curtain of what could only be described as *white fire*. It was just like the burning white forks of lightning from the storms he had witnessed;

a frantic dance of ripping light. The curtain stretched as far as the eye could see and the enormous entity was moving slowly but surely in his direction.

Wincing in pain, but determined to find out more, he moved closer to investigate the nature of the spectacle. It was only then that he finally recognised the curtain of fire for what it was; a moving electrical charge that was being generated by thousands of electric eels. They were spread out in a massive line that receded into the distance on either side. By constantly discharging their current together they produced a massive, impervious curtain of energy. It crackled and fizzed, preventing anything — solid or transmitted — from penetrating it.

At last, Findol understood the source of his pain and stared in disbelief, wondering at what it could mean.

So many eels together — but why?

He had a flash of memory from some time ago when he had witnessed an unusual gathering of the creatures. His heart had begun to race, pounding in his chest, because his thoughts were suddenly pursuing a path he had not prepared himself to take.

'Of course, why didn't I question it at the time?' He cursed himself for being so careless.

'Scared are we, little he-ro, Findol? *Ha ha!*'

Findol leapt out of his hiding place with the shock.

'Scaybeez! — I might have guessed you wouldn't be far away from all this. Been foraging in the festering drums for something suiting your taste buds?'

'Oh funn-eeee! Pardon me for not laughing, oh pale one, but your attempts at humour are wasted on me! So, now you believe, eh? *Ha.* Suddenly you are Findol the "not so brave!"'

'Watch it, Scabby or you'll regret it. Are you trying to tell me in your own pathetic little way that this is the work of Grampus?'

'Oops! Silly me. Is it that obvious? Did I let the catfish out of the clam? Ha ha! Oh dear — is that a look of despair I spy?'

'Shut it — I am not interested in trading insults with you, Scabby.'

'Oy, stop calling me that!'

'Or what, eh? Scabby by name and scabby by nature. Do you really think Grampus would have a place for little you in his scheming? I don't think so. Even he would see you as a waste of space — but then again perhaps you would both be well suited.'

'Ha. Now who is it making petty, empty threats, eh? Guess what? He *is* coming — coming for yooo-hoooo.'

'You make me sick,' said Findol, and he was telling the truth. What with the pain in his head, the deepening sense of danger, and the news of Grampus's return, he was starting to feel very nauseas indeed. 'You can go back to the bowels of Guano rock where you belong for all I care because you are not wanted here!'

'Go there yourself — I am not moving — I am the one with time on my fins. Your lifeline is coming to an abrupt en … *owww!*' Findol had slapped Scaybeez hard with his tail, and was now regretting it. He had managed to open up part of the old wound, and cursed himself quietly for his lack of self-control. Scaybeez, meanwhile, had rebounded off some nearby rock, leaving behind more of his flaky skin in the process.

'I will be seeing you again, Scabby, you can count on it!' Findol whispered menacingly in the injured fish's swollen earhole as it started to swim off.

Whatever the curtain of fire represented, Findol didn't like it and he wanted to get home quickly to warn the others. His mind was racing with a million thoughts; the damned prophecy, his absent friends, his family. He urgently wanted to speak to Cora, but first he had to warn everyone that Grampus was almost upon them. He needed to get them to safety. He couldn't allow himself the luxury of fear. Instinct told him he had to act NOW.

It dawned on him in a blinding flash that this was it; his Judgement Day. The accumulation of all the years of expectation for him was beginning to hit home hard. He was torn between wanting to go home or to his cave to just hide away, and his born duty. Then he felt the driving force of his growing anger welling up inside of him. It came from all the years he had been deprived of the father he had come to love through his mother's words. He knew that Grampus was responsible for it, although he had no idea of quite what to do about it. Facing his fear was so hard, yet he tried to remain focussed. Spurred on by adrenalin and the gnawing pain in his head and tail, he swam on with all his might.

Daring one last glance back, he noticed the electric curtain parting just like the one on the stage at Sea-Czar's Palace. As he stared, a huge moving mass could be seen through the gap, making its way towards him. With the barrier open he could now hear the sound of thousands of terrified marine mammals. They were fearful and screaming for their lives as they fell victim to the horde. The Electric Curtain had obviously trapped them and prevented any cries for help getting through.

Terrifying sounds of slaughter and mayhem assaulted Findol's senses and catalysed him into action. This was how Grampus had collected his armies together, free from prying eyes and ears. Now Findol could plainly hear and see the huge numbers of sharks, barracuda, giant rays and eels. He sensed the feeling of madness infecting each and every one of them. Findol had never felt so scared, and he swam with all his might, barely allowing his mind to give in to the images of death and destruction. Swimming like he had never swum before, he ploughed on, paying no heed to his aching muscles and bursting lungs. But he couldn't compete with his tired body. Try as he might, it was just not up to full strength or the demands he was making of it.

Despite his greatest efforts, he realised that the marauding army was gaining on him. Exhausted and fearful, he knew that eventually he would have to stop, if only to take some wattling beads. Agonising over what to do, he knew there was only one real choice. With tears blending into the sea around him he summoned up all his concentration and in the loudest voice he could muster, screamed: 'GRAMPUS IS COMING … HE IS HERE! DO NOT QUESTION! DO NOT HESITATE! LEAVE NOW! GET TO SAFETY! HE IS COMING! HE IS … "

Exhausted, totally drained and retching with the effort, Findol knew he had done everything he could for them. His tail was going into cramp-like spasms and he still felt sick from his headache. His one and only chance to save himself lay in taking cover. Findol knew he was near the Pumice Caves — an intricate labyrinthine cave system formed by the "running rock" eruptions, millions of years ago. He had never before entered them because of the very real danger of getting lost inside. His mum had often warned him about staying clear of them, but today he had no other option.

To make matters worse, there was no guarantee that he'd find any wattling beads within them either. Lost and without an air supply, he would drown. However, his situation was absolutely desperate and it wasn't as if he had a choice in the matter

He positioned himself just inside the entrance to the biggest cave and made a quick, silent prayer to the Moon God, Lunassis. He prayed for the safety of his family and friends, and lastly for himself, before he raced inside, hoping against hope that they had received his frantic message and would escape before Grampus and his manic hordes bore down on them.

Chapter 8
The Pumice Caves

Findol backed up as far as he could possibly go, eyes wide with fear and concern. He pressed his body tight against the rock wall, hardly daring to allow himself room to breathe or move. A few wattling beads lay discarded on the floor nearby and he instinctively reached down slowly and took them inside his mouth. The blood still pounded in his head; the icy, incessant throbbing almost too much to bear. He was so angry for allowing himself to over-react and yet he could not contain the rush of panic in his scared mind. Worse still was the strange silence outside, both ominous and terrifying, which seemed to last for an eternity.

Suddenly he was hit by a shock wave that sent him bouncing off the rock behind and caused small rocks and silt to scatter all around him. The cause quickly became apparent as the massive army of Grampus surged past. He watched with bated breath as the horde passed by, whilst he clung to his hideaway. His attention froze, mesmerised by the sheer horror of so many sea predators of different species coming together as one. He felt unable to move from the spot, whilst his tail kept twitching nervously. Each of the sharks and barracuda carried an ugly fixed grimace, both evil and terrifying. Many were still chewing on food, the source of which he had no desire to think about. They sniggered and cackled to each other and exchanged horrific threats that they swore to enact on all that stood in their path.

Findol's thoughts were with his family and friends. He again prayed that they had heard his urgent plea and quickly acted upon it to find safety in time. It was too much for him to consider the consequences if they had not. He thought of the magical enchantment that was supposed to protect the Lantica domain and all those living in it. It occurred to him that sadly it had either been broken, destroyed or gone past its expiry date. Thoughts of Cora were stirred and he wished she was with him, offering words of comfort and advice. All he could do now was to continue to hold himself tightly against the rock in the darkness.

As the dark shadows continued to rush past he became absorbed by a terrible feeling of failure. He couldn't prevent himself overhearing the terrifying words passing between them. It seemed to take forever as the army continued on their way and he couldn't begin to guess at the numbers involved. He allowed himself the tiniest of glimpses as he cautiously peered out of the cave entrance. It only served to make him feel terribly small and alone. He had never seen such numbers together, surging forward, intent on their cruel purpose. From far ahead, he felt he could sense the fear and pain of others less fortunate than himself who had fallen prey to the evil mass. There were distant cries of help that he tried to block out, but couldn't, because of his concerns. He was terrified he would recognise the poor victims, whilst being utterly helpless to assist.

Just when he felt close to despair, things managed to get even worse. A feeling of a truly terrible presence suddenly hit him — pure evil, cunning and heartless. It was without fear and like a huge black cloud tearing through his soul. Findol shrank back again trying to blend into the dark, knowing the massive bulk coming into view was that of Grampus.

The beast was flanked by smaller whales sporting similar crazed dispositions. His presence pierced Findol's heart like icy-daggers, causing a feeling of nausea to well up inside him. Findol watched him glide past, like a giant marine juggernaut, signalling instructions with the subtlest movement of a fin or nod of his head. More horrible still were his facial features, mouth distorted and twisted, making him barely recognisable as a whale. His eyes were empty and cold; devoid of compassion with thick scarred lids. There was something uncomfortably human about his look that sent a shudder down Findol's spine. The whale's body was lined with deep rivulets of ugly scars, the price of the violence he had once engaged in. Now he left the fighting to his followers. Suddenly there was a commotion getting dangerously close to him and Findol pushed back still further.

'Come on, will ya? Else we'll be late. Move it! I wanna catch up. Gotta be there for the kill!'

Fester Ling and the others were a gang of barracuda with more brawn than sense, always looking for dark deeds to satisfy their evil hunger. Grampus had granted both cause and protection for their simple minds to feverishly follow. They were practising their close formation skirmish swimming. From a distance it made them look like a large, writhing, multi-headed monstrosity that lurched this way and that due to the lack of any real coordination.

'Oi, yeh big oaf! Watch my blooming fin, will ya?' Pusstick was suffering a bad infestation of burrowing fin-lice that left him very sore and peppered with festering boils.

Magut was unfazed. 'If yeh just kept going in the right direction, I wouldn't have touched yeh, would I?'

'You just shut it, right?' Pusstick was getting suitably wound up and was not looking ahead as he snapped at his neighbour. 'Watch out! A*aaargghh!*'

The barracudas collided, full-on, with a large formation of loose rocks precariously balanced just above Findol's hideaway. The five of them scattered dramatically amidst falling rock, silt, and displaced anemones. They wasted no time in hurling abuse at whoever was nearest before reluctantly regrouping.

'I ain't swimmin' next to him again, that's fer sure!' moaned Magut.

'It don't bovver me if yeh swim on the other side of bleedin' Lantica fer all I care, yeh great Nudibranch!' said Pusstick.

'Just you wait till I tells me dad! He'll sort yeh!'

'You mean you've got one?' guffawed Pusstick.

Meanwhile, the avalanche of rocks and debris continued to cascade down, piling up in front of the cave mouth. Thick clouds of choking detritus billowed up and around. Findol could only watch and wait in silence, until it settled, stifling the need to cough and splutter. Then they had passed out of earshot.

The debris continued to fall for ages until finally there was silence. Findol waited for the silt to completely settle, coughing as quietly as he dared. He waited and waited until he realised to his horror that the darkness was not clearing and he was getting desperately short of wattling beads. All the time he had allowed himself to wallow in self-pity he had been wasting valuable oxygen. Worse still, the reason for the poor visibility was now all too apparent — he was blocked in!

He tried making an exploratory push at the large rock barrier, but there was no give whatsoever. This was the worst time to find out he was trapped. Once again he pushed at the wall with as much force as possible, but nothing moved. There was no time to allow panic to develop and he quickly turned around to carefully examine the wall behind him. In the darkness his senses detected a small opening, tucked away on the right. It seemed just big enough for him to enter comfortably and he ducked forward into it. He was already feeling his body beginning its demands for air. A thought briefly flitted through his mind: *Dolphins don't drown, surely?*

'Only those caught in Man's fishing nets,' his mother had once said. Findol's heart leapt as he thought of his lovely, beautiful mother and he steeled himself to find his way out. He couldn't afford to waste any more time and swam on through the opening.

Findol quickly arrived at a junction where a number of other, smaller tunnels led off, seeming to open up into even more space. It occurred to him how much light there appeared to be and he made a mental note to pursue the reason later — if there was to be a later. He chose what looked like the longest of the tunnels. He tested it with his echo, and raced along its length, only to come unexpectedly to a dead end. The need for air was now becoming urgent and he tried to suppress the fear that was beginning to well up inside. He reversed back with difficulty, taking too much time, repeatedly catching himself painfully on the rough walls before trying another route.

A cloud of anxiety grew within him, and an inner voice said, *try the next one.* Without questioning or thinking, he did just that and found a narrow outlet to the outside. A thin shaft of light teasingly shone through. It was agonising to be so close and yet the opening was far too small to pass through. Findol noticed that it did have a valuable clump of kelp, just within reach and laden with its precious cargo. He hurriedly pushed and pushed, squeezing in as far as he could. The rock scraped and squashed around his mouth but he just managed to reach the plant, nip it and pull it out. He quickly put all of its beads in his mouth and flicked them into the storage pouch in his cheek, immediately biting one as he did so. Stale air or not, it was a blessed relief.

A little feeling of hope was rekindled, but he knew he was still not free and the beads would only last so long. The network of tunnels was becoming ever more complex as he moved deeper inside them. He couldn't help but grow concerned at just how much further into the system of passages he would have to go. It was also becoming increasingly difficult to maintain his bearings and he recalled the metal disc with the moving needle back at his cave. He wondered whether it would somehow have been useful here, to help him work out his direction.

What's the point? he thought. *It's not here, is it?*

Any other time he would have relished this as a real adventure, but instead it was fast becoming a desperate struggle for survival. He just wanted to be outside, looking for his family, and this was wasting his time.

An object lay on the tunnel floor nearby; tiny, barely recognisable, but there was no mistaking it. Despite its thick coating of algae, the tanned leather could still be made out. It was an old human shoe. Amazingly, an anemone had made its home in it, tentacles drifting lazily around in the current. He was sure he could hear it humming a tune: ' ... *Hmm* ... *hmm* ... the I...rish r...o...o...ver.'

Isn't that one of Flaytus's songs? Findol thought.

Turning a corner he unexpectedly came to a central chamber where a number of smaller tunnels led off again. It was also getting noticeably warmer. Jets of bubbling, scalding water spurted out of tiny holes in the rock. The smell was familiar and disgusting, making him feel sick. Why it reminded him of Flaytus, he wasn't sure. He recalled the time when his mother warned him about the places to avoid and had spoken about the Pumice Caves. Apparently they had been formed many years before, from the "Hot Lava" or "running rock".

It was something like that, he thought. *When the seabed cracked and the water had boiled all around...*

Findol didn't like being in the hot, smelly place and yet again his thoughts drifted to his supply of wattling beads. The need to find more was growing urgent again and so he pressed on. All the tunnel entrances he could see ahead contained piles of rocks, dead weed and useless kelp. Some were almost completely blocked by rubble from collapsed tunnel roofs.

One tunnel, however, stood out from the rest for it was perfectly clear — abnormally so — and he chose that one. Its entrance was smooth and seemed almost to beckon him in. It had the look of being well used. Just inside, there were some small, broken, lion fish spines and cockle shells scattered on the floor. They reminded him of Flaytus's quills, and the shell pots Flaytus used to hold his inks. Suddenly Findol felt very sad and alone again. On the wall there was a shape that looked just like it had been deliberately etched there. It had five ... no ... four-and-a-half round shapes joined together by a central stem. From a distance it looked a bit like one of Man's propulsion blades that spun on the bottom of his boats.

He continued down the tunnel and found more of the markings on the walls. A little thought formed in his mind that quickly grew into an exciting idea. His mood lifted because Findol felt the markings had to be connected with Flaytus and his "four-and-a-half-leaf clover". He raced along the tunnel, twisting and turning to follow each of the signs. At one bend he turned and a flimsy wafer of parchment that was floating motionless in the water ended up covering his nose. He looked at it and could just make out scribed characters. They read:

Eye Rich Canapés.

Take half a pint of best ale … pickled truffles …

That was as much as could be made out; the rest of the flimsy paper had long disintegrated.

It has to be one of Flaytus's recipes, he thought. He cried out with delight as around another bend he found a large clump of kelp. The beads were even staler than before, but were usable. Moving with renewed confidence, Findol carried on.

Further ahead, the tunnel suddenly dropped downwards and then bent up sharply on itself. He wasn't sure if he would be able to get around it and to make matters worse he could not turn back on himself. Alarm bells started ringing again, but at that moment he once more sensed a voice inside himself.

Trust in your judgement and take courage!

He wasted no time and squeezed himself down into the passage. He was right; it was even tighter than he imagined … worryingly so. He pushed forward and tucked his head under the bend and up so that he was bent perfectly around — and then stuck! Frustratingly, he could see the end of the tunnel up ahead, but he couldn't propel himself out of the bend. There was no space to use his fins or body to dislodge himself. A terrible deathly vision came to him, which he instantly blanked out, yet it sent a nervous shudder right down the length of his body. His tail end twitched and amazingly pushed him precious inches forward. He repeated the process over and over again and then he finally broke free of the restricting wall, flipping and turning with delight in the extra space.

As he reached the tunnel's end, it bent around and opened up into a massive chamber. It was incredibly bright in there, and he had to screw up his eyes to see as the rock surfaces glowed a warm golden brown. The smell was not as strong — unless he was getting used to it. The sudden abundance of space was a delight and a little intoxicating. He twisted around and squeaked, 'Yesss!'

Around the edge of the large cavern, wherever there was a recess within the wall, grew clumps of Flowering Kelp — the like of which he had never seen before. The colours were amazing and the whole image was quite surreal.

I must be dreaming this, surely! he thought. *This just can't be real!*

Then everything was confirmed and slotted into place as he spotted an open storage clam. It was stuffed full of scribing quills and parchment. Findol's head turned and lifted as his concentration was taken by a noise nearby. He had heard some muttering up above and there to his absolute delight was dear Flaytus. The crab was resting upside down and was a very welcome, if not unusual sight.

'Now, now, before yeh be saying or thinking anything, don't even be going there! I can be guessing what yeh was going to say and, yes, t'is uncanny that I'm here t'be sure and that's a fact!'

'Well, yes! Though, actually Flaytus, I was going to ask why you are perched so high up on top of that rock, in such a strange manner?'

It was true. Flaytus was precariously positioned, rocking awkwardly on his shell as he leaned backwards, claws scrabbling for purchase on anything he could reach for support.

'Ah ha, yes, yes indeed, this be a strange sight I suspect, t'be sure, but there is a very good reason. This shell I appears t'be kissing upside down actually holds de blessed "Blarney Stone". Well not actually de real thing if yeh gets me drift but a small piece that I chipped off with me Dewson chisel many moons ago. I knows what yer gonna be asking next so I'll be saving yeh the trouble and tell yeh what it's for shall I? Talking. Talking, talking and more talking. Yeh see, even I lacks a bit o' the old self-confidence. By going through this ritual it binds me to m'past and me motherland and all the mystery that resides there. It also helps with me back problem — oh, this cursed shell!' He pointed despairingly underneath him and grimaced for effect.

'T'is not getting any lighter, that's fer sure. When yeh think what a nimble little elf I was. No, I mean "am"! It … it's why … It's enough to make your bark itch! Well if yeh was a tree that is. I … I knows from experience … but that's another story. Why, when I thinks about the Plague of Pustulent Knots it makes m'shell shudder. Sorry, I'm digressin' … '

'Flaytus, I have absolutely no idea what you are talking about, but I am just so glad to see you. Please come down.

Tell me how to get out of here. I need to find more wattling beads. I've got to find my family!'

And then a sudden and terrible thought occurred to him.

'OH NO! You don't know what's happened, do you? Outside? Grampus! My family!' Findol blinked away his tears.

'Bejaybers! Calm down, calm down, young 'un. Tell me … slowly now … come on … all the facts!' the crab quickly made his way down to him.

Findol slowly composed himself and bravely told Flaytus of the events leading up to his getting trapped in the caves and the desperate search for beads along the way.

'Now that's something yeh don't have to be worrying your head about!' he smugly exclaimed.

Findol watched through red eyes as Flaytus withdrew into his shell and re-emerged pulling out a large sack that he threw down in front of Findol.

'Call it the beads of Elvish kindness,' he smirked as Findol eagerly opened the bundle. It was stuffed full of them and he helped himself to as many as he could.

'Thanks Flaytus. You really are a life-saver!'

'Oh now, be getting away with yeh. I gets plenty from pruning my *Florus Kelpus Incrediblus* or Flowering Kelp to you and me.'

'You never fail to amaze me. I never knew about … well, any of this. I thought you just had the one home in Lantica. You know … . your studio. You hide a lot of secrets about yourself, Flaytus!'

'And that's the way I likes it, young Findol, thank yeh very much. I has me reasons fer having this secret abode, just likes yer own one, I guess!'

Findol smiled awkwardly.

'Yeh know, as a leprechaun I could do and be much more than this that yeh see before yeh. Why, I was almost on speaking terms with Mother Nature herself! There was magic that even I could control. Why I has even banished Tree Trolls from me wood when they tried to sneak up on me, one night. I was out with my two friends, Paddy Fields and Neddy Conkins. There were three o'them and they was climbing up the tree we were sleeping in. Luckily I was having trouble with me tummy and couldn't sleep. I heard their slobbering and whispered bickering as they prepared to pounce. I leapt up with me lucky four-and-a-half-leaf clover and shouted, "*Jalfrezi Entericus Exitus Acceleratum.*"

'This had the desired effect. It gave them the sort of tummy upset yeh would not believe … or forget in a hurry! They had to abandon their attack to find toilets with great haste. They never returned, but there was a terrible smell that lingered around the wood fer weeks.'

Findol smiled politely, unsure how much of the story was true, but grateful all the same for the distraction it gave.

'Flaytus, look, please. Don't think me ungrateful, but I can't stay here. I really need your help, just to get outside for starters; the way in is blocked! I have got to find my family. I need to know they're safe!'

'Curse me fer blabbering on and on about rubbish. I'm sorry, young 'un. Of course, yer family … Yeh must be worried sick to yer fins. But yeh must be philosophical also and think what's done is done as me third uncle twice removed used to say … twice removed from the local alehouse that is! I think he was referring to his mate Seamus Dunn who was having a wee bit of an identity crisis, but that is far from the point. I feel that you are lucky and fated to be alive. At this moment you're safe and yeh have to concentrate on the important things that concern yeh, right now. There will be plenty o' time t'be entertaining thoughts of today's events. You look like your needs are great at the moment and the best thing fer yeh right now … is food. So let's be getting some food inside yeh and getting yer strength back!'

'Oh, all right, Flaytus! Thanks. You're right, I guess. You are too kind.'

'Oh away with yeh, young scallywag. O*ooops!* A flotilla of bubbles sailed up from behind him and splashed against the cave's ceiling. 'Besides, you've not tasted me cooking yet. Yeh could live t'be regretting it!'

Findol laughed the best he could as he tried to settle and eat something. He looked around the cave and realised that there was no obvious source of light, yet it seemed so bright with all the glowing rock. His head flicked this way and that, amazed and confused. In fact, now that he thought about it, he realised it had been like that right from the cave entrance. He quizzed Flaytus.

'Ah yes. Now there is a clever thing. I believe it is the radiant crystals in the pumice itself that gives out its own light and what a wonderful gift it is to be sure and that's no doubt. T'is something to do with the heat that radiates through the rock itself, so it is!'

'Is this the same heat that causes the "running rock"?'

'If yer meaning the old "lava", then yes, I think so.'

Findol was suddenly concerned. 'Does that mean it is dangerous here? Are we safe?'

'Sweet St Pyronicus of Hotash, yeh surely are, have no fear there.'

As if on cue, a jet of hot gas erupted out of the rock behind, shooting a stream of microbubbles that chased each other to the ceiling. A sudden wave of heat washed over the two of them. Flaytus was relieved he was not the culprit for a change, however, it didn't stop him shooting a nervous glance in its direction.

'As I was saying, there is nothing t'fear. Now I knows yeh are wanting to be out of here!'

'Of course I do, Flaytus! Put yourself in my position! Try to imagine how I feel. Hunted … trapped … family all gone!' His voice was getting louder with emotion.

'Findol me lad. Do yeh not be thinking I don't know the pain and the anxiety coursing through yer body? I can tell yeh that I too have suffered that pain in me time. T'is a nagging pain that gnaws at yer soul and shreds yer heart. So yes, I does know how yeh feel, but I also knows how careful yeh got to be with yer judgement. It's clouded by your emotions. Now, do yeh think yeh can remember the way back? Shouldn't be too hard fer I have signed most of the way!'

'No, Flaytus, don't you remember? I told you I was blocked in. The entrance is no more! I can't go back that way. It's a wall of rock!'

'Ahhh yes, sorry it is the old maturing years … A touch o' forgetfulness. I don't think it will be a problem. Yeh can use me own means of getting out of this place. I calls it my "ejection-tube" since it's little more than a long narrow passage, but I do have a teensy concern with yer size.'

Findol followed Flaytus to the other side of the cave where some pictures had been roughly hung. There was one of Flaytus looking deep in thought with a large fat quill in his claw.

'What's that strange quill you're writing with in this picture, Flaytus? It almost looks like it is alive!'

'Ah-ha. Yeh spotted the deliberate mistake. It was painted by Lamp Wicks, the brudder of Lanky Wicks. He does like to be putting himself in his pictures.'

'What? You mean that is … ?'

'Yes, that's right. He could have been a little less obvious, yeh would think. By the way, talking of quills, look at this beauty.' He rummaged around in his shell and produced a huge Human's "pen".

'T'is platinum-tipped no less, and is real quality fer sure. Harder than a goblin's dagger I reckon. I found it over where you had your accident.'

'Erm, yes, very nice.' Findol winced at the memory as they by the picture. He could just see Lamp Wicks winking back at him with a smug expression painted over his tiny face.

They continued down a passage where tiny volcanic jets of hot water sporadically blew out from small holes and fractures in the walls. One caught Flaytus in the eye.

'Festerin' barnacles,' he blurted out. 'Here we are then!' he proudly exclaimed, claws outstretched toward a dark hole in the rock above them. Findol looked up and just made out the narrow passage that disappeared into the darkness. Way above, he sensed large eruptions of gas and a rattling sound as clusters of bubbles raced up and beyond to the exit.

Oh to be a bubble of gas, he thought as he looked at Flaytus

No matter how hard he studied the passage he couldn't escape the feeling that it was just a little too narrow. He knew he could squeeze in, but it would clamp his fins and tail so he would not be able to move and propel himself upwards. Once again a nauseous wave of panic returned at the thought of being trapped. It washed over him, draining the colour from his skin.

'Now, now. I know that look. All is not lost, by Froglet's eye, no. Where there's a hill there's some hay — as me mother used to say. I has no idea why she said it or its meaning. Anyway, look. I have the answer, but yeh will have to trust me completely!'

He looked at Findol with a serious expression that any other day would have appeared amusing.

'I will have t'be binding yer fin and flippers tightly to yer body so as they don't get in the way. Then I can be pushing yeh with all me might from behind. It will be working, I am sure, but yeh will need to be brave!'

'I don't think I have any choice do I?' Findol swallowed hard. 'Let's just go for it!'

His face steeled with the danger, jaw muscles visibly tense. There wasn't any time to lose. Findol was keen to get out and tend to other needs. Flaytus found some binding kelp that he skilfully worked into a loop around Findol. It could be pulled tight to draw his fin and flippers close to his body.

'There's no denying, it is gonna be a mighty bit uncomfortable, young 'un, but then I knows yeh can cope with that. You're a tough 'un!'

They positioned themselves at the base, just underneath the mouth of the opening.

'Are yeh ready then, me intrepid friend? We have t'be quick!'

'Ready as ever!' Findol shouted back, teeth chattering together.

Flaytus pulled tightly at the cord and Findol gasped,
'One, two, four … '

He pushed with all his might against Findol's tail and they were off up into the passage. It was a long, painfully slow process. Findol kept bumping and snagging on the side, the bindings catching on ragged outcrops of rock, tearing off loose stones that rained down onto Flaytus's head or clattered on his shell. Findol was getting scratched, battered and bruised, whilst thinking all the while that surely there had to be easier ways. Worse still, he realised, yet again he was down to his last bead. There was no way he could manoeuvre to replenish supplies from Flaytus's store and then a thought crossed his mind: 'Why does he need them anyway?'

He was just thinking about what dangers might be lying outside when he suddenly jolted to an abrupt stop. He could feel Flaytus's head collide with his rear followed by some intense pushing below — but he was not budging. A terrible thought came to him. He was trapped inside this claustrophobic tunnel, fast running out of air, in near darkness. There was some desperate shoving from below him, with many grunted curses. Underneath Flaytus, there was the sound of some gas erupting from one of the many fractures in the tube's walls. Large, smelly bubbles squeezed their way through and past both of them.

'They're nothing t'do with me!' Flaytus hastily shouted up. 'But wait a minute, that's given me an idea.'

Flaytus struggled in the narrow passage to turn himself around so that his shell opening was facing downwards.

'Whatever you're doing, you'd better hurry, Flaytus!' Findol anxiously called.

There were suddenly two more eruptions from below. An armada of bubbles came racing upwards and Flaytus skilfully steered himself as they approached so that they collected neatly in his shell. There was an immediate pulling sensation upwards that forced him tightly against Findol's rear.

'This is gonna work, I knows it,' he trilled, his voice getting higher.

Findol felt the pressure too and once more Flaytus tried pushing with all his might, without let-up, claws scrabbling for purchase on the surrounding wall. Findol could just feel himself shifting slightly. His skin was being pulled and scraped, and he ached from his old wounds as he was roughly shuffled up against the hard rock. The wait seemed to go on forever and progress became painfully slow. He was starting to feel woozy from lack of air, but then finally he heard another eruption … a big one this time!

The force of the bubbles hitting them was a mighty shock. Flaytus's shell almost filled completely with the gas, and the upward pull was enormous. Small bubbles skipped and scurried off any obstruction until finding their freedom and racing upwards. Flaytus pushed with all his limbs at the walls around him as a wave of euphoria started to build up within him. Finally it happened; a glorious juddering as Findol's body worked free.

They both found themselves racing up the tube, skidding and bouncing against the sides at an incredible rate. Flaytus tried as best he could to steer Findol away from the rough wall, but it was not easy. The speed of their ascent didn't help, making any sort of control almost impossible. By then, Findol was desperately short of air and he began to drift into semi-consciousness. He was dimly aware of the drum-like banging of Flaytus's shell on the rocky sides and of a soft, sweet voice gently singing in his head.

Go to sleep my little one ... precious little heart.

Fear not my love for missing souls ... we'll-not be long apart.

It sounded just like a Moon-Angel. Or was it his mother? He was too far gone to tell, if there was even a difference.

'I love you, Mum!' he whispered weakly to himself.

The two of them exploded out of the tube's exit in a spectacular cloud of bubbles and continued racing upwards. Flaytus was grabbing and pulling the limp body of Findol with him. When they broke the surface Flaytus went flying up and out into the air, returning with a heavy slap as he landed, shell first and squealing with delight.

'*Yeeee-haaah!* Now *that* was a ride! Takes some beating.'

He was laughing and chuckling hysterically as he quickly worked at freeing Findol from the restricting cord around him. Findol had instinctively taken a huge breath as his skin met the cool air. He lay on the surface, drowsy, but slowly regaining consciousness. His head was pounding and he was still thinking of that voice — or had he just imagined it? He couldn't be sure now! As he collected his thoughts and realised he was finally free, he suddenly remembered just why he had escaped into the caves.

He shook himself until he was fully alert and then warned Flaytus about the unseen danger around them. Nobody who knew him was safe and he quickly looked, listened and searched for any unwelcome eyes. Eventually he was satisfied that their dramatic appearance had gone unnoticed. He was, however, delighted he had made his escape.

'Flaytus, I am indebted to you! What can I say? You saved my life!'

'Now don't be starting on that, will yeh? I was just doing what anyone would have done for yeh!'

Findol glanced downward and then back at him.

'Look, I haven't really got any time to spare. I must get home. Now! I will go mad if I don't find out if they're all okay!'

'Right, I quite understand. But be careful, will yeh? I thinks that there's still a lot of evil about. Trust no one, yeh hear! Fer sure there is a pretty price on yer head. Be alert! I will take a rest and be waiting down below. I'll see yeh when yeh get back, and remember: take care!'

Findol raced off towards his home, cautiously scanning ahead for any unwelcome attention. It was a fair distance, but fear and his nagging concern gave him the strength and determination to hurry along at an impressive rate.

It wasn't long before his worst fears started to take form, for down below, he could dimly see, lying on the seabed, the torn bodies of less fortunate souls. They were the victims of the cruelty that went in Grampus's name. Their bodies brutally savaged by the wave of evil that had descended upon them. The lingering smell of death was choking all around. He had no desire to look closer; he did not wish to find any of his family or friends down there. He wasn't sure that he could cope with the terrible sights anyway. It strengthened his resolve and encouraged him to swim faster. Soon he was within range and, throwing caution to the current, he wasted no time in shouting with all his might: 'Mum, Wippit, Splinter, Lotus, Pipsqueak!'

There was not the slightest hint of an answer, only a terrible silence that seemed to whisper back an emptiness that was somehow loud and shocking. Eventually he became desperately exhausted from the effort of swimming and shouting. Findol was getting more and more anxious as panic started to rise within him. He approached the entrance to his home, heart pounding with the dread of what he might find within, but was shocked when met with nothing, inside. Not even any signs of a struggle which in its own way was such a relief.

That has to be a good thing, he thought, trying to reason the situation and reassure himself.

He swam around, confused and unsure, not knowing what to do, or where to go. Part of him just wanted to go back inside and just nuzzle up on his sleeping shelf and hope everything would magically work out fine. He would wake up later and see his brothers and sisters playing down below. His mother would be casting him a stern glance as she pretended to be angry with him for not getting up sooner. The smell of the food … the Scavits bickering as always …

Try as he might, he knew there was no sanctuary in fantasy, so Findol stopped daydreaming and pulled himself together. This was his reality and he had to deal with it, no matter how hard and unpleasant it was. He lay on the great feeding clam, still smelling as if it had just been filled. The extreme silence in the room that was normally so full of hectic family life was, in its own way, deafening. Even the Scavits had disappeared.

It wasn't long before his fear and worry turned to anger and rage. How dare he be made to feel so wretched, to have his family and friends taken away from him. His defiant mood welled up into a fury as he swam outside. He forced his way out through the kelp screens, throwing his body around in great exaggerated movements. The rage within spilled out as he jerked violently around. Without a care or thought, all the pent-up frustration surfaced and burst out as he shouted with all his might: 'GRAMPUS!

This is not over! I will come for you and I will give you an ocean of pain!'

His words carried far and wide, echoing through the distant blue as they bounced off the seabed and rocks until gradually dissipating into a whisper. Most of the smaller sea creatures that bothered to listen couldn't be less interested.

Exhausted and crying, Findol sunk to the seabed as he finally gave in to his despair. There was absolutely no one around whom he could ask for help, or for news of where his family were. He felt very, very, lonely. The ocean — his ocean — seemed suddenly so much bigger and darker!

It was quite some time before he picked himself up, after reluctantly chewing everything over and weighing up his options. He stretched himself out and took a wattling bead, filled his chest and lifted his head. His face carried a steely expression of single-minded determination as he collected his thoughts and put everything into perspective to prepare for the dark days ahead.

Okay, if that's what everyone wants! Then so be it! From here, it all starts! he thought.

He looked back at his Lantica home, wondering when he would see it again and under what circumstances, before kicking hard with his tail, as he raced away back towards Flaytus.

Chapter 9
From Guano Rock to Cora's Atoll

Findol realised, firstly, he needed time to think, and so swam as fast as possible over to his cave to avoid being in the open for too long. It was just about his only sanctuary and the place where he at least knew he was safe and free from prying eyes. He was delighted to see a familiar face; Wichita was still there, huddled in a corner looking sorry for himself and supping on some Seachum's Chowder.

'Hey, Wichie! You look a lot better. Are you all right now? How you feeling? I guess you probably know what's happened? Tell me everything you have seen or heard!'

'Hold on. Hold on, Findol! Too many questions!' he said. 'I am so sorry, but I don't know what to say. I haven't heard anything. I don't even know what you're talking about. The FlemDip you recommended knocked me for six. I've been sleeping for ages!'

'Oh no! Sorry, Wichie, I never gave it a thought!'

Findol had to go over it all again (which was painful) as he explained all that had happened and some of what he could only guess at.

'So you see I have to hope that Mum and the family heard my warning and got out in time. I know they are alive. I feel it in my heart, but now I have no idea where they might be. Even Whitlow's gone and she never strays far, normally.'

Wichita listened, both fascinated and horrified, the news only making him feel worse. It reminded him of when he lost his own family and he felt the pain deep inside again. He hoped that Findol wouldn't have to confront his greatest fears and suffer the same loss as he did. He did his best to reassure his friend that no news was good news and to trust in his inner feelings.

'Okay, well I guess I'd better go then. Can't hang around. Gotta find out what happened somehow!' Findol grabbed some food and beads and glanced at the metal disc with the pointer, as he raced outside.

'Bye Wichie, catch you later, and take care!'

'You too, Findol. You are gonna need it,' he said, a look of grave concern written on his little face.

Findol raced back towards the Pumice Caves feeling a little more positive than when he had left. Even though he was no further ahead, he convinced himself that no news really was good news.

Exhausted, it seemed like he was back in no time. He found Flaytus where he had left him on the seabed. He was now talking to a small group of sea-horses. He animatedly gestured with his claws and feelers, punctuating guffaws that resonated in his shell. His small audience looked highly impressed and gushed *oohs* and *aaaahs* in all the right places, at least as far as Findol could make out. As he came into view, Flaytus spotted him.

'Sweet Mother o' Pearl, here be the little fella himself.'

They turned as one and looked impressively at Findol, nodding in appreciation and actually clapping their tiny fins against their sides.

'Errr, thanks. Can we talk, Flaytus? In private?' he nudged Flaytus aside from the group. 'What was all that about?'

'Ah, there's nuttin' to worry yer head about. I was just telling them about yeh being trapped, and the big escape.'

'That's all very well, but don't you think the fewer who know about it and my whereabouts, the better?'

'Err, yes, yer right of course, but it is the power of the Blarney Stone that keeps me blessed tongue wagging all the time. I'll be trying to put the brakes on it a bit I will.'

'Yes please, Flaytus. I definitely think you should! Hold on a minute, I have an idea.' Findol turned to face the group. 'Look. You lot could actually help me!'

'Sure! We will if we can. Just name it,' said Otis Saddlesaw. He looked to be the oldest and possibly the wisest of the bunch. Findol looked intently at them.

'There are three friends of mine that I have lost contact with. You may know them: Pinkerton Gallop, Piebald Fetlock and Lippizana Stirrups. I arranged to meet them over a month ago now and was unable to do so. I have had no contact from them whatsoever and need to find them. If you know or hear anything please can you get news to me quickly, somehow?'

They appeared to go into a group huddle and there was a frantic verbal exchange between the three of them. Eventually Otis swam up to Findol with a concerned look in his eyes.

'These three you mention are indeed known to us, but we cannot give you good news. Pinkerton and Piebald saw us many weeks ago and said something rather vague about an important mission and a Hint-at Net — whatever that is. They said they had been far away and they were travelling up to the Northern Seas to get some news. About what, they wouldn't say, except to be aware of Grampus. If we heard any news, we were to contact Lippizana as soon as possible. He was going elsewhere and was supposed to be keeping us informed of his whereabouts. He was going to be circuiting the far Outer Lantica Rim to pick up on any information over there. However, we haven't seen or heard from him or indeed any of the other two since. It all seems very exciting, but rather worrying too! Just what is actually happening?'

Findol explained all that he knew whilst Otis and the others listened, mesmerised as their little tails tightened around the kelp they were holding onto. He explained how he had been involved in the terrible accident that caused him to miss his meeting with them and all that had happened after. When he had finished, they swore they would do all they could to help and would contact him somehow if news came through. They raced off, wishing the two of them good luck.

Flaytus was scribbling his notes down when Findol came over to talk to him. 'It is grand that yeh be getting back safely. I does not need to be guessing that yeh found nothing of yer family. I am sorry for yeh Findol, but not surprised.'

'What do you mean, Flaytus?'

'Now look, don't be taking offence, but I just knew yeh had to see fer yourself. I thinks yer family has a lot of friends and so I am sure they were helped and warned in plenty of time to be getting to safety. Me telling yeh that, would have made no difference. Yeh still would have wanted to see fer yourself and I can't be blaming yeh fer that. Why, I would have done just the same, so I would.'

'Yes. Thanks, Flaytus. You are right as usual. There was no sign of anything, not even a struggle, so at least I have hope for them!'

Flaytus had begun getting his writing equipment out and proceeded to start scribing away some more notes. 'It's no good, Flaytus. I can't decide what to do on my own. I don't know quite where to start first, that's the problem. I need some more of your wisdom to help steer me in the right direction I think. After all, I guess there is only so much time before Grampus makes a return visit!'

Somewhere, not so far away, an ugly creature was listening in and also thinking of Grampus. Even though he was considered "small-fry" and had been left behind by the horde, Scaybeez still knew the power he could wield. Some suitable, highly prized information that Grampus desired would be rewarded most generously.

Information concerning the whereabouts of a certain much sought-after dolphin maybe! he cackled to himself, rubbing his flaky fins together in glee.

Flaytus gazed intently at a small sea-fern that to him looked just like a lop-eared rabbit with a hare-lip and braces on its teeth (he had a very active imagination). He was reminded of the time he had joined the quest for the Coney Quail; a bird steeped in legend. He had first spotted it standing beside a fern that had looked similar to the very one he was staring at.

'Sorry Findol. Bejaybers! I was a trillion miles away. What a stupid turnip I is and that's fer sure. There's you askin' me fer wise words and I am off on one of me daydreams. It seems to me to be obvious who yeh must be finding to talk to. Only yer one true guardian angel that's who!'

'Flaytus, stop talking in riddles! Who do you mean?'

'Fer goodness sake, young' un, do I really have to be spelling it out? There's only one who has always been there for yeh, not always when yeh realised, I wager. CORA, of course. If anybody knows who, why, when, where, which … it has to be her.'

'Of course, yes! YES! Cora! How could I be so stupid? She is the obvious choice isn't she? Why of all Cetaceans did I not think of her immediately?'

'Yer a wee bit stressed out, that's why. Yeh needs to get yer cool back, that's what.'

'I guess you're right, but one massive problem immediately springs to mind! Where do we find her? After all, isn't she supposed to live as a recluse or a hermit or something? And she is so secretive.'

'Oh slap me on my thorax fer not thinking. Yer right of course. There will be someone who knows, I am sure of it. We just needs to be thinking fer a minute! I had a mate once, Feargal O'Riley. He used to drive everybody mad with his knowledge. Yeh know ... bit of a know-it-all. We could do with him now and that's fer sure. The best thing we can do is to be getting something to eat. Yeh might not be thinking yer hungry, but I wager yeh will be glad of it and yer not knowing when yeh might get another chance once yeh be setting off.'

Flaytus produced a kelp packet from within his shell. 'These are me favourites, MantaMunch Crunchy Krill Chips. Take them and enjoy, young 'un.'

'Thanks, Flaytus — *scoff, scoff* — they are delicious — *munch, munch* — really tasty!'

'There. See. Yeh was hungry and yeh didn't even know it! Yeh can't be thinking on an empty stomach.'

Flaytus also gave Findol a couple of squidling patties that he had left in the recesses within his shell.

'Do yeh know, things always seem to be getting lost or mislaid in there, but on this occasion I am well pleased to be finding the patties for yeh.'

'Me too, Flaytus,' burped Findol. 'Sorry. Pardon me! Look, I have an idea. I am going back to my cave. There's something I should have picked up when I was just there. Just might be what I'm looking for. Maybe something to point me in the right direction.'

'Alright, I am sure I don't know what yeh be talking about so take care. I will wait here fer yeh again!'

Findol was off in seconds.

'See ya soon, Flaytus.'

The crab watched him race off and immediately collected his scribing parchment and quills and began writing again.

This is going to be a mighty big book, he thought.

Findol didn't know quite how he was going to find Cora's home, but could only trust to his instincts. It was the round artefact in his cave he had been thinking about and decided he should take it along. Surely it would be useful somehow and all too often his hunches had paid off. Eventually he arrived back at the cave with Wichita still looking a sorry state in the far corner. Globs of glue had splashed on the floor around him and thin wispy trails snaked from them in the current.

'Not much better then, Wichie?' he said as he moved carefully to avoid them.

'Er, no, Findol! Still, I don't complain, does I?' He blew his nose loudly on a kelp tissue. He didn't have any more news for Wichita, so Findol decided to try to clear his head and just allow himself to think. He lay there on his favourite sea-sponge mat and tried to put all thoughts of his family and friends to the back of his mind. This allowed him to focus on the matter in hand. Where was Cora and who would know?

As in moments of crisis, crazy things happen. Strange things are done, irrationally, which is probably why he found himself humming a song, slapping his flippers on his sides to the beat. It also explained why he had then thought of Sea-Czar's Palace and Barnacle Groans. The harder he tried to remove the image from his brain, the more he could actually see him. He scolded himself and thought how stupid he was being.

Curse me for being so birdbrained, he thought. *Hold on! Birdbrained. BIRD! That's it, Tegan. Of course, Tegan. If he doesn't know where she is then surely he will know someone who does!*

He felt a warm flush of positivity wash over him as he revelled in his optimism and the first tiny piece of hope in his heart. Findol did a backward flip that knocked a few ornaments off a shelf, not that he noticed or cared, such was his good mood. He went over to the curious round artefact and placed the strap of it over his neck. Within seconds, he had said his farewell to Wichita and was back outside again. All he now needed was to get his bearings and somehow find Tegan's home. He aimed for Guano Rock (the rocky prominence on the small island of Spinney's Folly) and glanced down at the round object hanging below his neck. He could see the needle pointing just off to the right. As he moved around obstacles he kept watching the needle's movement.

This really will be useful, he thought. He swam to the surface, took a large gulp and continued to swim just below the surface. He rose regularly to check for any sign of the small island and any hint of unwelcome eyes.

Eventually, what had started as a small dot on the horizon rapidly became the towering form of the white-stained Guano Rock. It had a seething mass of screeching birds, circling around and covering the surface that he could just see through the swirls of sea-mist that hung around the top. Braver birds could be spotted, clinging to dangerous outcrops on its sides. They held on tightly, choosing precariously crazy locations for their nests, amongst small clumps of vegetation that also seemed to be desperately hanging on. The birds themselves were everywhere, soaring, circling, ducking and diving. Their noise was deafening as raucous cries echoed all around.

Not the place to come when you have a headache, he thought. He then realised he had yet another problem. How was he to find Tegan amongst all these birds?

Just to his left there was a small group of them scrapping amongst themselves over a pathetically small carcass of a fish. He seized the opportunity to get their attention with an idea.

'Hi guys, sorry to intrude, but can I ask a huge favour?'

'Oh yeah, so what's that then, eh? What's your game?'

'Yeah, tell us whatcha want?'

'Look, look it's very simple,' said Findol. 'I just need to find someone. He's one of your lot, actually. Tegan?'

'Ha! Don't know a Tegan. Hmm … Hang on a minute! Has he got white wings, a beak wiv a yellow flushed face and black around his eyes?'

'Yes. Yes, he has,' Findol excitedly replied.

'Ha! Well there's about 30,000 to choose from up there.' The gannets collapsed in a cacophony of cackles and whoops.

Findol stared back at them impassively.

'Yes, okay, very funny. Now do you want to help or not? I can make it worth your while! I know roughly where he should be located.' He reeled off Tegan's address from memory. 'Guano Rock … Row 24 … Aisle 6 … just right of the large guano stain on a broken periwinkle!'

They were still laughing,

'Cor, couldn't yer have been a little bit more exact? I mean what colour or type of periwinkle? There's maybe loads and loads of them, eh? Anyhow! Just how yeh gonna make it worth our while then?'

'Well, it's simple. I can chase a shoal of fish right into your waiting beaks! Is that good enough for you?'

'Hmm! Regular little starfisher ain't he guys? Go on. Guess so!'

'So you will do it then?'

'Yeah alright, but only if we catch some big 'uns, okay? And only if we finds the right periwinkle!'

'Fine, fine!'

Findol wasted no time in swimming away to prepare to harvest the gannets a suitable feast as they circled above. The artefact was bouncing on its strap around his neck. Every now and then it caught the itchy spot and on one occasion struck him square on the nose. He was oblivious to it though, such was his resolve to hurry and get the information he needed from Tegan.

He spotted a small shoal of sea bass and thought, *Ideal!* He circled around them and in no time was herding them upwards towards the open bills of the greedy gannets. Without warning, there were suddenly hundreds of mini explosions as bird upon bird plunged into the water all around him to feast on the fish. Garibaldi, a small yellow fish, was watching all this from below as he tucked into his jellyfish snack.

Crumbs. A dolphin feeding gannets! Whatever next? he thought.

Eventually the birds had finished eating and many of them were now floating on the surface, their bodies fat and replete.

'Well are you going to honour the bargain or what?' Findol asked.

'Yes, yes. Okay. I don't wanna get indigestion, do I? Plays havoc with my preening it does.'

A couple of them struggled to fly off. Their wings strained at their heavy bodies as they slowly lifted out of the water. They disappeared for what seemed like an eternity until Findol spotted Tegan's unmistakeably erratic flying. He rapidly descended clumsily from above and came to a rest on the water.

'Findol, Findol, an absolute delight to see you again, dear boy. I have been so worried and feared for your safety. News of events below have not escaped me. I hope you have not been too put off by these coarse upstarts. They are not as bad as you might think. They are sadly not blessed with my intellect and wit … '

''Ere, watch it you festerin' nudibranch!'

' … or vocabulary!' he added. A mis-timed kick from one of them swept past his head.

'Ha, they joke! Funny lot, aren't they? Look, let's find somewhere quieter, free from that lot. I am anxious for your news of just what has really been happening down below! My friend Snippitz the pelican said something about an army, a battle and huge groups of eels. So come on, he may have a big mouth, but what he says is never far from the truth!'

Findol motioned to him to follow and so they moved far away from the rock and the other birds. Tegan flew behind as Findol swam, and landed on the surface beside him.

'Dear Findol, put me out of my misery. I have heard so many silly rumours and a lot of them not nice at all. I hear names, the like of which I have not heard mentioned by others, except yourself and Glycol. Names like Grampus, Hamrag, Kreegan and others. I have done as you asked and tried to be aware of anything developing below, but until I spoke to Snippitz, I had nothing worth reporting to you. It would seem that by then, I would have been too late anyway! So you are going to tell me it has finally happened then?'

'Yes, I am afraid so, and don't feel bad. I really think you wouldn't have been able to help. It all happened so quickly.'

Findol explained as briefly as he could, all that had occurred since his accident, already an event that seemed such a long time ago.

'Tegan, I don't think there's much time. I need to find Cora urgently and I really hope you can help me find where she lives. Without her help I have no idea what to do!'

Tegan went quiet and thought for a long time. 'Old Cora! She's a bit of a mystery for sure. I shall have to go and ask around. Stay here while I go back up to the colony. I shall be as quick as I possibly can.'

He was gone a long time while a group of birds moved closer to Findol as they concentrated on a shoal of fish they were plundering. He had to put up with the noise of their incessant squawking and calling. Not to mention avoiding the occasional mis-timed and mis-aimed attempts by younger birds to plunge into the depths for their food.

'Oi! Watch it, Mr Blubber!' they would cheekily shout if he appeared too close. He ignored them as he reflected on recent events. It was during his daydreaming that he realised to his horror, he had completely forgotten all about his friends Sterbol and the Kriblings. He had been so focussed on those nearer to home that he hadn't given them a second thought. They too might have been attacked for all he knew. All he could do was console himself with the thought that they would be okay. It was almost certainly only specific Cetaceans, dolphins in

175

particular, like himself, that had been targeted and so they were probably okay. It was still annoying to him, though, that he could so easily have overlooked his best friend. He wondered what the Kriblings would make of all this. With their long history of trouble and strife it would probably have not made much of an impact on them. But then they did have principles and would probably have been outraged at the cruelty of it all.

He lay there gazing up at the high cliffs, watching the birds going about their business, but not really taking it in. The immense rock with its crawling feathery carpet was quite hypnotic and he found himself imagining what it must be like to be so high up. What would it feel like moving around, out of the water, supported by nothing, feeling the cool wind all over your body? The thought of floating through the air, performing amazing manoeuvres, then landing on two feet and walking around was weird. It was hard to imagine the sensation and he could only guess that it would be amazing. He was mesmerised by the skill of the birds as they wheeled around, banking and diving, pulling in their wings at the very last moment just before hitting the water. It was the first time he had ever really looked at them and just what they could do and he couldn't help but be impressed by their grace and agility.

Just then, he slipped out of his daydream as he saw that one was coming right towards him at quite an alarming rate. It was Tegan! Findol dived at the right moment as the swaying bird totally misjudged his landing. His feet connected too soon with the surface and way too fast, pulling him over in a series of undignified somersaults at breakneck speed. His back slapped hard on the sea's surface and he reeled from the impact and came to a halt, coughing and spluttering.

'*Ouch*! Can never get the hang of these "high-speed, auto-deceleration, negative back thrust stops", you know!'

Wincing still from the sight, Findol replied, 'So I noticed,' as his mouth trembled with the effort of trying hard not to break into laughter.

Tegan was shaking himself free of some of the water and trying to straighten a few bent feathers.

'Anyway, it's great news, Findol. I put the word around and old Shyneez Wispaz came up trumps. He might be a nosy so-and-so, but this time it's certainly paid off. It would seem that up north, there is an atoll that Cora uses as her home. It's partially hidden from view by semi-permanent sea mist, difficult to get into and apparently very difficult to find. Shyneez overheard a conversation between two frigate birds that were discussing the atoll. Seemingly they were wondering why someone was blocking up the entrance and forming some sort of wall around it. It doesn't take a genius to figure that either it's been blocked to stop someone getting in or more likely to stop an individual getting out.'

Findol was looking intently at Tegan.

'So who is doing this and how?'

'Findol, come on, do I have to answer that?'

'No, of course not. It's obvious isn't it?' He was looking sad and awkward. 'But sometimes I guess I find it easier to avoid the glaring truth.'

'That may be so, young one, but this is not a problem that is just going to disappear, is it?'

'Yeah, I suppose not.' Findol felt a little foolish, realising he still had a lot to learn.

Tegan continued.

'So anyway, this must be where you will find Cora. It's got to be worth a try!'

'Yes, you're right Tegan, and thanks. I do wonder though that surely Cora would have tried to get a message out somehow! Wouldn't she?'

'Yes, but I haven't finished telling you everything. You will find this hard to believe perhaps, but the whole atoll is apparently surrounded by a closed wall of electric eels, positively revolting thought.' Findol nodded as he thought back, whilst Tegan looked sternly at him.

'Apparently they call themselves "The Gridlock" because the power they generate collectively stops everything, whether it be individuals or any form of communication passing between them. Cora could have shouted and cried for all she is worth, but no message would have got out.'

Again, Findol felt a surge of anger that Grampus could do this to one as revered as Cora.

'That's it! That ... is ... it! Don't you see? I have been puzzling how I — how WE — were all taken by surprise by him. He must have had something like that Gridlock preventing news of his movements coming from my Hint-at Net.' He shuddered as he remembered the sight of it just before he hid in the Pumice Caves. Tegan's face was a picture as the thought hit him.

'Yes, you are right. It does explain the lack of news' His voice softened ' ... and the absence of your Sea-Pony Express chums, doesn't it?'

'You heard then?' Findol looked sad. 'Come on, let's get going before I lose my nerve.'

They wasted no time in setting off, Tegan above and Findol just below the surface. He regularly leapt up to snatch a breath and a quick word with Tegan.

'Oh my gosh — *splash* — Tegan — I have completely forgotten — *splash* — Flaytus. Stop!'

'I'll have to send him a message somehow, so he doesn't worry.'

They resumed and forged ahead. Findol had never travelled so far north and at such a fast pace for so long. His old wounds were still throbbing and his muscles complaining. Soon, he was worn out and just had to rest. Tegan wasn't sorry as he too was not getting any younger and his back and wings ached. They spotted the faint outlines of some small coral islands on the horizon and decided to rest there. It meant they were close to the atoll and they would need to get as much rest as possible before looking for Cora and whatever lay ahead.

They stopped at the first islet that barely broke the sea's surface. It had a small, but very convenient shelf just above the water, which was dry and was perfect for Tegan to roost with a sheltered area beside it for Findol just below the waterline. Findol pulled some weed together and made a rough, but usable kelp mat that he worked over some exposed rock to give him a more comfortable sleeping shelf. 'Home from home!' he whispered to himself. He had barely settled down when he heard a rather disgruntled voice, right up close, beside him.

'Young sire, dost thou not know the noble art of etiquette?'

A large harlequin shrimp was looking straight into his eye and appeared to be rather upset. Findol had obviously invaded his space.

'Oh, I am sorry. Let me move over here. I didn't see you. I am Findol of Lantica Down, and above is my friend Tegan of Guano Rock. We are not here to upset or inconvenience anyone. We just need somewhere to rest for the night!'

'Verily thou knowest the courtesy of polite introduction, carrying a warm tongue upon thee and for that I will reciprocate!'

Findol was struggling to understand the strange creature, as it continued.

'I am Jethro Trawl, the minstrel shrimp of King Neptune's Gallery. My music once graced the Great Halls of Residence, for truly there was a time when I was the official minstrel in the Gallery.'

Findol was confused. Although he had often listened to stories of King Neptune, it had been suggested that they were pure fantasy — or so he had thought! Tegan was asleep so he didn't disturb him, but carried on talking with his rather fascinating companion.

Jethro was seemingly far older than he looked. He put his youthful looks down to a lifetime of healthy eating and good living, with a dash of good fortune. He had played his silver shell-flute all his life, touring the whole of the Big Blue, much to everybody's appreciation. When he took up residence at King Neptune's Court he had played in the mighty Imperial Orchestra. He certainly enjoyed talking about himself and explained how he had even played at Sea-Czar's Palace.

Findol listened, fascinated, but confused. Was this the truth or was Jethro just a good story-teller? Either way, it was a nice distraction. Eventually it was his turn to relate his own story and Jethro listened, mesmerised. It soon turned out that Jethro was not in the area by pure coincidence. He had a talent for writing tunes and folk songs about current events and was monitoring the situation with Cora over at the atoll. In its own way it was terrific news as it meant that they were definitely right about where Cora was and that she was alive. Jethro would be able to show them the exact way too. The shrimp was however a little unsure about the idea, since he had taken his life in his hands on a number of occasions and had nearly paid the ultimate price. He made it clear that the eels were cruel and heartless and thought nothing of "frying" any poor unsuspecting individual.

'If you intend doing all that you have told me then you need as much rest as you can get, young Findol. Wits alone may not be enough to see you through!'

Findol settled down and gazed up through the water at the full moon, whilst Jethro played some songs on his flute. Findol couldn't help but peep at the little shrimp on his right. Jethro was balancing himself on one row of legs with the others bent and tucked up under him. He stood precariously balanced on a flat rock as he played, looking rather uncomfortable in the process. Findol decided to leave the little one to it and continued gazing upwards.

The moon's image stretched and danced around in an almost playful manner as the water gently lapped around the coral. Findol surfaced for a few seconds and listened, bobbing slightly in the swell. He looked up at the moon and thought that she had almost become an embodiment of his mother — or maybe Cora. *Pure and white, a guiding light. Always there, when in despair,* he thought.

Tegan was snoring off to his right, with an irritating whistle exiting his nostrils. Ahead on the distant horizon the last rays of light were already creeping over the edge. A warm, deep crimson glow remained, slowly oozing over the surface as flocks of birds crossed the dark sky in silhouette, before the darkness finally consumed all in its path.

'So much beauty in a world of hurt,' Findol whispered to himself. He slipped into a deep sleep almost as soon as he returned below to settle near Jethro, who thankfully had stashed his flute and was snoring quietly. His last conscious thought as he looked at Jethro was about the female Kriblings.

'Wow! They really are girly tights! Still, it takes *a*ll sorts, I suppose.'

Then he fell to sleep.

Chapter 10
Storming the Net

Findol did not sleep well. He wrestled throughout the night with all manner of terrible images until eventually he rose late in the morning to chuckling and guffawing from Tegan and Jethro who had struck up quite a friendship. Tegan had already been awake for some time and had long since caught and ate his breakfast. But he had also stashed a few fish for Findol on a nearby rock.

The young dolphin remembered some strange and disturbing images from his dreams. There had been a beautiful full moon that had smiled down at him before morphing weirdly into the face of Cora. But then the image had bizarrely split open to reveal a gaping hole in the sky through which his family and friends were attempting to swim. He had swum forward in an attempt to touch them, but they just seemed to dissolve right before his eyes. As he had desperately searched around for them, the ocean parted and became the giant jaws of Grampus. His red-stained baleen plates were clumped together into sharp terrifying teeth, his strange bulk far larger than in real life. And he looked … almost …

He couldn't tell for sure, and fear certainly had a way of exaggerating things, yet the beast appeared almost human!

Then there was poor Sterbol; he was trapped, forced into a corner by a group of evil barracuda. They were cruelly pulling him apart, limb by limb; his pitiful screams had stayed to haunt Findol's mind, long after he had awoken, confused and scared and shaking. He snapped himself out of it, refusing to recall any more of the night's horrors.

'It was just a dream, that's all!' he reminded himself. Suddenly though, he remembered a moment of pure joy; another thing from his sleep. Something wonderful. His attention had been drawn to a brilliant flash of light, or so he had thought. Even now he could not be entirely sure if he had seen it for real or whether it had been just inside his head. But he was positive he had woken up and there in front of him had been yet another vision of Cora. This time she had looked terribly aged and weak, yet still seemed to glow as she struggled to speak to him. She had looked anxious and was obviously concerned with the message she was trying to relay to him:

Take care Findol, take care. And remember, dive deep, dive deep …

There was yet another dramatic flash, and then she was gone as quickly as she had arrived. He had sensed an intense pain in her. The sort you got from the dreaded electric eels, for he too had suffered it before and it confirmed what he already knew and feared. But at least it also proved that she was alive, as long as the price for sending the message had not cost her too dearly!

Findol felt they had no time to lose and they would have to act right now. They hurriedly finished their breakfast and made off with Jethro clinging to Findol's back just like Sterbol used to do, though thankfully he was a lot lighter.

Jethro insisted on making sure they were on the right bearing to arrive at Cora's Atoll. Clutching tightly to his fiddle, he was looking forward to composing a new jig or reel about all he had heard. He also informed Findol that the thing around his neck was called a "Camposs" and was indeed a tool of Man for assisting with travel. Findol felt rather impressed with himself for getting it right. He thought of Sterbol and hoped he was safe. He hated to think of him as only a memory, and especially as a horrendous flash from his dreams. But somehow he knew that he would see his friend again.

Tegan flew ahead, in the direction Jethro had given them, keen to get any news as quick as possible. It wasn't long before he was returning in an extremely excited manner, flying erratically, dipping this way and that.

'Findol … *gasp* … *gasp* … it's all true! The … *pant* … atoll is not far ahead … I flew over and I am … sure I saw Cora, down below, under the surface. But … *gasp* … the worst of it is … the eels … thousands and thousands of them, just as we thought. They look like they have completely surrounded the entire atoll in a tight, closed circle. There is a massive wall of light and energy that extends all around and out of the very water. It is a curious sight — it crackles and burns; you can smell it in the air!'

'Yes, I know what you mean; I have experienced it in the past. It's like tasting the very panic between terrified thoughts!'

Tegan looked at him, confused. 'Yeeessss! … Right, I think I see what you mean!' he said.

Jethro was looking agitated. 'Look, if it's all the same to you stout fellows, you now have your destination firmly in thy sights and one really must be going. For I fight with my words, music and deeds. For truly, violence is not my forte and my talents are required yonder. Fare thee well!' He was pointing south.

'Yes, we understand, Jethro — and thanks. History and music teaches us many things, I know. I hope we meet again because there is much I would like to talk with you about.' Findol was still keen on learning more about King Neptune.

With that, Jethro swam off and was gone, leaving Findol and Tegan to themselves.

Well, here comes the scary bit, Findol thought. 'Okay, Tegan, how am I going to find the entrance and get past the Gridlock? In my dream Cora had said something about "diving deep". Is that a clue? I just don't know! All I can do is try and go down deep as I can and see if there is a way in below their barrier!'

Tegan was floating beside him, wings tucked in, head cocked to one side as he listened intently.

'Yes, I'm sure you are right. She has great powers, still, and I feel this really was a message from her to help you! I think there is a problem though. You are going to need some sort of distraction because those eels are not going to let you find the entrance without a fight. If they get the slightest suspicion of your presence ... You can't afford one of them spotting you, it would be your end! Worse still, you don't want certain individuals to know you are here either, do you? There is no way you can possibly consider to take on even a fraction of their number. I will have to find a way of occupying them, to divert their attention from your true purpose.'

'Thanks, Tegan, I hadn't thought of that.'

Tegan clasped his wings over his head as he bobbed on the sea's surface, in deep thought. 'I have a crazy idea that just might work. I am not the most popular member of the colony, but there are many who owe me a favour or two and it's time to call them in. The colony's hunger can be turned to our favour. Trust me, I will be back as fast as my wings will carry me. Take care and keep yourself out of their sight, won't you! Make sure you stay here, okay?'

'Yes, thanks Tegan. See you soon!'

Tegan raced back to Guano Rock as if his very life depended on it. There were still a lot of birds loyal to him, back from his days as leader of the pack.

The twins, Bile and Flem had rather surprisingly grown up to be two individuals that he could almost always rely on when in a fix. Grissel had left to try and form his own colony, whilst Nostrul had a run-in many years ago with a fish eagle that involved possession of a large fish carcass. He had come off considerably worse, with a torn wing that had never fully healed. Eventually he was unable to fly well enough to be of any use and couldn't catch his food. Natural selection dictates the rules and he was forced out of the colony to fend for himself. No one knew of his fate since that day.

Tegan wished now that he had Nostrul around. Nostrul hadn't particularly liked Tegan, but would have jumped at the challenge that presented itself, despite his handicaps. Bile and Flem were not hard to find; they were always running errands for others, which was good for their business and also meant they were well known.

'Hiya Tegan. 'ow's it going?'

'Er, fine thanks. Listen chaps, I really need your help.'

He explained all that they needed to know with the promise of a banquet with food-a-plenty, at a time when the colony was yet again desperate for a big catch. There was indeed going to be a very "big catch" though and not necessarily the kind they wanted. They would have immediately jumped at the chance, but for their concern over the huge numbers of the eels. A few on their own was not a problem, in fact they would be a positive delicacy, but when thousands were involved and fighting back, then the situation changed. It didn't take them long, however, before they both were thinking with their stomachs and racing round the colony looking for volunteers for an exciting mission. They said that it guaranteed a large food payout, glossing over the little matter of the danger involved. They had asked Tegan to remain where he was and let them do the talking since they felt that their word maybe carried a little more clout. He didn't care though, if the end result was the same. As long as they achieved the necessary distraction for Findol, then that was all that mattered. Job done!

However, time dragged and it seemed to Tegan like they were taking forever. He was precariously sheltering behind a particularly moist, guano-stained rock on a ledge over a massive drop. Old age was giving him intermittent vertigo which was very inconvenient and he looked giddily down at the birds beneath, swirling around and then quickly up on thermals.

'That was me once,' he reminisced and for the first time he felt a frail vulnerability in himself as he realised that age was indeed catching up on him.

Eventually the two birds returned, clearly delighted that they had amassed so much interest. Behind them shuffled a very impressive army of famished birds all keen for a go at the promised shoal of "fish"! Tegan took the two aside.

'Am I right in saying that they all think they are going after fish?

'Well, yes … so what? I mean they is sort o'fish are they not? Just got a bit of a sting to them, that's all. We're just being a bit frugal with the truth.'

That's the story of their lives, thought Tegan.

'Yeah, Bile's right. I mean they really is just fish without fins. Sort of unFINished yer could say!' they cackled to themselves. Tegan wasn't going to argue the point.

I just hope they don't change their minds when push comes to shove, or in this case "dive", he thought.

'Listen, Tegan, you know our motto, don't ya? Blood 'n' guts 'n' glory!'

'Yes, yes, yes,' he sighed. 'I know all three of them although I prefer not to! I hope you are right though, I really do! Because more depends on this than you could ever imagine!'

Back at the atoll, Findol could not control his curiosity any longer. He just had to have a tiny peep. He made a wide sweep around it, just keeping the edge distantly in view. From this far out he could just see through the low wall of energy and, through it, the irregular surface of the coral walls with the belt of eels writhing around its girth just under the surface.

The energy field was massive and Findol hoped it would come to an end before he hit the bottom. He popped a bead and dived deep, way down to the seabed. The Gridlock thankfully ended some way above so he carefully dared to venture closer, glancing up, all the time. The coral down there was so old that years of silt deposit and calcification had caused it to harden to almost rock, whilst a hazy fog of dust and detritus hung around in a foggy carpet. He came up to the walls and cautiously swam around, scouring the hard surface for any signs of an opening. His echo worked overtime whilst he nervously looked up to check on the eels.

As he crossed a large outcrop, the wall unexpectedly disappeared below him into darkness and down a deep trench. This perhaps was where Cora meant. It was ominously dark and murky with no clue as to what lay beyond. Yet it was reassuring to dive further and increase the distance separating him from the evil above. The lack of light was worrying though and he wasn't too sure about the growing sense of foreboding he felt. His gut feelings were usually not far from the truth and yet evil often had a way of being able to avoid detection.

He spotted a small clump of kelp and used the opportunity to nip some wattling beads from it, storing them in his mouth. Cautiously he swam down into the blackness, using his echo as best he could. Before long what little light that was left had all but gone, making it hard to see and forcing a greater dependence on all his other senses.

Without warning he came upon a large opening just beneath him and around a bend. He warily moved forward and could sense what appeared to be a huge cave entrance extending deep into the wall of the atoll. Findol was shaking both with fear and nervous excitement.

This has to be what Cora meant, he thought. *Fancy leaving such a large entrance for me ...*

He had just been about to enter when he felt a dramatic change in the water pressure as something exceptionally large moved towards him. It came silently from within the darkness, and at that moment his heart leapt a beat. He felt it pounding heavily in his chest as his senses alerted him to terrible danger. His blood ran to ice and all muscles tensed as he cautiously withdrew backwards. Like before, he was pulling himself against a wall, trying to find somewhere, anywhere, to conceal himself and avoid detection.

The reason why such a large cave entrance had appeared to be left open was now apparent. A massive conger eel was slowly uncoiling itself as it oozed out from the inky blackness within. Even in the poor light it was not difficult to make out its hideous form. He could tell it was far bigger than any he had ever previously seen and could only stare in horror at the fixed grimace and razor-sharp teeth. Its massive head shook from side to side, working out the stiffness in its muscles, as it struggled with its poor sight. There was a smell that it carried which made Findol's stomach urge. He instinctively clasped the Camposs tight to his body to prevent any sound.

If evil had an aroma then this is it, he thought. Findol was close to despair as he now thought he knew the identity of the creature.

Kreegan. It has to be. It fits the description. What do I do now? With the eels up top and Kreegan below, how do I get in? This can be the only other entrance and yet, surely Cora would not have mentioned it, if she had known Kreegan was here. She couldn't have had any knowledge of it! It's down to me to figure a way of getting him out long enough for me to sneak in!

He continued to slowly reverse, nervously looking back to where Kreegan had gone, until finally satisfied he was far enough away and had avoided detection. Findol swam up to the surface, careful to avoid attracting unwelcome attention, not even risking the pop of a wattling bead.

He returned to where he would meet Tegan and the wait seemed agonisingly long. It was all made worse by his latest find, and the longer it was left for him to ponder, the worse it appeared. He spotted a ship in the distance. It was one of Man's war-ships, a distant shape, sunlight blinking off its gun turrets, far away on the horizon. There were little white puffs of smoke that could just be made out, billowing out from its funnels. It put his own reality into a clear perspective. There were wars for Man to deal with too, on land as well as in the Big Blue. Even Mankind had occasion to live and work in fear and dread. Findol had learned about the battles that had occurred on the seas in days long gone by: the massive destruction of human lives, and all for what? Even the wisest of the wise could not explain the terrible waste, or the very desire for it, deep in the Human Psyche. His mother had told him that as Cetaceans they were lucky to be part of a species that had evolved beyond that.

As his mind wrestled with it all, a small, unusually-dark cloud appeared over the horizon. It was heading quickly in his direction which was strange, for it appeared to pulse and sway much like a fishball. It was the only one in an otherwise clear blue sky and it was moving much too fast to be a cloud. Before long, Findol understood its true nature and watched in fascination.

It was Tegan and his army of helpers. The massive flock must have numbered thousands of individuals and came closer and closer. He was delighted that there were so many and it warmed his heart and boosted his confidence. They quietly landed on and around some of the many small coral outcrops close by, but distant enough to avoid attracting attention. It created a huge white blanket on the surface, eerie because of the absence of any sound. Strict instructions for silence were keenly adhered to. Tegan flew over to Findol when all his followers were settled.

'Hi Tegan, well done! I guess you've more supporters than you thought!'

'Don't kid yourself, Findol. They are here for one thing only and that's food. Hunger has a way of persuading the coldest heart. I had a spot of bother on the way over the actual nature of the catch. We had previously left that bit out, but they are still going through with it.'

Findol explained how he had found Kreegan below and the need to change the plan, for it now seemed the Gridlock was not the main problem. Together they thought long and hard as they hatched a plan, choosing to launch the attack at twilight when it would be least expected. Furthermore the poor light would give just enough visibility for the birds needs. Hopefully it would add to the confusion to maximise surprise. The plan, however, required that the birds would have to dive really deep to create enough noise, and commotion. It would need to disturb and attract a curious conger like Kreegan, drawing him out of his cave. The danger for the birds involved would be immense. Both from the sheer force of hitting the water so hard and from the very eels that they would be attacking. For Findol, down below, it would be really dark and he would have to rely more than ever before on his echo and his wits. Tegan looked sternly at him.

'Look, Findol, I really believe in you! It is not something I say lightly. I am old and maybe too long in the beak. Nothing surprises or worries me anymore. But I see something very special before me. You are honest and true. You have courage in your heart. I know your purpose and your need to stay true to it. I think my followers would understand that, if they could only look past their own stomachs. I will make sure we do all we can to help you achieve this, no matter what or at what cost! You have my word!'

Findol swallowed hard. For all his bravado and attempts at wisdom he was always humbled by the total trust and loyalty placed on someone so young by those older and much wiser than himself.

'Thanks, Tegan, I will try not to disappoint you!'

He left early to give himself plenty of time to get into position, glancing back at the bird and exchanging looks that said more than words. It was an unspoken bond of courage, hope and determination that crossed the boundary of their respective species. It spurred him on to swim down to the seabed stocking up with as many wattling beads as he could carry.

Cautiously Findol made the long, slow trek over to the coral wall, snaking along, tight to the seabed, before dropping down the side until he sensed (rather than saw) the huge cave entrance. Once in position he waited for Tegan to start the initiative. It seemed like time had stopped in the countdown to action. He nervously chewed on the beads and quietly toyed with small pebbles on the seabed as he tried to occupy himself. Suddenly he sensed movement, far behind him and in the distance a tiny voice, barely audible: 'Oh fer Pete's sake, me nib's snapped!'

He was about to move towards it when up above, all hell broke loose. A spectacular thunder of muffled thuds began to puncture the near silence as the gannets launched their fierce attack on the Gridlock. Findol was a little stunned by the sheer ferocity, judging by the growing wave upon wave of deafening explosions. The birds attack got progressively louder as above him he could dimly make out an ever-increasing cloud of bubbles. It was caused by the many violent plunges and frenzied mayhem ensuing, with bodies of gannets writhing and floundering in a sea of eels.

'Just how many followers did Tegan actually get?' he wondered, and, 'Just how high must they be diving from to achieve such an effect?'

Above the sea, the birds were indeed taking their lives in their own wings as they reached giddy heights before plunging like lead weights into the dark blue below. Many died, with necks snapping instantly as they panicked, trying to pull up at the last minute. Those that broke the surface and line of eels had the air punched viciously from their lungs by the impact. They urgently launched themselves back up towards their prey in streams of turbulence, snapping desperately as they did so. The Gridlock was taken completely by surprise and the ring of order broke down spectacularly as it disintegrated into chaos and confusion almost immediately.

Tegan returned to the surface with the remains of an eel in his beak when he was joined by Tewna, who had at least four smaller ones hanging from either side of his large bill.

'Er, look, Tegan. I'm a Walrus!' he joked, as he shook the dead eels in his mouth like giant whiskers.

The surface was becoming littered with thousands of dead sea-birds and mutilated eels as the battle raged on and on. Despite all order breaking down, however, there was a hard-core group of demented eels that remained. They were fixed to purpose, completely covering the now obvious entrance to the atoll regardless of danger. A menacing arc of electricity whipped up and around, as it surrounded them.

Far down below, even in the darkness, Findol could still see and hear the battle raging intensely above. The sea was boiling with violence, interspersed with spectacular wild arcs of electricity. All the time, there were terrible sounds of suffering. The flashes created silhouettes of gannets and eels caught in frozen snapshots of death.

He moved ever closer to the cave mouth, senses on high alert to any movement or sound nearby. Never had he felt more focussed, as yet again his heart began pounding heavily with anticipation. He was so close that he felt giddy with the tension. A noise, somewhere behind made him suddenly hit and mould himself tight to the coral wall, causing a cloud of silt to settle over him. Before he could move any further, just up ahead, barely twenty feet away, the massive bulk of Kreegan re-emerged, heading right towards him. He felt paralysed with fear as the creature was nearly upon him. Sniffing and searching, his head flicking back and forth, the enormous tail with its scars and pestilent sores just barely brushing past Findol's head. He had to stifle a cry, as his stomach churned.

Instinctively he cleared his blowhole of silt that sent a sudden jet of bubbles upwards. Kreegan lurched around, his poor eyesight hindering his search as he paused. Thankfully the intriguing noise above finally won the battle for his attention. As he looked upwards, the enticing smells and sounds of death invited him to investigate. His powerful body moved effortlessly as he whipped his torso and tail and left to join the mêlée.

Findol wasted no time and seized his opportunity, springing forward straight into the cave. The smell was appalling, with scattered bones and pieces of rotting carcass floating around. He had not even given consideration to the possibility that anything else could have been waiting in there for him. Thankfully the cave was devoid of life. There was no knowing how long Kreegan would be otherwise occupied, and he certainly didn't want to be around when he returned, so he quickly looked for other passageways. He travelled the full extent of the circular cave until he eventually found an area where it receded further back. It became deeper and narrower, reducing down to a place that was just wide enough for him to pass into. He put his head inside to investigate. Worryingly, it appeared to veer up and back on itself so that he couldn't see exactly where it went. It reminded him of the desperate situation he had encountered back at the

Pumice Caves. Without warning, he heard the dreaded sound of Kreegan returning, a low, deep growl preceding his entrance. Findol could feel the change in water pressure as Kreegan's bulk moved around inside.

'There is trouble afoot. I smell it!' his loud gruff voice boomed in the narrow passageway. Findol froze, not wanting to go back, but worried about the way forward. As if answering his fearful thoughts he felt Cora again reaching into his mind:

Quick now! Follow your instincts.

There is little time. Be brave, young Findol!

He urgently swam into and up the passage, but had to twist himself tightly around. The Camposs snagged and made progress difficult as he awkwardly negotiated the difficult bend. Once around it, he could just see dimly ahead for a short distance. He raced quietly along, panicking as the space narrowed to barely a body width in places. Annoyingly his fins kept catching and scraping against the sides, yet he was always fearful of the menace behind him.

If I have to try and turn around now …

He didn't dare think about it.

Instead, he thought about Tegan and the others and hoped they were okay. There was so much silt in the narrow passage that his efforts to move forward whipped up great clouds of the stuff. It clogged his eyes and nose, nearly causing him to choke in the process as he squeezed into the narrow space. Eventually, swimming slowly through the gritty clouds he came to a dead end and his mood plummeted. The silt settled and he saw that his way was truly blocked by an enormous rock. There were tantalising tiny streaks of light just seeping through the few gaps around its irregular edges. The thin filaments of light flickered as something was obviously moving behind. His desperation was suddenly interrupted by the sound of great effort as the rock juddered and shook, disturbing more silt into another cloud of dark debris. He stared as it was finally scraped, pushed and somehow pulled to one side.

Findol's disheartened face looked up astonished, as a dark, menacing shape appeared and pushed its face close up to his. The enormous jaw full of razor sharp teeth came ever nearer as he struggled to collect his breath.

This is it. I am without hope! he thought.

The mouth closed in and clasped around the Camposs, pulling him through the gap. He closed his eyes to await his fate, but dared to slowly open just the one. The image that met him caused him to squeal in delight.

'CORA! It's you! I've found you! You're alive! Wow, this is fantastic! It really *is* you!'

If he'd had room to dance he would have.

'Goodness, child. What did you expect? A ghost?'

Chapter 11
Cora's Wisdom

'What kept you, child? Have you been dilly-dallying again? Wasting time?' Exploring as usual!' she laughed.

'*Oooh*! You little scamp! *Owww*!'

Findol had swum out of the passage and nuzzled up close to Cora, planting a big kiss on her cheek. She winced as he pressed, without realising, against a raw patch around her neck. Findol embraced her massive girth with his fins and stared into her eyes almost delirious with happiness.

'Cora. I have felt so lonely and helpless! I have been so scared and so desperate to see you!'

'Now, now. Who do you think has been looking out for you all this time, young one? I have tried to guide you as best I could, but have not always had the strength to make contact. I paid badly for my last message to you yesterday as I tried to breach the cursed Gridlock outside. She displayed the hideous burn that travelled fully all around her neck. The skin had gone, leaving open flesh beneath. It looked terrible. There were smaller ones all over her body that he was only now beginning to notice. He couldn't disguise his look of horror, but was so pleased to see her, and yet saddened at just how old and frail she appeared to be.

'I know just what you are thinking, young one. Do not be fooled by an appearance! Ever! These wounds are of no consequence and like so many, I have yet to play my biggest part!'

It was a curious thing to say, but he wasn't going to question her about it just yet. After all, he was just thrilled to see her and finally have someone to answer his questions.

'Cora, I am so glad to have found you. There is so much I need to ask you that I am afraid I may never stop talking; I don't know where to begin!' he said frantically.

She smiled. 'Patience, child. Slow down and try to calm yourself! I can guess at much that you wish to know and there is such a lot I must tell you too … before it is too late.' Her voice broke with restrained emotion. It sounded ominous, almost like she had "Final Plans", which suddenly gave him cause for concern.

'Before we start,' said Cora, 'we must do things right. The big priority is for you to eat as much as you can. You must be starving. Free your mind and allow yourself time to indulge your body's needs for you are going to need all the strength and reserves you can muster. There are terribly dark deeds in motion that are not good for you. Yet take strength and good cheer from the fact that you have many allies and the very courage you possess will be your greatest weapon.'

Rather than feel hungry, Findol was rapidly beginning to lose his appetite, what with all the talk of dark deeds and he knew only too well who was behind them. As for courage, he certainly didn't feel he was spilling over with that either!

'Err, would yeh be pardonin' me if it's all the same, but I think I needs to be a bit closer to catch all the important stuff, yer be saying!'

'FLAYTUS! Flaytus Gurning. I don't believe it!' Findol fairly squealed with delight as the crab shuffled out of the passage behind him, flicking silt and detritus off his arms, legs and shell.

'Yeh has no idea of the risks I has to be taking in the name of me work. I should be paid danger money I think. Do yeh realise that sneaking past that stinking big worm was scarier than the time I had to retrieve me lucky four-and-a-half-leaf clover. It were from the hall of Madrigal Blooz, the Elven King of the Evergreen Blueberry Forest. But then, like everything else, that's another story.'

Findol was still open-mouthed with surprise.

'What are you doing here, Flaytus? How did you know where I was? I thought I had left you safely behind. Why risk your … ?'

'Findol! Findol, that is enough!' Cora smiled at him as she moved between them.

'Flaytus has come here because I asked him to. You are not the only one I have been trying to keep in touch with. Now before any more idle words you need some rest, if not food, and then we will talk!'

'How can I sleep with so much going on in my head? I feel like it's going to explode, like that poor puffer fish, whatever his name was!'

'Obi-Sness, that would be!' a passing elephant fish added, as she darted past them.

Cora ignored the interruption. 'Everything will start fitting into place after you have slept and we have spoken. Trust me!'

Findol had underestimated his exhaustion and now he was safe in Cora's presence, his eyes became heavy, stress lifted and he gave in to sleep as he settled on a bed of kelp. Cora took Flaytus to one side and spoke to him quietly.

'There is not as much time for us to talk as I would have hoped. When he wakes, there is much I must pass on to him. You must remember, however, to stick to your own path and the task I have set you, please. Do not be dissuaded by his protestations. He is still very young and full of the impetuousness of his youth. It will not be easy for you, with the fears he harbours for his family let alone the realisation of the prophecy. I feel he needs you more than he realises and you have yet to play your part!'

'Ah, yes and what might this here part be I have been wondering? Fer if it's close encounters of the Grampus kind then I think you've got the wrong crab. Yeh might just be noticing the white line that runs down me blessed back. Let alone the small issue of the size difference!'

'For goodness sake, Flaytus don't be ridiculous. You will hardly be expected to combat Grampus. The worst you could inflict on him is hiccups I'd say, or maybe a stomach-ache. Now listen: the Fates have cast their plans for each of us. We all have parts to play that are beyond our control. Just trust to honour and justice for all, and pray for a bit of your Irish Luck as you call it!'

She winked at him and he did his best to smile back. They stayed close to Findol, talking in whispers, like two old friends reminiscing about the past.

'Look, I am sorry. I know I only asked for you to just document all that you could, but things have now changed. I did not anticipate the Dark One taking my role in all this so seriously and for that I feel foolish. I should have been more aware and have been better prepared, but I am getting old and cannot escape the fact. Sadly I am not infallible and yes, I too make mistakes. My mind is not what it once was. It is because of my failings that you will have to take my place escorting him to the Vortex of Karn!'

'W-w-w-whoah! Now, holds on there. What in my mudder's name is the "Vortex of Karn" when it's at home and why can yeh not be takin' him?'

'It is complicated. I am old and slow. Besides, there is unfinished business and on that I will say no more, so please just trust me.'

Time passed as they exchanged small talk. Cora would not be drawn on any more news until Findol was awake to hear it. Flaytus, meanwhile, alternated between scribing and nervously chewing his claws as he stewed over his new role, desperate to change the subject. He ended up telling her about his embarrassing time at Sea-Czar's Palace. Even though she seemed distracted and in a lot of pain, she chuckled and shook with laughter at the thought of poor Flaytus being harangued by Old Barnacle Groans. She knew Groans from long ago when he was just starting out on his career. He used to tour with a band of travelling minstrel shrimps that Jethro Trawl had originally belonged to before they developed into the famous Flat Lees.

'Yes, he certainly has a mouth on him, old Barnacle, but deep down he's not so bad. Just part of his act I guess!'

She was gazing dreamily at a particularly colourful bloom of coral. 'Yes, I had so much fun when I was young. I do miss it! Old age can be cruel. It sneaks up on you and robs you of your faculties when you are not looking.'

Flaytus himself was no youngster and was beginning to feel uneasy with all the doom and gloom.

'Now, now, let's not be having any of this melancholy. Why there's plenty of life in yeh yet. You will soon be tripping the light fantastic, fer sure!'

'I really do not think so, Flaytus, for I am far older than you could ever imagine and I know there is more to you than meets the eye. Magic has a way of preserving its keeper, but once the magic fades … ' She glanced across at

Findol. 'But thank you anyway for your kind words. Oh! Oh, look! The little prince is waking!'

Findol stretched out and chewed a bead. He flinched and looked around at the two of them staring at him, a big dopey smile working its way all over his face.

'Hi. Everything okay?'

'Yes, yes. Now listen. Have something to eat.'

Cora passed him some Sushi Pemmican, which was like concentrated chewy fish. 'Now settle down,' she said. 'We have a lot to discuss.'

She cleared her throat and inflated her chest in dramatic fashion. 'Now, young Findol, is the time for you to let me talk and for you to listen with no interruptions please. There will be plenty of time for questions at the end, although I hope I will have already answered most of them. Firstly, the reason why Flaytus is here and why you have seen so much of him is simple. He is documenting your life, which I know sounds odd, but then it's just like having a diary written for you, isn't it? All details of what has and will happen must be preserved for all to see. I have my own good reasons for this that I have not time to go into now, but he is also going to escort you on your continuing journey'

'Hold on! What jour–?'

'That will do! Just listen, please!'

Flaytus was poised over a fresh sheet of Albinokelp parchment, a new cuttlefish-bone-tipped scribing quill (one of the best you could get, apparently) quivering with anticipation. Findol watched Cora, the frailty of her old age and wounds palpably disappearing as she stretched herself, and she seemed to grow before his very eyes. She looked strong and proud, as a light blue aura glimmered around her body.

'What I tell you now are the most important parts of the history of our world in the Big Blue. Some you will already know, though not in the detail you need. You will find some of it hard to believe, but it is important you listen and try to understand. There is only time to tell you once, so please focus and concentrate hard.

'Long, long ago the various universes of creation were formed, each one accessed by Spatial Gateways. They were linked together yet inaccessible to all, for each world remained a separate entity, holding its own ecosystem within. It was not possible for inhabitants of one world to move to another. When life first evolved on this planet there were created the twin powers of Light and Darkness, Good and Evil, whatever you wish to call them. They coexisted as opposites, yet each required the existence of the other to survive and maintain the balance. Their names have changed throughout time but not their nature! Over thousands of years, countless battles and wars have been fought in some form or another in the name of both. Each force trying to dominate and outdo the other to claim victory. They have shared the land and sea over all time until the entity of Evil found a way of gaining easy purchase and commitment. By penetrating the very soul of Mankind it could hide within him, ready to manipulate, coerce and wreak mayhem at any given opportunity.

'The spirit of Good (from our blessed Lantis) tried to combat this, seeking refuge in good heart. It was, however, a futile war for there would never ever be a satisfactory resolution. By the time Man had evolved into the creature he is today, it was far too late. Evil had become insidious and firmly embedded within his very soul. For all the good that he started out with, there would always be a bad side that remained hidden. It would lie dormant, waiting patiently, but always there, ready to seize an opportunity.

Some Men were worse than others; more receptive to the seduction of the Evil ways, welcoming its rise to the surface. Others seemed to possess an ability to combat it and live their lives honest and true. They would be ever fearful of the Dark forces that could be allowed to grow from within them. It remained, however, that there would always be those, vulnerable to its seduction, who preyed on the weaknesses of others. They would greedily take all that their desires asked for, be it land, lives or resources.

Life on Earth became hard, brutal and fraught with danger with the uncertainty of fellow Man's cruelty and hidden purpose. But there was always hope and there existed in the Big Blue something special. In our glorious Blue, there was a life free from the fears and anxieties from above on land. An Order, overseen by the Spiritual Guardians, or the Fates as we know them. For it is they who have controlled the great game of Life and Death. They have jealously guarded the fact, being ever fearful of the repercussions should the wrong mind be allowed to make certain considerations. For they have no power over Good or Evil directly and can only influence the parameters of life. They decided that there was a way that the problems on land could be partially solved. It would give a chance for those who wished it to escape from the terrors they feared. So it was that they created the Portals of Lunasee, which you will have no doubt heard about. The magical Portals allowed Man to pass from land into our Big Blue to live as a Cetacean. This power was harnessed from our Sister Moon, Lantis, herself, using the great powers of magic that existed back then. When Lantis was full and complete in the sky, an individual of true and just heart, who so wished it, would find a Portal. They would then be able to pass through it and emerge into the Blue. The Portals always appeared on the surface of the Big Blue, near the seas edge. Their appearance was created by the very desire from within the person themselves. The Human would pass through and reappear below the surface out of the Portallic tendril as a Cetacean — just like you or I.' Cora smiled at Findol as she popped a bead before continuing.

'Once free from the greed and cruelty above, it was tempting for many of these "visitors" to stay. Some did, and eventually became the wise "Lingerons". The majority, though, chose to return to land and in doing so acquired a greater understanding of our life. A few tried use the knowledge from their experiences in a positive way. They demanded the cessation of the barbarity and cruelty so prevalent everywhere above. Sadly, though, the protestations often fell on deaf ears for the cunning of Darkness is great and its power intoxicating to many.

Sadly, and to our despair, the Portal's power seemed to weaken over time. They were never designed to permit access to the dark of heart. Perhaps it was a lack of supervision by the Fates that weakened them. Whatever happened, the consequence was the same. Evil saw its big chance and found its way in. These twisted Humans that passed through the Portal found suitable representation in their sea-dwelling forms. They manifested as berserker barracuda, evil whales, malevolent conger eels, giant octopuses with poisonous ink, and many more. The disruption in the order of things helped lead to holes forming between the universes. The situation allowed the passage of monstrous mutated sea-creatures from Lejendta. Suddenly the Hydras, Krakens and Sea Trolls gained entry. They appeared at the time of the Scourge and the Big Blue was thrown into chaos … '

Findol could only stare open-mouthed at the names he had heard at school.

' … until Ichabod the Unsure saved the Big Blue with his great armies of mighty warrior shrimps and his magic petrified starfish … '

Now Findol was wearing a permanent frown, for his teachers had portrayed all he was now hearing as mere fantasy. Cora saw his expression and paused before continuing.

'I can see you are looking confused, so please try to concentrate! You have to understand that at that time, our planet had passed through the tail of the giant Sailfin Comet. It temporarily tore at the weakened Spatial Gates, creating the holes that allowed universal leakage. In a short time many different creatures crossed the barriers between the worlds, some appearing in the sea and some on land. This resulted in a total breakdown of order and chaos thrived. It would have nearly spelt the end of the planet and maybe all of the other worlds. Humans could not cope with the creatures of their dreams and nightmares any more than we could with Hydras, Krakens and such. The Fates had to step in and help restore normality by banishing the creatures back to their own worlds. They had to set to work repairing the Gates whilst further enchanting the Portals.

'You need to listen carefully and know that entering the Portal is only part of the story. Once entered, it transports you to the most important place in creation — Lymbow. For it is only there, where the Spatial Gates exist and can be chosen, depending on where you are travelling. As I have said, many of these Gates are closed to those from other worlds. Despite best efforts, accidents have still happened and so there have been cases of bizarre individuals still appearing outside of their own worlds. Even recently! Yes, I know I am looking at you, Flaytus. Sorry! I tell you this, though, because you will need to know the importance of choosing the correct Gate!'

Findol flashed a quizzical look at Flaytus then back to Cora.

'You must also remember that the events that I have spoken of happened long before Mankind's real involvement. His history has consigned much of this knowledge to fable and legend. There is an arrogance in the very spirit of Man that makes him believe in his own importance and denies the existence of other worlds. You do, however, need to be aware of the thin line that exists between each of them and the problems that can occur!'

Findol was both fascinated and fidgety. There had only been rumours of all this at Dolphin School. He still had many unanswered questions that were building up and were a lot closer to home:

'Why do I need to …?'

'As I said, you will have your turn to speak. Patience please! I know you were only aware of the link between Man and the Big Blue and knew nothing of the other worlds, but it has become essential that you see the wider story.'

Cora continued at great length whilst Flaytus feverishly scribed away, trying to capture all the important details. He wanted to ask just how he himself would get home, but thought better of it. There was yet more talk of the power of magic that was passed down to the Descendants of the Fates. It was given to help control the path of Evil as well as benefit the cause of Good.

'Good does have a habit of eventually overcoming Evil, but that victory sometimes comes at a very high price. It was partly because of this that so much of the magic freely used was either contained or destroyed.'

Hello now, I think we're coming to der nitty gritty, Flaytus thought, resting his little clawed wrists for precious seconds.

'Those wielding the power in misuse were banished and stripped of their powers. The stronghold and depository for the very essence of this magic became the original City of Old Lantis. For this was where the spirits of the Fates dwelt in physical form and the magic of Lantica was bound.'

Flaytus listened keenly as Cora described the spectacular city, wondering just how she could know so much. When Cora mentioned golden furniture and jewel-encrusted cutlery however, he got very excited.

'Now that's a place I can relate to fer sure and would not be minding visiting too!' he exclaimed.

'Flaytus, you are quick to be impressed by the smell and taste of opulence, but never forget that nothing is more valuable than the riches within a person's heart.'

Flaytus felt a little foolish and decided to curb his tongue. *I should have known better,* he thought.

Findol, meanwhile, was wanting to ask why it needed to be built above sea, but decided better of it.

Cora continued: 'At this time, Mankind was forever fighting his battles, on land, occasionally at sea, but all for greed or honour. The end result was always the same, ultimately leading to unprecedented death and mass destruction! The Portals that once had seemed so perfect were still allowing destructive, evil elements into the Blue.

'Stories of rampaging groups of sharks and berserker barracuda were becoming all too frequent. Bands of wild swordfish and giant mantas were plaguing everyone's safety. The continued strife was beginning to threaten the very ecosystems that existed. There were real fears for the survival of many Cetacean species of dolphins and porpoises. Many of the allied whales too, for so it was that the Dark forces found easy sanctuary in the foolish and weak-minded. Sharks and barracuda seemed to succumb easily, though not all did. The near perfect balance that once existed in the Blue was finally gone and fear had crept into the hearts of all that lived there. It led to the Great Day of Reckoning, although in effect, it took longer than that.

'Through a growing lack of use, mainly due to fear and the curse of dark deeds, the Portals diminished and many were lost as their magic dried up. The locations of the remaining ones were known to only a select few and yet darkness still thrived and continued to invade the Big Blue. A meeting was called of the Ruling Council of Old Lantis, formed by the children of the Fates and also the 'Lingerons'. They discussed at great length the turbulent times and the persistent scourge of Evil. Even before my great grand Orca mother existed, there was a human "warlord" called Gasprum Fangtooth. He had learned of the Portals' existence, finding one by chance when he saw some individuals re-morphing before his very eyes. It provided him with the knowledge he sought. He cruelly dispatched them before waiting for the next full moon to allow the entrance Portal to form ... '

'But I thought you said they only allowed the pure of heart to pass through!' Findol quizzed her.

'Child, are you not listening? The power of the Portals had been so greatly weakened over the years and the cunning of Evil has twisted the parameters. It was not so hard for those with strong purpose to pass through regardless of their blackened hearts. Please let me continue, there is not much left!' She swam around the two and resettled.

'So, originally allowing only the pure of heart, the Portals were responsible for the creeping death that seeped into the Blue. They allowed Gasprum's twisted form to slip through. He passed through a Pacifica Portal where he found unlimited scope for his evil ways. It was not long before he had easily built a huge army that he was able to turn and twist to his every whim. Gasprum was charismatic, cunning and an attractive leader to his simple-minded minions. He was responsible for massive destruction and killing on such a scale that the Ruling Council had to take quick and drastic action.

'Now he is known as Grampus the Grey and much of his doings you already know. For, protected by his evil dark magic, he has survived even to this day despite the many times we have thought that we had finally beaten him. Back then, the Council was not gifted in the "Art of War and Battles". They debated long and hard about the one course of action left to them. The only solution to rid the Big Blue of the disease that was Grampus and all of his kind was to close permanently the few remaining Portals, after banishing him.

'The council elder Karn reminded them all that there would have to be one left open, for emergencies. More importantly it was needed to keep the connection with all the other worlds, so maintaining Global Harmony. To achieve this, the price would be high. Old Lantis and all of its magic would have to disappear by sinking it and absorbing its magic in the sealing of the Portals. The one remaining Portal was left hidden in the kelp forest of Kelpathia. Karn constructed an enchanted Vortex that would be used to help prevent its detection and deter most. It would only allow the most brave and true-hearted of individuals through. He alluded to another hidden one, known only to himself, but said no more on the matter. Now, Karn possessed a truly prized magical artefact, known as the Morphing Stone. It was a small purple stone worn around his neck'.

Findol scratched at his own neck involuntary.

'It was created at the same time as Old Lantis, so its value could not be guessed at. Its purpose was to effectively act like a key, locking and unlocking the doorways of the soul. Its powers still remain unclear, but in essence, it was like a catalyst that could re-awaken a Portal. The wearer of the Stone could also, with practice and intense concentration, morph an individual into his or her alternative form, permanently. It was a very powerful and dangerous tool that could cause great harm through misuse or lack of self-control. The success of the plan to banish Grampus lay in someone getting close enough to use the Stone and return him to his human form forever. It would be a way of permanently land-locking him.

'However, it would require an incredibly brave individual to draw him through the last Portal. There would be no guarantee of success or survival before the Vortex of Karn was put in place. The chosen one would then use the Morphing Stone to return. It was a complicated plan and depended on so many things happening correctly and at the right time.'

Cora now looked exhausted and needed some moments to compose herself.

'Now, young Findol — listen closely to your dreams made real. Feel great pride, for if you had not already guessed it, you have much to feel blessed in your blood. Your father, Kai-Galant, unknown to your mother at the time, was the one chosen by the high council for this very task. The true blood nephew of Karn, he spent most of his life travelling. His adventures had taken him far away in other, deeper waters when he was not around the Lantica domain. Karn had searched for and found his elusive brother and nephew, discussing the Big Blue dilemma with them, knowing that Kai-Galant would be an ideal saviour.

'It was in the long weeks spent in Lantica, whilst finalising the plans for the Great Day of Reckoning, that he and your mother met. So it was then that they made their vows and were drawn together to become as one. She had no idea of his secret task, for it was deemed forbidden for anyone else to know of the plan. Its success lay in the element of total surprise.'

Cora settled herself for her final words.

'So you see, Findol, it was your father, Kai-Galant, who was entrusted with the Morphing Stone in the hope he could find Grampus and remove his threat forever. It is known he succeeded in chasing Grampus through the Portal before the Vortex was completed. There, however the story of what we know ends. As you know he never returned, though sadly Grampus did. I cling to the belief that somehow he is still alive somewhere. Although I do have to accept the fact that he had the tool of his return hanging around his neck, so I have to question why he never made it back.'

Now, all I have told you is the essence of the Big Blue's history. There is more, but it is all well documented and you have been told all that you need to know for now. You are probably quite tired; I certainly am!'

Flaytus took some time to finish scribing his notes, whilst Findol lay still, quietly mulling over all the information in his head.

'I had no idea that he carried so much of everyone's hopes with him. And for what? Where did it get him?' Findol felt rather upset. Cora snuggled up close and tried to soothe his anguish.

'He bought us all precious time and in doing so saved many lives! Take courage and hope, child, for he was a very brave dolphin. You have his blood flowing through your veins. I think your mother secretly knew or guessed at your father's true bloodline, even though he was sworn to secrecy to protect those around him. I am sure she saw through his pretence even though they were not together for long.'

It suddenly hit him; 'My mother, my brothers and sisters. Cora, tell me now, please! I cannot wait a moment longer. What has happened to them? It's why I came here to find you! You are my only hope. Please!'

She looked down at him proudly, and gently settled him onto the sea bed as she whispered:

'Child, be brave — and prepare to be astounded!'

Chapter 12
An Adventure Begins

'Now hold on, hold on! Calm yourself! Firstly, let me say, that just as you surely sense it in your heart. I too believe your family are alive. You must be strong and brave, but most of all you will need to use great courage and patience in equal measure. For you must see that many have lost their lives in the cruel hunt that Grampus has set for you. Make no mistake about it, this is all about his fear of you and your potential to destroy him and all he stands for. He also carries an intense desire for bitter revenge at the Lantica name.

'It is a hard and difficult course that you must follow, for dear Findol, you are still so young. You will need to grow a strong resolve to carry the weight of your quest. But you must prepare yourself. Be brave and accept the fact that some of your friends and maybe your relatives too, may not have survived. There was, after all, only so much news I was able to pick up before I was imprisoned by the Gridlock and cut off from all outside communication. Luckily, a friend of yours, Lippizana Stirrups made his way in here a few days ago.'

Findol's eyes widened.

'He managed to sneak past Kreegan and brought me the terrible news of the events outside and also his fears for your safety. I reassured him that I was certain you were alive and knew that you would make your way here to find me. Apparently, together with Piebald Fetlock and Pinkerton Gallop he was supposed to meet with you some time ago and had not been in touch since your unfortunate accident with the boat. It seems they had good reason for not communicating. They were called away unexpectedly, far away to northern waters, and got themselves tied up in a situation there. He didn't say any more on the matter, but wanted me to reassure you that they were desperately sorry and would explain it all when he found you. He told me of the devastation caused by the scourge of Grampus and their fears for your safety. He was on his way to try and find you, but I sent him away to find his friends and seek shelter. I knew they had greater work yet to participate in. Trust me, you will all meet up again!'

The agitation that had been visibly growing in Findol's face gradually disappeared as Cora continued.

'Shortly before I was imprisoned here it became my task to resolve a dispute between two families of porpoises. They had allowed a situation to blow up out of all proportion and were not allowing any other Cetaceans through their waters. It was all due to a serious squabble over jealously-guarded ownership rights of the area for food stocks. Whilst there, however, I had the good fortune to speak with a Sea-Pony Express by the name of Colt Chaser. He had arrived in the area in a desperately exhausted state. It appeared he was affiliated to your Hint-at Net and had been routinely delivering some urgent Jellygrams a week before. It had been a huge journey far north, when he had stumbled by luck on some important information. He had been travelling with two friends when they came across a sleeping scavenging party of berserker barracuda. Apparently they were resting after a particularly large meal, dozing and seemingly very pleased with themselves. He overheard them breaking into laughter in their sleep and caught Findol's name being muttered by one of them. He risked his own life by carefully swimming right up close to them. He clearly heard two of them dozily discussing Scaybeez and how he had told them of Findol's whereabouts. How Scaybeez had got news so far north I cannot begin to guess at. The barracuda wanted to find Grampus before Scaybeez beat them to it. For, doubtless there would be a huge reward for passing on fresh news.

'Unluckily for Colt's two accomplices, however, he had backed into a Regurgitant Anemone that belched out a vile cloud of its semi-digested seafood. Their sounds of alarm and surprise had attracted attention from the barracuda who immediately took chase. Colt got away, since he was much faster than the other two. What happened to them he couldn't say, except that he didn't stop swimming until he found me and that had taken him many days. He hoped I would pass the message on to you quicker than he could. Sadly, I have, because shortly after that he died of exhaustion, such was his overriding desire to get the information to you.'

Findol felt stunned for yet again someone had actually died for him. All the years of being treated as "special" were weighing heavy in his heart and he still felt uncertain about his cloudy future and destiny. Flaytus was moaning just loud enough to be heard;

'I tells yeh, if the pace does not be slowing down, then I will be suffering from RSI (Repeated Scribing Injury). My poor joints; why they're swelling up bigger than Neddy Conkins' Elifant Bunions and let me be telling you, they was big!'

'Okay, okay, we get your message, Flaytus, but time really is of the essence. We have little of it and there is still so much to ... '

There was a sudden splash above them immediately followed by cries of:

'Don't panic, it's only me, simple me, but with a message for ya. Quick, come on, where are yer all?'

They all looked up expecting something rather large, judging by the overbearing, booming voice. What they found was a small sea cucumber descending in a spiralling fashion and settling on the sea-bed just to their right.

'Cor blimey! Perfect positioning, though I says it myself. Like to introduce myself, if I may? Chester Nutz, cousin of Wichita Grub an' currently his last surviving relative!'

'Pleased to meet you, Chester. To what do we owe the unexpected pleasure of your company, only, with respect, we are busy and extremely lacking in free time?' Cora asked.

'I've just got in from old Wichie's place. Your cave, Mr Findol, sir. We was having a nice chat like, when some sea horse called Stirupz or something, arrived. He were jibber-jabberin' on about you. Said you were going to Cora's place. Wichie had some news about your family that he overheard whilst collecting his FlemDip or whatever!'

Findol immediately surged forward to catch his every word. Cora looked a little awkward and tense.

'Seems Rayno Plastee, a cuttlefish with a reputation for sniffin' out gossip had some dealing with Scurf Fungalfin, a friend of Scaybeez. They had been talking about the plan to get yer, and more importantly, Grampus's special surprise for yer family!'

Findol froze at the words as the first true link between his family and Grampus was made. He couldn't stay quiet any longer and immediately interrupted.

'What special surprise? Come on, what?'

'Look, I only knows what Wichie heard. He said they hadn't been specific and that all he heard was that it would be better than death itself.'

Findol juggled his thoughts, mind racing and interrupted, 'So? Then it must mean that they really are alive then, yes?'

It was Cora's turn now.

'Yes it appears so. If I had been given a few more moments I could have told you, though. I fear you may have had a wasted trip, Chester, but we are still indebted to you. You see, Findol, I know that when Grampus was nearly upon you, a desperate message was sent to your family. I felt it and did the same, for my voice carries much further than yours. They needed to understand that they had to leave, there and then. There was no time for collecting artefacts, keepsakes, trinkets, or trying to reason the situation out. They had to leave and that is what I believe they did. After Lippizana left me, I set myself the task of trying to find out just what had happened and searched for any word of Findol's family. I risked my life listening in as close as possible to the Gridlock at the entrance. It was the only way I could pick up on their thoughts and words.

'Luck was with me when two days ago Grampus returned, and in a foul mood by all accounts. He made no secret of his presence, seemingly revelling in my imprisonment. I dare say he has some plans for me too, but his arrogance will be his downfall. I heard him gloatingly urging the Gridlock to double their efforts to entrap me. Just before he left, Kreegan appeared from below and I picked up on the conversation between the two of them.' She ushered Findol close.

'Now, be brave and strong and listen, for this is what you have been wanting to know. It is no surprise to learn that the massed army of Grampus descended on your family, informed of their escape by evil spies. However, they took great care in herding and steering your family in exactly the direction that Grampus wanted!'

Findol's heart was racing. 'What are you saying? What happened? What do you mean? Herding? Steering? Wippit. Splinter. Lotus. Pipsqueak. They … they … Cora, tell me!' his body trembled, tears blending with the surrounding water.

'They were herded straight into the nets of one of Man's ships! I'm sorry, Findol.'

'W-WHAT? … I don't understand!' The pain of separation was agonising. His brothers and sisters … gone. He so desperately wanted his mother to hold him, to kiss him, to cuddle him.

Then Cora was holding him between her fins.

'This is not the end of the story, but a beginning. Listen to me. They are alive, we both know that. The task now is to find them! Just let me finish.'

Cora had agonised over the cruel laughter as she had listened in on the story until Grampus had finished and left. She had barely been aware of the pain it had cost her, as she ventured too close to the net. Her neck throbbed and prickled as if to remind her.

It was a while before the fury and despair within Findol had been focussed into something stronger. Flaytus and Chester had felt awkward, like intruders on poor Findol's despair.

'Now you listen, young 'un, cuz I'll tell yeh what. If I sees this here Grampus I'll punch his lights out I will. That's after I gives him serious Shynees Burnz on his fins.'

Findol looked at the tiny green sea cucumber whose face was contorted with aggression, and managed a smile.

'Thanks, Chester, but save him for me too. I feel I have one or two things to thrash out!'

Cora looked sternly at them.

'Now listen up, because our time has almost run out. If they were captured by Man and are still alive, then I feel that I know where they are heading. For there is only one type of place where they can be kept without raising any suspicion. My mother once mentioned a friend who had been caught by Men, taken away and put into a large pool. There, she was held captive with no way out into the Blue. Sadly she was kept there for many years whilst the Men made her perform strange feats and do stupid things that seemed to entertain them. Separated from her family, the humiliation was only made worse by her loneliness. Her health quickly deteriorated and she lost weight, losing interest in life itself. For without her family she was nothing, so she stopped eating and ultimately, performing. I guess she became no longer of any use and they eventually released her back into the Big Blue. She was extremely fortunate that it was not long before she was re-united with her family.'

Findol understood how that must have felt. To be with the ones you love most. To return his life of normality. To wallow in the triviality of cleaning, tidying, bickering and playing. How he ached for it all now; a hunger he had never experienced before. Cora was going to continue the story, of how the poor whale had sadly died shortly after that. The damage having already been done during her imprisonment, but thought it would have been unwise to do so.

'I am convinced that is the sort of place where you will find them, Findol. At least something like it!'

It was as if he was snapped out of a daydream.

'What do you mean? Me? What about you?'

'As I have said, I have my own part to play and that is to be here!'

Chester's loud voice suddenly boomed: 'Look, I had better be off! Erin will be waitin' up top. Got her to thank fer bringing me here. Said I'd only be a few minutes! She's a good old bird, but she does flap so! I don't want her to get peckish either, whilst I'm around, if yer get me drift! You lot take care and if yer ever need a hand or rather a foot, if I can, I will!'

He swam to the surface and they watched as he was picked up carefully by a large white bird and was suddenly gone.

So that's how he got in here, thought Findol. *Must have been one of Wichie's Gull-friends.*

Cora caught his attention.

'To continue,' she said, 'if you want them back, which I know you do, then you are going to have to do something you may never have even dreamed about. There is no alternative. You will have to pass through the last Portal to become a Human.'

'I will have to WHAT?'

'Look, I know it's something we have not done for many, many years. Remember that, in our history, it was such a commonplace practice. A fact of life, if you will. I fear it really has to be. I see no alternative!'

'Cora, I know nothing about the life of Man, or even where to find a Portal!'

'Look child, I am afraid there is such little time for debate and if you want your family back badly enough,

223

then this is the only way. I can help guide you to where the Portal is in Kelpathia. But it will be left open much to your wits and skill as to how you fit into the world of Man and find your family once you are Human. I have every faith in you, though!'

Flaytus was as surprised as Findol when Cora first mentioned the Portal, and a large explosion erupted from his rear. 'Errrm, sorry about that! T'is shock!'

A few aromatically-challenged cleaner wrasse rapidly retired from behind his shell and immediately considered serious career changes.

Findol was a little stunned by the events and news he was receiving. It was all happening way too fast; his life felt like it was rushing past in a blur. It was just like when he rode the current through the Slalom Straights two seasons ago. He had come dangerously close to being severely injured on the ragged walls as he raced past, caught in the vicious tide.

His father a hero, his family alive and now the prospect of having to pass through a Portal himself. To find what? Strange thoughts of dry land, moving on limbs, hair, clothes … suddenly he felt very giddy, sick and extremely apprehensive.

'It's okay, do not worry, it is only natural. I have seen those a lot older and wiser reduced to nervous wrecks at the thought of morphing through a Portal.'

Flaytus was still trying to catch up with his notes and he moaned about his wrists aching. There was little point in entertaining his whining though, when so much needed to be done. Cursing everyone, he made a mistake. It was a tricky business erasing and correcting errors.

'Sweet mother of Paddy's knock-kneed goat, could yeh please be giving some consideration to poor me, thank yeh very much!' He cracked his knuckles as he stretched his claws.

Cora was concerning herself with telling Findol as much as she could about living on land. "Dry" land. 'Remember you will be having to breathe out of water all the time. It will feel strange at first, but you will soon discover it is easier than here. You will not have to think about breathing as well. Also breathe slowly, no matter how excited you get! You will of course have arms and legs. Make sure you know which is which and take time practicing the use of both, before you make contact with others. The last thing you want to do is to attract unwelcome attention. Get used to what you do with each. We do not need you being distracted from your purpose. Too much is riding on it, but then I don't have to tell you that!'

Findol constantly wondered where and how Cora got her information. He decided that when you got to be as important as she was, then the need to explain yourself was abandoned. Besides, she had probably used Portals countless times in her long life.

She continued, 'You will have noticed that Humans prefer covering their bodies with material of all sorts. Whether they are ashamed of their bodies I do not know, but I guess who would not be when compared to the beauty of the Cetacean form.'

Findol certainly couldn't disagree. He had been very taken with Afrodite Speckles, a female spotted dolphin he had developed strong feelings for, back at Podling school. A sickening thought passed as he pondered upon her fate.

'Your first task, when you have mastered the art of walking, is to somehow find some of the materials that they wear. I feel that they will treat you with untoward concern if you are not covered as they are. I cannot tell you much more because it will be a learning process that you will have to go through. You will need to discover much of what is right and wrong yourself. Draw hope from the values of our Cetacean society and hopefully you will not go far wrong. Be careful too that you are not seduced by the huge change in your lifestyle. Trust will be a difficult thing for you to find, not least because you will be a stranger in a strange land.

'There is one more important thing I have to mention. If there is any chance that Grampus hears of your plans, then he may well try to find a way to get to you on land. I feel he had a far bigger part to play in the capture of your family than we realise. He is cunning and his fins reach far, maybe even beyond the Portal, though I do not know for sure. He still may yet believe your father is alive and be looking for the Morphing Stone. There is much trouble he could cause by using its power. His evil has no boundaries.'

'Could it get much worse, Cora? I mean here I am, feeling pretty desperate already. With no family around and you want me to find a Portal somehow and then cross through it. Next, become a human and conform to their expectations, try to locate where my family are, all by myself and in the knowledge that Grampus could be behind me at any moment!'

Her face glowed with pride as she saw the feisty young adult peeping through the youngster's exterior. She looked into his eyes as she spoke.

'Yes. Yes I do, and I also know you can do it. You will be most excellent. It was always written that this time would come for you, remember. All you need is self-belief, determination and a little bit of luck!'

She explained the route he would have to take that would lead him to the great Portal of Lunasee. He would have to cross into the kingdom of Kelpathia until he reached the weed forest. The long, green, thick filaments of kelp grew in abundance in the nutrient rich waters. The forest stretched over a vast area and would need careful negotiating to locate the Portal in the Vortex of Karn. Precious time could be wasted wandering aimlessly around in the near impenetrable forest, if its exact location was not known.

Findol realised that he had suffered with nightmares about the very same place. Could they have been premonitions of what was to come? In the dreams he was playing in the forest, swimming in and out of the filaments, hiding behind thick bunches and surprising his brothers and sisters as he leapt out. It always ended with him hiding one last time as he sensed his mother and the others coming around, for him to startle them. He would leap out, but no one would be there. All around there would be just darkness closing in on him. Strange unfamiliar voices and sounds would resonate from all directions. The long tendrils of kelp would twist and snag on his fins, clinging and tugging, not allowing him to leave. Then he would unexpectedly be in a clearing, surrounded by the kelp, looking for a way out. As the long filaments parted before him there would appear the enormous mouth of some Giant Sea-Dragon. Or maybe it was even Grampus, jaws wide open, inviting him into its vile depths. If there was one place in the Blue he would least like to look for, then the kelp forest was probably it.

He realised that Cora was watching him, probably guessing at his thoughts.

'Maybe you need some help; someone to go with you whom you can trust with your life.'

She slowly got up and swam over to the other side of Findol. Flaytus was cleaning the inside of his shell, whistling to himself. Out came all manner of bits and pieces as he eventually settled down. He looked up, aware of a sudden silence that was beginning to ring alarmingly in his ears.

'Ahhaaargh. Now hold on, why yeh looking at me in that manner, because from where I be standing, well sitting, then, it looks like it spells trouble with a capital F fer Flaytus. I can see what's happening, oh yes! Here is der clever plan so it is. Yeh gets me in a lemming frenzy recording this here book for yeh and then yeh land this on me. Well methinks it was danged sneaky of yeh — so it was … !'

He paused and thought: 'But then I suppose I won't be turning yeh down either. If it means I be getting a chance at returning to the old "Terry Firma" then I guess I has to jig to it. Oh to see the green, green shamrocks of home!'

'So we can take that as a "Yes", can we?' she said.

'I think yeh can, but then I don't think yeh would have accepted a "No", would yeh?'

Cora smiled to herself and flashed him a knowing grin: 'No, probably not. Excellent! But remember you are going first and foremost to help and advise Findol in any way you can. He will need to be able to depend on you!' She was looking sternly at him.

'Ah don't' yeh be worrying about that. I will be giving the youngster all the help he needs. Then and only then will I return to me beloved home!'

'Hold on, aren't you forgetting something?'

'Ah yes, that would be the book, would it not? All right — when the book is finished, okay?'

Findol was beaming right across his face. The thought that Flaytus was coming too made it all seem much easier to bear and prepare for. He realised that everything was making sense now, what with the furtive way that Flaytus had been writing, with it actually being about himself all the time!

Cora hastily apologised.

'I am sorry, young Findol, but I really wanted to keep the book a secret. I didn't want to alarm you in any way by making you aware of it. It seemed right to me. I wanted it to be written as free from bias and distortion as possible. I thought that would be achieved so much easier if you were unaware of its very existence. It is my belief that in years to come, its content will be an inspiration to all and an important record of all that is to come. For you must try to put it to the back of your mind. You do have more pressing things to think of; the exit for one!'

Flaytus wandered over to the small entrance that he and Findol had slipped through earlier. Cora took Findol right over to the main entrance/exit to view just what they were up against. Through the large hole in the coral wall could clearly be seen the large electrical curtain generated by the Gridlock. It pulsed and gyrated like a living electrical entity, swirling and flicking around, crackling with energy, right in the opening itself. It was intensely bright and Findol's eyes stung with gazing at it, yet it was strangely hypnotic watching its lethal dance. Cora's wounds though were a serious reminder of its cruel power. All around, there was the constant spark and fizz as it burnt away, leaving a strange metallic taste tainting the water.

'I tried to break through to send you a message the other night. I guess you must have received it to have found your way in. It did however nearly cost me my life. I had no time to warn you of Kreegan, but thankfully you made it.'

Findol could see she was in some discomfort from the dark, ugly wound that surrounded her neck. It was an evil looking oozing wound that showed no signs of healing. He felt so humble that someone so wise and powerful would have risked her very life to send him the message.

Cora suddenly looked very agitated as a look of great concern washed over her and she swung around to face their rear. 'It is time, young Findol!' she all but shouted, moving away from him.

The sudden intensity of her reaction made him jump and he looked around in startled confusion, scared not knowing quite what she had sensed. There was a low rumbling sound coming from the far wall where she had helped break him in. Something began moving quickly towards them, scuffing up silt in front of it like a smokescreen making identification difficult. Unbelievably it was Flaytus!

'I've never seen you move so fast on your little legs. They were almost blurred!' Findol said.

'Ah there is more to me than meets the eye, oh yes. I can move when I has to and I'm telling you there is good reason,' Flaytus replied. 'Something is stirring over there that I'm not liking the look of! It's mighty big and I thinks its mood is none too good!'

'Stay here,' Findol shouted as he raced after Cora. He caught up with her as they neared the hole he had used to get in. There was indeed something making its way through it and Findol looked in horror as he recognised the fish pushing its way through the silt.

'Scaybeez! I don't believe it. Or maybe I should do! Yet again, I should have finished you off when I had the chance.' He wondered why Flaytus had over-reacted to such a pathetic creature.

'Ooh, ooh, little Findol upset is he? Oh, where's Mommy gone now, eh?'

Findol lunged towards him, but Cora blocked his attack. 'Stay calm, he is not worth it,' she barely whispered.

Meanwhile, Scaybeez continued.

'Think you're safe, do you? Think that Grampus doesn't know you're here? Did you really think your eelbait friend's attack would go unnoticed, like it was the most normal thing in the world? You are more stupid than we gave you credit for! You should have seen them, so many dead and for what? A pathetic little dolphin who's lost his family ... *tsk, tsk* ... how careless!'

It was all too much for Findol. He skirted quickly around Cora and jack-knifed sharply to reach Scaybeez, who had already leapt back into the hole. He almost followed, blindly enraged, but stopped himself just in time as he realised now what Flaytus had been so scared of. It was obvious now just what had caused the noise that was getting louder still. Kreegan's massive bulk was pushing and shoving its way through the narrow route from the cave below. His flank was rilled with cuts and gouges from the rough walls. He had forged on, driven by the blind madness of his evil purpose. The beast seemed oblivious to the pain and damage that he was inflicting on himself. Cora looked intently into Findol's eyes and something unspoken passed between them. She had said or rather shouted in his head: *Get ready to leave! … No questions. Please! Go! Wait over there and move only when I say!*

He didn't need to look where she was subtly pointing, for he knew exactly where she meant. Her large sad eyes looked at him imploringly. What he had felt had been much more and he suddenly craved the time that he no longer had with her. He had an uneasy feeling, as if another door in his life was closing and he could only hope that it would be shortly replaced with the opening of a new one. Everything was happening far too quickly. He seemed to have no time to take in one thing before something else occurred.

He hurried over to the far entrance, just as she had asked, and then looked back. Kreegan had now pushed himself fully through the hole, pulling and tugging himself free as large lumps of rock fell away. They crumbled and crashed around him, thudding on the seabed. Dark patches of bloodied water bloomed around the enormous eel's as he drew his body completely out. Seemingly he was unbothered by the wounds which made the sight all the more horrific.

Scaybeez pathetically skulked tight behind the eel's body, looking anxiously from left to right. Cora threw a quick glance back at Findol and Flaytus before launching herself forward in an immediate attack upon Kreegan's neck. The eel thrashed its tail this way and that in a desperate attempt to free itself, all the while trying to coil his bloodied tail around her. Cora was old and weak and could not hold on for long, but what little strength she had was staggering. Kreegan knew her weakness and picked his moment. He suddenly pulled away, her sharp teeth leaving deep ugly wounds in his tattered flesh. He quickly twisted his body around hers in an attempt to suffocate and immobilise her. His jaws snapped together as she pushed and pulled, each time barely managing to avoid the ugly, fetid fangs. She was gasping with the effort, but managed a massive swipe with her tail that sent him sideways, hitting the rocky walls and causing further cascades of broken rock and silt, as fractured branches of coral scattered in the turbulent waters. Scaybeez cowered pathetically, hiding under some debris. Kreegan meanwhile paid no heed to the damage done to his sides as his blood continued to flow clouding the waters around them, a furious madness in his wild eyes.

Findol looked on helplessly. He was scared that Cora would lose and he would be next. He hated the feeling of weakness and wished he was able to help. There was no escaping the fact that he was no match for the size of Kreegan though, which made him doubt his own threat to Grampus.

'There will be a way, I just know it,' he thought. There was pure insanity infecting Kreegan as he lunged forward, solely intent on destroying Cora, whilst she was seemingly oblivious to fear. He was getting desperate, bested by an old female! Cora was labouring badly though and was now swimming towards the entrance. She was tiring and looked desperate for air, unable to find wattling beads. Findol was unclear as to just what she had planned, why she was bringing the fight towards them. Kreegan was severely wounded from her teeth, they could see that and it was welcome. But then Cora's strength was fading fast too and they could now see gaping wounds on her flanks that left Findol shuddering with a deep sick feeling in his belly. There was an unrelenting madness in Kreegan's eyes that said he would just not give up and would rather die trying to stop them all. It was scarier than the creature itself, for it meant he had no fear or care for his own life or the consequences of his actions. He had wrapped his jaws around the top of Cora's tail and she screamed with the pain.

Findol, without thinking, acted purely on impulse, shouting, 'No!' and propelled himself forward as fast as he could, aiming straight for Kreegan's head. Flaytus was dumbstruck, mouth open, staring wildly at the young courageous dolphin. Findol gritted his teeth as thankfully Kreegan's eyes were still squeezed tightly shut with the effort he was applying.

Please don't look, please don't look. Stay shut, stay shut!

He was almost there, metres away, the eel growing bigger and bigger as he got closer.

Do not open, do not open. Nearly … hurrrrraaaggggh!

He hit the eel full on the side of its head and felt its jaw snap, immediately releasing his grip on Cora's tail. It was both a beautiful and sickening moment.

Kreegan instinctively flipped violently and managed to hit Findol hard in the chest, as his evil eyes bore down on him:

'I will kill you,' he hissed. 'And, so sssslowly! Tearing your insides out!'

Findol! Get back now. Take Flaytus and get ready to leave when I say! Cora was shouting, and yet her mouth remained closed. It was in his head again. She looked terrible.

'How … how can we leave? What has changed? Look!' He was staring at the Gridlock's electric bolus, bobbing and swaying in the entrance. It appeared bigger and fiercer than before, but then there were more eels huddled there. The largest ones, each jostling for a view of the battle within.

Findol gasped with the pain in his side and popped a bead. There they were, trapped between the Gridlock on one side and Kreegan on the other. He could see the hideous shape of the leering Scaybeez hiding someway beyond the eel. Cora was blocking the path of Kreegan as Findol shouted at Scaybeez: 'It's not over between us. I will see you again! You will pay!'

He saw Cora steel herself and move forward towards her adversary. She was almost spent, gasping and desperately weak, clearly in a lot of pain. Yet she suddenly seemed to fill up with a hidden strength and a subtle aura appeared, glowing around her as she swelled and commanded: 'Now, Findol! Ready yourself and remember, love is all!'

A tear formed in her eye and disappeared just as quickly. She seemed to invite Kreegan upon herself, motionless and submissive, as he leapt forward and hit her hard, allowing his full force to carry them towards the entrance. It was something she hadn't expected and she latched onto his broken jaw. Using her last drop of energy to swim back as hard as she could, avoiding Findol, she pulled him straight through the entrance. It was a terrible sight to see Cora dragging herself and Kreegan into the very heart of the Gridlock. The realisation hit him too late as Kreegan saw her true purpose at last.

'Now, Findol … now, sweet child … '

Findol carried Flaytus and surged through the gap behind the jerking tail of Kreegan. The intense electrical bolus had splashed around the couple, creating a small gap and little could be seen through the intensity of its light, thankfully! Cora had no intention of allowing Kreegan to escape and had chosen to buy Findol's freedom with her own life. Findol surged away with all his might, stunned and unaware of minor burns. He was not sure of the direction, but just wanted to put as much distance as possible between himself and what he had just witnessed. His head was screaming with blind panic and his body working harder than he had ever known. There had been no time to react as he refused to allow any of his emotions to catch up, knowing he had to stay focussed on their escape.

He corrected his course to the route she had suggested and eventually dared himself to glance back quickly to see if they were being followed. When he could go no further without breathing he surfaced to draw on fresh air, gasping and gulping frantically. It helped clear his head, which was now pounding.

Flaytus was able to relax his grip a bit and quietly agonised over the pain in his claws. Sensitive to his friend's feelings, he dared not say a word for he knew it was time to wait until Findol was ready to talk.

The young dolphin suddenly stopped and turned, the motion causing Flaytus to swing out wildly as he held on dearly, with arms stretched near to breaking point. It was then that Findol had let out a terribly long and agonised cry as the realisation finally hit him.

He had just lost his most dear and beloved Cora and all the love and wisdom that went with her. His whole world seemed to have suddenly drained away with the terrible, unbelievable thought:

Cora was DEAD!

Chapter 13
of Sadness and Hope

It was many hours later and Findol stirred from a hopeless sleep. They had been forced to stop, totally exhausted, at a large rocky outcrop with a small cave, covered with seaweed and just big enough to hide the two of them. There they had rested, perhaps for too long, but Findol was drained, both from fear and despair. The terrible memory of the last images of poor Cora, lingering and haunting him. Her despairing look and yet the sheer courage she had displayed with her actions and words were playing around in his mind.

His fears extended to thoughts of Tegan and the others as he recalled the dead bodies that he had sensed (and soon after seen) above them during their escape. There had been no time to go searching and he could only hope that most of the birds were okay and that dear Tegan had survived.

He was angry and bitter for he still wished he had got rid of Scaybeez, long ago when he had had plenty of chances. If he had, then maybe things would have been so different right now; Scaybeez wouldn't have been able to lead Kreegan to them. Grampus wouldn't have received the news he had sought of Findol's whereabouts. More importantly, he thought, he would not have caused the death of Cora.

Cora … *dead!* It was still hard to take in and the words weighed so heavy in his heart. When he finally found his family, as he was sure he would, they would be devastated.

The sun was setting and he realised that they had spent too much time resting and it was time to move on. It was probably safer to travel in poor light. He woke Flaytus who was just in the middle of a dream about one of the fairy handmaidens he had met many moons ago and shared a flagon of Old Foxglove with. There was a silly grin that danced over his face — until he was rudely awoken.

'Sweet Mother of mine, have some consideration will yeh? She was just calling me her prince, so she was … and she was gonna be showing me her royal treasure collection with the golden dragon giblets and all. And then yeh goes and spoils it by waking me up … yer a cruel 'un and that's no mistake! Yeh be getting no marks fer yer timing!'

He flicked his head around at Findol, then back down in shame. 'So sorry, Findol my lad. I forgot myself there!'

'It's okay. Come on, Flaytus. We don't want to be here any longer than we have to!'

It was quickly getting dark and though it was not ideal travelling by night, the poor light would hide them a little. It would also allow them to put some distance between them and whatever horrors lay behind.

As his thoughts drifted, Findol sadly felt that he had barely spent enough time with Cora. Her last, lingering look at him had seemed to flood his head with all manner of knowledge like a lightning bolt of data. He silently resolved himself to justify all that had gone with "Action" and "Deeds". The Camposs, he now knew for sure was used for guiding Men during their travels. It would help them steer in any one particular direction.

With the guidance of Cora's knowledge, and the Camposs around his neck, he confidently swam on in the direction he believed Kelpathia to be. He decided it would be best if he carried Flaytus on his back. Flaytus's alternative form of propulsion using sea-squirts would have drawn unwanted attention.

It was eerie swimming in the darkness of night and Findol was glad of his companion for diverting his attention from his rather overactive imagination. It was strangely quiet, too, which made every move they made and word spoken sound so much louder. Shoals of fish appeared from nowhere out of the darkness as if slipping through a shroud, silent and nervous as they caught sight of him. Distant, mournful whale-song resonated around them as an unseen pod passed them by, calling out for lost loves. It sounded like a symphony of delicate emotions in an ocean of pain.

They had been travelling for some time, chasing the moon above as its light splashed on their bodies, flickering through the surface. It had been a while since they had last seen or even sensed any living creatures nearby. Findol had one of his feelings that something was not quite right. Usually he could travel safely by scanning ahead and would know what lay before him, but that night he sensed something sinister lurking beyond in the darkness. It was like nothing he had ever encountered before, for he had now become aware of a terrible, disgusting taste in the water. It made him feel sick, and all around them was a strange absence of life as far as his senses could detect. If there had been a nearby cave he would have gone there and hidden until daybreak before tentatively venturing any further. Instead, he felt more vulnerable than ever before and nervously whispered to Flaytus: 'I don't like this, Flaytus. It's like being in the very breath of Death itself!'

'Yer not one fer mincing yer words, are yeh, youngster? I mean don't be trying to scare me or anything, will yeh?

This makes me think of the Plagues of Duchelm that Great Grand Goblin, Sappy Willows, used to be talking about.'

As they cautiously continued forward they were suddenly cloaked in total darkness. Findol instinctively began to dive, unexpectedly bumping into soft lifeless objects. They glinted and flashed as they were caught by random blades of moonlight that broke through the dark veil above. It teasingly offered tiny glimpses of the obstacles. Findol had somehow, through lack of concentration, missed detecting them.

The pair of them gasped at the sight when they realised just what had happened. They were in a huge submerged graveyard of fish corpses, eerily floating in their deathly decay. Lifeless shoals of large bass and small mackerel hung limply together in the eerie blackness. The strange silence was almost deafening whilst slight movements caused by the current merely added to the horror. Findol was at first confused by the sudden blackout above and the terrible taste in the water.

He was about to surface to find out the cause when Flaytus screamed, 'Don't go up fer the sake of all things that has life left still in their shaky bodies! That's us in case yeh were not realising!'

'Flaytus, what are you talking about? How else can I?'

Flaytus extended and pointed a claw at a large black fish. Once silver-white, it was now covered in a suffocating film of thick, dark, sticky sludge. A lifeless eye stared back at them.

'Now you understand, eh? This be the work of Man. Methinks this poison has been dumped from one of their Longships, I is sure of it! Either that or t'is one of his "accidents". Can't yeh be tasting it now? T'is the muck that comes from the cursed things!'

'Now that you mention it, yes. I recognise the taste from when we are chasing their boats.'

All around them, the flashes of moonlight breaking through the oily mat would highlight yet more of the pathetic corpses. Findol increased his speed and dived deeper in an attempt to avoid any more contact. They both had to find some kelp to wipe the disgusting splashes off them from their collisions with the soiled bodies.

'I should have known … shouldn't I? Sorry, Flaytus. It's disgusting. Just look how many have died. There must be thousands … and for what?'

'T'is a terrible waste, and that's a fact. I am afraid this is how it is. Man is a selfish creature who pays little heed to his home … and I am talking about the Mother Earth now. T'is bad enough that he cares so little fer the land and the sky, but even yer Blue cannot be escaping from the foul muck that he pours into it … (*Parp!*)… Oh bejaybers! Pardon me, I didn't see that one coming! Anyway, when all is said and done I will be glad to be returning to me beloved homeland … t'is where me heart is and also somewhere untouched by Mankind.'

Findol was cleaning the Camposs. 'Flaytus, this will be our salvation in the Kelp forest, I am sure of it! I am also sure that I was meant to find it.'

How else could I succeed? he thought. He was getting quite excited that maybe things did happen for a reason and it gave him an inner strength that helped fuel his confidence.

They swam on as quickly as they could, keen to put some distance between them and the area of death behind. Soon, the moon's juddering image could be seen clearly above them and they took the opportunity to surface.

Findol took long gasps of fresh air and they decided to eat the next chance they got and also to rest somewhere. The sun would soon be coming up and they could already see a deep redness bleeding over the horizon. Far away, they could see the silhouette of one of the Longships. Findol wondered if it was responsible for the spillage and destruction they had seen.

Hunger got the better of them and there was no sign of any shelter, so they resigned themselves to floating for a while and picnicking on the surface. Findol caught some small fish for himself and some shellfish for Flaytus who whipped up a Big Blue salad with some salad bream. It was a welcome comfort break; lying there, tucking into the food, while the early morning sun warmed their bodies. Only the realisation of what lay ahead coloured their mood.

As he lay there, stomach full and creaking with satisfaction, Findol looked up at the sun and wondered just what his family were doing right then. Could they be wondering the same about him? Maybe at that moment, they were looking up at the sun too. The thought warmed his heart and he wished there was some way he could send them a message. If he could just reassure them that he was on his way and would somehow find them. To let them know that he was alive and hadn't abandoned hope.

As he looked at the golden sun he shut his eyes and thought of his mother and it seemed he saw (or perhaps felt) her presence. It was a very special warmth that glowed inside and lifted his spirits. Surely it was his mother's love shining down on him, wasn't it?

'Did you see that, Flaytus? ... Did you? ... It was my mum. Up there. Up in the sky!'

Flaytus looked up and then back at Findol with an understanding look on his face. 'Are you sure yer not thinking its yer heart's desires showing yeh what yeh be wanting to see?'

'No, it was her. I made a connection, I know I did. Somehow I got to her, I'm sure!' He squeezed his eyes shut again and tried to repeat it, but there was nothing.

'Maybe yer just trying too hard, young 'un!'

It was not easy just switching off, though. It was all very well for Flaytus with his own life and the characters in it, but Findol felt he still had all the others to think of too. His friends as well as family that he had to consider. He had been so wrapped up in missing his family that he hadn't given a second thought to many of the others; the friends that he had no way of knowing whether they were okay. He could only console himself with the thought that it was himself that had been Grampus's prime concern. With luck, Grampus would not have wasted any time in trying to deal with the others.

Flaytus was precariously balanced on Findol's back, thinking it best to let him rest while he kept lookout. He knew there was much troubling Findol, and the lad needed to work it out in his head.

After a time, the young dolphin drifted into a deep sleep. In his dream he was playing Finball with all his family. There were brothers and sisters, cousins, his mum and even Whitloe, who normally didn't seem to have the energy to pop a wattling bead, let alone play a game. Here in his dream-world she was leaping about like a newborn pup, flipping around and leaping out of the water. There was somebody else there too. A large, powerful dolphin that looked so strong and, as his mother would say, 'andsome. He was too far away to see clearly and every time Findol swam closer, he would appear the same distance away. Not being able to get near to him was driving him mad because Findol realised it was his father, Kai-Galant!

Suddenly Kai leapt out of the water and hit the Nautilean Disc straight towards Findol. Findol immediately leapt up to catch it, and as it approached it started to change shape before his very eyes. It was moving in slow motion, which didn't seem to be at all unusual at the time. The Disc had changed into a small metallic ring on a chain with a deep-purple jewel heavily set in the centre. The jewel seemed to possess its own fiery aura of light that radiated off it. He caught it easily with a flourish, showing off, as he leaped out of the Blue. He was startled by a flush of warmth that flowed from the ring and coursed through his body. As he dropped back into the water he looked for his father, but found he was now alone. All of the players had gone.

Findol turned to leave, but as he did so, there in front of him was the massive bulk of Grampus. Findol's heart raced and he made to escape, but he saw that Grampus was staring intently at the small ring, now in Findol's mouth. He actually looked scared, which was something he had never seen before in any of his dreams. Grampus unexpectedly turned to swim off in panic and as he did so a frightened eruption of bubbles escaped from his rear ... except that it wasn't Grampus anymore ... it was Flaytus.

'*Tsk, tsk.* Sorry, Findol ... terribly sorry ... I think it were some trapped wind from earlier. It's the flaked breams or something. Did I wake yeh?'

'No, I don't think so. I was just coming round.'

He was still thinking of the ring, which Grampus had seemed so terrified of … could it have been the actual Morphing Stone, within it, he wondered?

'Okay, Flaytus. Let's do it! As they say: *When the going gets tough, the tough get going.*'

Flaytus looked up, puzzled, from stashing away his scribing equipment. 'Now who is it that says that then? That's what I be wanting to know, so I does!

'Okay, Flaytus I reckon that with some hard effort and serious swimming I could get us to Kelpathia in a couple of days. It will slow me down with you on my back, but I think it's best you stay up there.'

Flaytus thought to himself: *He thinks that me sea-squirts would draw attention to us, but thinks nobody notices a dolphin with an 'ermit crab on his back … tsk, tsk … that's rich!*

All the same, he caught hold of Findol's dorsal fin and held on tight. 'Yee Haaa! Yer know, this reminds me of the time Finnegan attacked Herrapin the Tree Goblin's hideout from the back of Dromma Dree the Humpback Tree Slug. It didn't work, but he sure left a nasty trail all over the front door. So he did!'

They covered a lot of sea that first day, powering on mostly in silence, only slowing once in a while to check the Camposs for their direction. As long as they followed the W they were okay. Eventually they stopped at a floating mat of kelp. And there they rested. Findol was exhausted.

The second day, the weather was not so kind to them. It was cold, and a strong wind was making the surface very choppy. Findol went down deeper where it was easier to swim, even though there was a powerful current that he had to swim against. He had been moving along at a terrific pace when he was aware of something strange that was going on up ahead. There were plainly a lot of sea creatures up in front, yet they appeared mostly lifeless and barely moving. As he slowed down and cautiously swam upwards he came into contact with a very fine net that he had not even detected. The fibres were so thin it was nearly invisible. The sudden contact made him jump and Flaytus had to increase his grip as he swung out to one side before regaining his footing.

'Bejaybers!'

Findol skirted the net as best he could until he was happy he would safely avoid it. Above him he could just see the top, lined with hundreds of small coloured plastic balls. They were much like the ones he collected and they bobbed around just below the surface as they were tossed around by the waves. It was obvious that a lot of fish were trapped within the net, and many were in the last moments of their short lives. He could see shapes of a few sea-birds that had died foolishly trying to catch the fish, unaware of the danger hiding within. They had found out, too late and to their cost, the reason for the easy pickings. Now most were stiff, feathered corpses, ugly and pathetic.

Further ahead, along the massive net's length, he could detect other shapes. The sea was shallow and he could see where a part of it was caught tightly around a rocky pinnacle. The choppiness had caused large clouds of silt and debris to swirl up and around. Where it was shallow, visibility was very difficult, if not nigh-on impossible.

'Do we have to be looking at this?' Flaytus whined. 'T'is as bad as that oily graveyard!'

'Yes, I don't like it either, Flaytus, but I want to check for survi- ... Aaargh!'

A large shark suddenly loomed out of the murkiness, directly in front of him, mouth wide open in a deadly yawn, rows of jagged teeth bared. Findol instinctively swerved, almost losing Flaytus again in the process. As he frantically turned to check its progress he could see it was not following. He realised that he had been surprised by it because it had no life force. As he went back he could now see the shark, twisted in the agony of its death throes, entwined in the undiscriminating net. Unable to swim and breathe, it had died a slow, cruel death. Scarred from its desperate attempts to escape, and from opportunistic feeders, it was a pathetic and sickening sight.

They travelled further along the eerie net, morbidly taking in each macabre sight. It hung like a curtain of doom that spared none, regardless of species. Findol sighed as he looked in sadness at a pair of snared porpoises and wondered if one had died trying to help save the other; their empty eyes stared back at him with unanswered pleas.

'If yeh asks me, this is not the best place to be fer someone with dampened spirits as it is!'

'It makes me sick, Flaytus, it really does. To think that we are related, no matter how distantly, makes my blood run cold. Cora always said that Mankind was intelligent, yet everything I see makes me think otherwise. Look at all this senseless destruction!'

Each part of the net that revealed itself in the murky waters brought new images of horror to them. There were sharks and rays, dolphins and porpoises, even a small baby whale that had probably got separated from its mother. It looked like it had spent its last few moments of despair hopelessly entangled in the net, far from its family. It struck a terrible chord with Findol.

'I have got to see if there is anyone with enough life left to survive, there must be a chance. I owe it to myself and my family as much as anything else. You understand, don't you, Flaytus?'

'Now of course I does. Are yeh not thinking there is a heart tickin' away inside this hard exterior?' he said, tapping his thorax with his claw for effect.

They continued along the length of the net in silence, with Findol keenly scanning ahead. It was far bigger than they realised and had obviously been there for some time, for lower down they could see where it had been colonised by thick weed, slime and strings of goose barnacles dangling below. There were some small crabs that were hanging on for the ride.

And for the buffet, no doubt, Findol thought with a shudder. It was becoming an ordeal for him as the sheer scale of the numbers became apparent. There were just so many dead or dying, and even Findol found a reluctant compassion for the sharks that he hated so much.

This is no way to die, he thought.

Flaytus was just about to suggest that maybe they were onto a loser when suddenly Findol cried out and put on a sprint. Flaytus slid backwards on Findol's shiny skin and only just managed to grab hold of his dorsal fin in time.

'Whoah! Now will yeh give me some warning before yeh is doing that!'

'Up ahead, Flaytus — there's movement, I'm sure!'

Findol frantically scanned the net as they raced along it until it started getting smaller and smaller, tapering to a point. At the very end of its length they saw a giant female Leatherback turtle caught in some bindings. It was obvious that the turtle was desperately exhausted and close to death. But she was alive and making slow, powerless attempts to strike at the ropes with her free flippers. They barely made contact with the ropes that held her so tightly at her rear. Though only a few feet from the surface, she was in danger of drowning.

'Trust us and please try to relax,' Findol whispered in her ear.

Flaytus jumped onto the turtle's back and started rummaging around in his shell. He knew exactly what he was wanted. Findol set to work trying to bite through the hard rope. He then decided to position himself under her and swim upwards. The rope clung to her tightly, pulling and cutting further into her flipper, causing her to whimper. He stopped and swam up to Flaytus.

' ... Now here it is, just what I be needing ... a life saver so t'is.'

He produced a razor shell that he used to sharpen his quills and immediately set to work on cutting the ropes. It was a joy to watch the cut strands springing apart as he worked his way frantically through them. Eventually, he was almost finished and Findol got underneath her again to take her weight when she was released. It caught him by surprise when it happened, as she had little energy to help and weighed an enormous amount. He pushed and pushed, swimming as hard as he could, but making slow progress.

At last they broke the surface. The turtle gasped and gulped great lungfuls of air and stared at her two saviours with tears pouring from her eyes. It was some time before she was able to talk clearly and when she did, it was in a sweet fragile voice, totally unexpected for her large bulk.

'Thank you! ... Thank you both ... so much. You have no idea how grateful we are ... you are both truly "Knights of the Seas". My name is Tannin and we are forever in your debt!'

'It was nothing really. I mean, I am just so glad that we were in the right place at the right time! I am just sad we were too late for the others!'

'Yes, I have been tortured by the terrible sounds of the poor creatures that didn't survive. I curse myself for foolishly getting in this predicament in the first place. I have crossed these waters all my life and have travelled thousands of miles. Maybe I risked my life once too often and should have known better. This season I have been too idle and left myself with little time for the Great Crossing. I rushed and exhausted myself before I even got caught up in the thing, and as you see, very nearly paid the price for my laziness. Look over there and see how close I was.'

They both looked in the direction she was pointing and saw a small island.

'So why were you going there and why travel so far?'

'I am sorry I didn't explain myself. I carry the eggs of my last brood, for I fear I will not be able to make this journey again!'

'So that's what you meant when you referred to yourself as "we".'

'I can see yer gonna be needing some lessons on basic ecosystems and such like, young 'un. Did yer mother or Dolphin School not be teaching yeh about the blessed turtle beaches?'

'Well, I suppose not. But I think, maybe, I wasn't concentrating at the time. I guess some things are going to have to change!'

'They certainly are … oh yes, begorrah. I can see that I am gonna be having my work cut out with yeh!'

'Now steady on, Flaytus. Cora said you only needed to help me until I find my family!'

'Now are yeh thinking that's gonna be happening overnight … I don't think so!'

Tannin suddenly interrupted.

'I am sorry, but did you mention Cora? She is an old and very dear friend of mine whom I have not seen for many a moon now. How is she?'

Findol glanced at Flaytus before he looked at her with sadness pooling in his eyes:

'I am so sorry. We have terrible news! We were with her only a week or so ago, but we fear sadly she is no more. She has been lost to the maw of Evil'

Tannin looked crushed. Findol and Flaytus told her all that had happened and of Cora's brave sacrifice.

'How typical of her,' she sobbed. 'She was a good, kind and loyal friend. There have been so many times that she helped me and I am heavily in her debt. If I can repay that debt in any way by offering you my help, should you ever need it, then please accept it. I will miss her greatly!'

'We all will, Tannin … we all will!' Findol looked down and Tannin smiled, lifting his head gently with her flipper.

She looked right into his eyes, and spoke again.

'There is something special about you, child. An aura of greatness that envelops you. No doubt Cora could see it and so can I. I pray that you find that which you seek, and remember my offer will always stand. Take care for I feel my time is fast approaching and I must leave!'

She turned and laboured on until she found her stroke, then ploughed steadily ahead through the gentle waves and surf towards the turtle beach.

'Bye, Tannin … take care … best wishes for the little ones!'

'Yes. That goes fer me too, so it does, and especially der little flipper-nippers. We calls 'em "Muddy Dugs" in me homeland, we does.'

Findol turned to him. 'Really? … That's nice. Muddy Dugs. I like that.'

They bobbed there, watching the old turtle disappear with surprising speed toward the distant island. Findol was thinking more of the little future hatchlings, the power of Tannin's motherly love and the strength it obviously gave her. It made his heart yearn to feel that same strength from his own mother.

As if reading his mind, Flaytus choked: 'Ah, it gives me goosebumps all over me carapace, just to be thinking' about it!'

'Come on, Flaytus,' said Findol. 'We can't afford to waste any more time. We have to keep moving.'

And with that, they were off, passing the island to their right and casting a glance at the far-off beach that some time in the near future would be teeming with little ones.

Chapter 14
Towards Kelpathia

It was hard swimming for so long with both Flaytus on his back and the Camposs round his neck dragging against the flow. Findol had to make frequent stops to rest and could feel the old wounds in his fin and tail throbbing with the exertion. He couldn't help but make frequent glances behind to reassure himself that they were not being followed.

'Don't you think it's strange, Flaytus, that we haven't had sight or sound, let alone a whisper of any news of Grampus or Hamrag? I bet he will be going crazy when he hears of Kreegan's death.' He allowed himself a smug smile. 'Don't get me wrong. I mean I am hardly keen for any sort of meeting, but it is odd, isn't it? I don't know whether to be grateful or suspicious!'

'Bejaybers, will yeh be careful with the things yeh be saying? Yeh don't want to be tickling the fancies of the Fates. Don't be putting things in their minds that are not there already.'

'Do you know, Flaytus, I sometimes haven't got a clue just what you are on about!'

'Look ... t'is good that we are having trouble-free travel ... so far! ... And that's the way I is liking it, okay? I is certainly in no rush to be worrying and fretting again. The sooner I have me arms and feet back, then the better I'll be feeling. Just to be touching the grass between me hairy toes is a desire that's difficult to convey to yeh! All this water ... t'is causing rising damp in me brain and tench-foot in me feet!'

'Yes, I hear you, but what really is the attraction of living on land? I mean what have you got there that you haven't got here?'

'Well, fer starters, there's me lucky four-and-a-half-leaf clover … somewhere … I hope. I thought it came with me, but I never did find it. Then there's me home at Great Oaks Copse. It's not the biggest, but t'is the cosiest, and, more important, t'is dry. Most of all, I misses Snuggles me pet Boar. But there's also me pots o' trinkets that I've acquired over the years. A bit like yourself in that respect, I has a love fer bright and sparkly things. Guess they are me weakness. I does find it comforting to be running me fingers through them!'

'Sounds like you would get on well with my mate, Sterbol,' Findol remarked.

'Do yeh know though, me greatest loss was me pot o' gold? I'd spent years trying to get to the bottom of a rainbow, but I could never get there quick enough before it vanished. Ruddy Plecshun sold me a pair of two-and-three-quarter league boots, that he said could cover vast amounts of ground in a blink of yer eye! In a single stride I tells yeh! I waited fer the next rainbow. It seemed to take forever. When it finally happened I put on the boots and leapt the distance with me spade ready at hand. I dug furiously … down, down, deeper and down … and then … *Eureka*! I shouted, for there it was. Me own pot o' gold. That's when me troubles began — though there's not nearly enough time to be telling yer all about 'em!'

'Oh, you have me intrigued now. Some other time then, eh, Flaytus?'

Findol was always mesmerised by the talk of land and places alien to him, especially where Flaytus was concerned.

'I tells yeh young 'un, once yous tasted life outside the Blue, it will be a tickling tease in yer mind to be not coming back here!'

'Are you kidding, Flaytus? Have you already forgotten the reason I am doing this?'

'No, look … listen … I didn't mean anything by it … it's just … well — t'is a very different way of living. Not nearly as bad I'll wager as maybe yeh been taught or think!'

'Look Flaytus, I can safely say that no matter how enticing living on land might be, it's my family I will always want to be with and nothing will ever change that!'

'Good. Good, because yeh will need to be remembering that. Trust me!'

Findol was a little concerned by the nature of the conversation. Any suggestion that he might be distracted from his purpose, he took very personally and it made him uneasy. There was nothing in his world that would live up to the joy of being reunited with them all, that was something he knew for certain!

'Hold on there, Findol … stop!'

'What do you mean? I wasn't saying anything. Oh I see … you mean stop as in … STOP!'

'Yes, yes … down there if yeh please. See the clam?'

'Okay.'

They dropped down to where a large clam sat proudly on a soft bed of silt, quietly filtering its food. Flaytus excitedly jumped off Findol's back and scampered over to it where he proceeded to fiddle around behind the partly open shell.

'Ha-haargh!' He proudly displayed two large sea-squirts that looked decidedly unimpressed with being forcibly evicted. He exchanged them for the smaller two, hidden in the recesses of his shell and smiled at Findol, obviously pleased with himself.

'Now these are "turbot-charged" … just wait till yeh see these things go!'

Not far away he spied some bushes of Propelting Grains and took the opportunity to stock up. A good clawful of grains would last for an hour or more.

'I guess you might as well use them. I really have had enough of carrying you, Flaytus. My back is killing me!'

'Quite right too. I does so prefer driving to being a passenger. These big 'uns can be tricky to control though. They will wriggle so and make it difficult to be holding on. If I keeps a good supply of the grains, and holds on tight, they will keep going fer hours.'

It certainly sounded good to Findol and he looked forward to taking it a bit easy.

Suddenly Findol stopped and waved a flipper, beckoning Flaytus to be quiet. Far away he could barely detect the sounds of distant dolphin-song. It was a joyous sound, something he had forgotten just how much he missed. He didn't recognise the owners and they were quickly moving out of range. It was so tempting to go after them, but he could tell they were probably from Northern pods, judging by their dialects. They wouldn't be able to help him with his quest anyway, yet it warmed his heart to hear the sound again.

Flaytus had managed to get a couple of clawfuls of grains, placing a good supply in each of the squirts and saving the rest in a sponge pouch. He held on tight and watched as each inflated at its base. The large swellings rippled up the length of each tube until a jet of water belched out, quickly repeating the process. The trick was in getting both sea-squirts to work at the same time, since using them out of sync would lead to a nightmare journey. They would end up moving forward in a zigzag, meandering manner, resulting in severe motion sickness as each pulsed out of time with the other. He surged forward with each expulsion until he had built up a pretty impressive speed that even rivalled his dolphin friend. Findol was amazed at just how fast the large squirts could make the crab move, as he was forced to swim hard just to keep up.

Flaytus was able to steer with ease by a gentle turn of his shell and Findol was able to focus more on checking their route whilst struggling with the pace. They journeyed with ease for two more days, stopping frequently to recharge Flaytus's sea-squirts and to eat and sleep. The days passed quickly and soon it was nearly two weeks since the loss of Cora, yet it felt like an eternity. For the two of them, it still weighed heavy in their hearts. They had put a huge distance between themselves and the atoll, but their terrible memories were still raw.

The cold winter seas were actually feeling warmer as they continued moving further west, which helped with their moods somewhat and made the journey a little easier. Apart from one occasion when they had hidden from a party of large reef sharks, the time passed without any real incident. There had been a moment of panic for Flaytus when one of his sea-squirts developed a blockage, causing him to spin around violently. He eventually turned the remaining one downward so that it sent him spiralling up to the surface. There he had waited cross-eyed and giddy, until he regained his composure and was able to clear the other one's tube.

'That was not funny. *Ffhoooarr.* I've not been feeling this rough since I over-indulged on Seamus Gob's

Tatty'n'Gherkin Ale (which was even stronger than Old Foxglove). Now that was bad and no mistake … I am telling yeh I wuz greener than the grass around me!'

Findol just nodded and waited for Flaytus to get his head together before carrying on. As they moved off, they became aware of some small kelp rafts drifting on the surface. There were also blades of kelp scattered everywhere that had almost certainly broken off from the main forest. It had probably occurred during a storm and it suggested that they were getting close. Below, on the seabed, where the sunlight made contact, they spotted a group of circus shrimps. They were busy rehearsing in a large clearing. Microlite Brewno and Harribald Tieson were boxer shrimps and were currently practising their carefully choreographed stage fight.

Over on their far left, there was Flat Lee, the famous dancing shrimp, being very loud and over-animated. He shouted instructions and wildly gesticulated to the rest of his dance troupe as his tiny green cape flapped around.

'Watch and learn, will you!'

He had two pairs of arms hoisted up on his thoracic hips, elbows perfectly in line. Each of his legs was kicking and twisting in a peculiar manner as he bobbed up and down in the same spot as if he were stepping on something hot! Tiny shell-bottomed clogs tapped away on the pebble surface beneath him. This was performed by music supplied by a small band of very bored-looking bagpipe fish. They had witnessed his star-struck rants and raves on countless occasions. Curiously, he was now moving in a very intense and unusual manner from left to right. Legs flicked out at regular intervals, then he swivelled his thorax, whilst tightly holding arms on his hips. His head whipped from left to right at appropriate moments in time with the music as the frantic tapping beneath him continued. He maintained a manic grin on his face at all times, almost as though he were stifling a belch.

Suddenly his concentration was distracted by the audience of two above him. As he raised his eyes he failed to notice that he was trampling over some volcano barnacles.

Findol thought, *this should be fun*, as he keenly waited to see what would happen.

The barnacles spectacularly erupted into a loud shouting match of protestation and irritability.

'Ere ... get off us, will ya! Lava bread feet!'

'Yeah, what's his game? The whole ocean not big enough for yeh!'

Flat Lee carried on dancing as if their words were simply falling on deaf ears: 'So sorry, plebs, for the disturbing stance ... for I am truly Lord of the Dance!'

With that, he jumped up, twisted three times whilst holding a leg over his head and landed doing the splits with his remaining ones. This was achieved totally unfazed by their outbursts as he raised his arms and nodded his head to receive imagined applause!

'Thank you! Thank you! You are too kind!'

He continued to dance his way to the climax. His arms were still tucked tightly into his sides, whilst his legs kicked back and forth with ever-increasing speed. The Bagpipefish were straining with the effort, red engorged cheeks swollen with the increased puff! Suddenly Flat Lee disappeared behind a large rock and re-emerged. He was trailing a line of emerald shrimpets, each copying his movements to perfection. It appeared that there were at least twenty of them, legs, arms and heads moving in perfect synchronisation.

'Did yeh see that? Oh, the timing! T'is something else. Sends shivers up and down me shell it does. Makes me think of home … What with the Irish Frog Dancing and stuff!'

Flaytus was clearly impressed for there were tears welling up in his eyes, whilst Findol was putting the situation into context.

'Yes, Flaytus it's really spectacular, but I think we really need to be pressing on now. Don't we? This is a bit of a distraction.'

Reluctantly, Flaytus literally dragged himself away as he followed Findol, his neck straining to look back. They raced on again, to cover more sea-miles before looking for somewhere to stop when it was dark enough to rest safely overnight.

'I suspect this could be our last night in the Blue, Flaytus. Tomorrow we should get there. What do you think about that? Are you scared, nervous, apprehensive? Anything at all? … Only you seem so calm. You just sort of accept things with ease as you encounter them!'

'Are yeh kidding me? I've got Belugas doing cartwheels in my stomach so I has!'

As if to punctuate his point, large bubbles trumped and rippled out from behind him. 'There is a way of thinking though that says that Fate takes us regardless of what we does. It's like we can't be hiding from our own destiny.'

'You know, Mum would have said you sound like old Plato Scubbings'

'T'is true though, young Findol. What we be seeing as the great unknown future is tomorrow's history. Bejaybers! I'm thinking all this philosophical thinking stuff t'is doing me head in, t'be sure! '

As they slowed down to stop for the night, Findol looked solemnly ahead; a cold shiver ran down his back and settled right at the very base of his tail.

'There it is. I don't believe it! Look! Tomorrow we are going to change our lives! … Maybe forever!'

Ahead of them, they could clearly see the dark oppressing wall that throbbed and swayed menacingly in the heavy ocean current. It was the beginning of the massive Kelp Forest of Kelpathia. The ever-increasing darkness of night only added to the foreboding that welled up in Findol's heart. It was as if each dark strand seemed to snake towards him and scream: *GO, leave before it is too late!* a sniggered hiss tormenting him.

There was a single thought that gave him strength: *If my father did it, then so can I!*

He had, however, forgotten that back then his father had not had to negotiate the mysterious Vortex of Karn, for the Portal had been virtually unprotected. Cora may have given him plenty of information, but she had also been a little economical with the fine details. She had offered no clues about its nature and just how exactly it served as a deterrent to so many.

What's to stop it deterring me? he thought.

He waited for an answer, but none came, only the speedy wall of tiredness that comes after a hard day's swim. It descended on him quickly, sweeping him up and away to the land of dreams. His last thought was of Flat Lee and Sterbol bizarrely dancing together. They were matching each other's arm and leg movements perfectly, crossing to the left and then to the right, spinning each other around. Sterbol's crazy bandana seemed massive and flapped all around him, which made the image all the more surreal. Flaytus was there too, attempting his Irish jig, shell colliding with any fish that was not watching where it was going.

Findol smiled in his sleep, enjoying the silliness until the images suddenly stopped. A loud slapping applause seemed to fill his head from somewhere. It was followed by an unexpected deep voice that boomed all around.

'Bravo. Bravo indeed young Findol Lantica! But then, what a dance you have led me!'

And the awesome bulk of Grampus moved into view from behind a large rock wall and crept menacingly towards him...

Chapter 15
Into the Vortex

He awoke with such a start. His heart was beating faster than a conch with the hiccups. All he could see was the dreadful image of Grampus and his head whipped around, looking and searching frantically. It was some time before he could convince himself it really had just been another bad dream. He tried to get back to sleep, but it was impossible. His mind kept racing between fear of the unknown and nervous excitement of what lay ahead. He desperately wanted just to rest, to feel refreshed. The more he tried to drift off, the harder it became.

In the end he decided to relax by focussing and thinking his happy thoughts. He turned his attention to his family and the last time they had all been together, the night before Grampus came upon them. It was the same day he had spotted Flaytus and Whitloe together and he took time to wonder how dear old Whitloe was. She was certainly no speedy mover, but equally she was hardly a threat to anybody. Not that Grampus cared about such things.

'I hope she was left alone. I really do,' he thought. As he remembered the last game of Finball he played with his family he finally drifted back into a troubled sleep, where images of Grampus were never that far away.

Flaytus woke him a few hours later with a large breakfast of Flurriton Crabits's Canapés. He had purchased them before his speedy exit from Sea-Czar's Palace. He also had hidden away a re-sealant draught of Pickleberry Juice.

'Aha now … it's the breakfast of champions, so it is. Will be putting scales on yer chest and tendrils on yer fins, so it will!'

'I'll be happy sticking with my plain old dolphin skin, thanks all the same, Flaytus!'

Re-sealants were one of the newest inventions from the Kriblings, consisting of old mermaid's purses made into very efficient fluid containers. With the help of Trevor Tronkee the Elephantfish and some of his friends they inserted the fluid via their thin pointed mouths.

Findol was forever amazed at the endless supply of knick-knacks that Flaytus seemed to accumulate inside his shell. 'For someone who doesn't like it, you certainly make good use of your shell, Flaytus!'

'Ah well it comes down to a question of survival, doesn't it? Me mother would say "never look a gift horse in the mouth". I've always got her to thank fer drumming into me the importance of making the best of what yeh got, so while I needs it, I uses it … see? After all, most of me furniture and kitchen stuff is made from acorns, conkers and their shells.'

'Yes. Yes. But don't forget, Flaytus … I have seen what the Kriblings can make and do. So I do understand.'

They were soon as ready as they were ever going to be. Flaytus had spent time securing everything in his shell and Findol checked his Camposs was securely fixed around his neck and that the pointer was moving freely. They would be relying on it completely to find the Vortex of Karn once they entered the thick forest. Once again, Findol's heart was pounding. All the months of anticipation and the adventures on the way had finally brought him to this moment. The sun was high up in the blue sky and time was pressing on.

Findol lay still for a moment, quietly, reflecting on things, when he had a sudden overwhelming urgency to find the Vortex as quickly as possible. To pass through it and get on with finding his family, maybe even his father and free them all. There was such a potential for so much good and happiness to be achieved that he was giddy with the sheer thought!

Meanwhile, there was a nagging, uncomfortable pressure at the back of his mind. Even Flaytus, who had been waiting patiently, was fidgeting and biting his claws. Something made the crab quickly turn around, almost doubling up on his own shell. He looked at Findol with a pale, worried expression etched on his face.

'Err, I say ... Findol ... would I be right in thinking that there is something following us ... something mighty big ... in fact it's ... *Saints preserve us!*'

He was now staring, eyes wide, mouth open. Findol spun round to see what was agitating him, and his eyes froze upon the horror. Behind them in the distance was a swirling, living mass approaching at a steady pace. No longer did electric eels dominate the throng. Now, impossible numbers of sharks, barracudas, small whales, rays and worse, made up the horde that was fast descending upon them. It was made all the more terrifying by the total silence with which they were all moving. Findol and Flaytus would have been none the wiser if they had not looked back and the dolphin could not believe he had not detected them at all.

'This is the work of Grampus's evil and whatever cloaking magic he has been able to conjure up, I shouldn't wonder. And I can guess who helped them pick up our trail! Scaybeez! This is his doing, I have no doubt. I curse the day I let him go. He will cost us dear if we do not move quickly. Come on, Flaytus … let's go!'

Flaytus quickly fired up his sea-squirts with a large clawful of grains in each, and surged forward. His head was thrown back with the speed, whilst Findol closely followed, as they raced on towards the Kelp forest.

'There's no time to find the correct entrance. Just follow tight behind me,' Findol shouted, as he overtook. 'But you must stay really close. You cannot afford to lose me!'

'Yeh do not have to be repeating yerself on that, fer sure. I will be like barnacle gum!' agreed Flaytus, as he pressed up tight against his companion.

Findol had to leave his dread and apprehension behind, casting it aside as they punched their way into the Kelp mass with Flaytus frantically steering close behind. Just before they entered, Findol looked back with morbid curiosity at the huge army that was following them. They were no longer silent. Their jeers and evil laughs, together with wild guttural battle cries rung loud and heavy within him. It only further increased his resolve.

'Come on, Flaytus! Let's get in there and do our job. I'm not going to let them have the satisfaction of even a sniff of victory!'

It was however, easier said than done for the going was treacherous and desperately hard work for the both of them. The thick blades grew far closer together than even Findol had imagined and he hated the way each one seemed to cling and tug at him, as he brushed past, slowing him down. It made it difficult for Flaytus too, with his large shell constantly snagging on the kelp. To avoid losing him, though, Findol was forever looking back to check on his position, and looking for signs of their pursuers.

'Now don't yeh be worrying about me. Just yeh be keeping yer mind on the direction. I will keep up with ya … *awwwwwwwow*!' Flaytus had collided with a large clump of calcified barnacles attached to the side of a thick kelp blade. His head was spinning, tiny starfish dancing before his eyes.

'Stop messing about, Flaytus … come on! … Now's not the time for your jokes!'

Drat the youngster, he thought, biting his lip, his head throbbing.

There was a terrible pressure of panic and desperation that was pushing them both on — but worse, Findol knew they had no real idea where they were going. All he could do was follow the correct point on the Camposs that Cora had instructed him to take, although not from the entrance she had suggested due to their hurried departure. His fear was that they could easily miss the Vortex by only a few feet, such was the density of the forest. It was exhausting, pushing through the thick, heavy blades and Findol knew it was only his nervous energy that kept him going.

It wasn't long before he could hear the sound again of the horde behind. The noise was so intense with loud, crushing and snapping as the massive army pushed its way through and broke the Kelp with ease. It was a constant incentive and kick to both of them to find the little bit of extra energy needed to keep going.

Neither one dared entertain the thought of not finding the Portal, because that meant there would be no escape from the pursuers. The niggling worry of perhaps just missing it was agonising and Findol was forever looking at the Camposs to check their direction. At one point he looked down and was horrified to see the pointer spinning around wildly until it froze and started pointing towards the right. He changed course again until it was pointing in the correct direction, and then swam on. Once again, the same thing happened and he found he was constantly changing direction to keep the needle pointing directly in front. Thankfully the sound of Grampus's Army didn't seem to be getting any closer.

I wonder if maybe they will miss it, he thought, but then he remembered that Grampus had been there before and probably knew the way. How he would remember though, in such thick, unrelenting kelp, was beyond him.

'Does yeh know what yer doing there, young 'un?' Flaytus cautiously asked. He was getting rather concerned with the repeated change of direction they were taking.

'Of … course … I don't … Flaytus!' Findol stammered, emotionally … 'But Cora told me to believe in my inner feelings and that is what I am doing. It feels right so I have to go with it!'

'Ah sure, now, well that's fine,' Flaytus muttered as he added more grains to the sea-squirts. 'I'd be hating to think we was on some terribly wild goose-barnacle chase or something.'

Findol was beginning to find it hard to concentrate. He'd noticed the sound behind them getting louder again, which meant that their purusers were closing in. Flaytus's whingeing was now becoming irritating and Findol's heart was still racing away for all it was worth. He was no longer certain of anything, not even of finding his family.

Up ahead he thought he could see movement through the tiny gaps between the blades. He was becoming scared — really scared — in spite of his brave words. In spite of everything! It was dark. It was cold. He had no mum or dad nearby and yet again he had the feeling of just wanting to find a dark hole to swim into and hide. He could wait until his mother found him, cuddling up close and reassuring him with a great big kiss and a hug, and telling him that everything would be all right.

But it was not going to happen. This was Real Life … Real Danger and Real Evil. It was his moment, his time to offer proof for all those that had placed so much trust in the belief that he was special. His courage was reignited a little and he concentrated, but it was just so hard to make real headway. The constant buffeting by the kelp was draining and the rapidly dwindling self-belief, forcing the same old question that kept recurring: 'Why me? Why me?'

Findol realised he was actually shouting out loud when his words bounced back at him. It was an echo from just ahead. It could mean only one thing: a large space. And here in the middle of the forest it could be only one place.

The Vortex of Karn.

He was refuelled with extra energy as Flaytus bumped into his rear. They made a final push through the huge blades, finding it easier almost to twist around them. Suddenly, there it was, in all its glory, assaulting their senses full on, infusing them with a blaze of triumphant joy and relief.

Before them was an amazing ring of intense bright light that burned their eyes and made visibility difficult. It was simply huge, its power intoxicating. They became aware of a terrific roaring, rushing sound caused by the massive, swirling Vortex just in front of them. It was a giant underwater whirlpool, with the huge ringed Portal just above the centre, slowly rotating.

The Vortex whipped around furiously, and they both felt its terrific pull trying to draw them inwards, towards its centre. They held back, both terrified and yet elated. The pointer of the Camposs was spinning wildly and it too was being pulled towards the centre of the whirlpool, tugging at the chain. Findol was staring wildly at it, shouting at Flaytus above the deafening roar.

'This is it! This is really it!'

'Well now, yeh could have fooled me!' he shouted back.

They could see clearly now that their eyes had adjusted to the intense light. They were in a massive clearing deep within the kelp forest itself. The huge Portal that dominated its centre was a ring of unquenchable fire, its bright light glowing in orange and yellows on the walls of kelp surrounding them. Beneath it, the enormous whirlpool whipped around; a dark, swirling Vortex of magical energy, both horrifying and hypnotic. At its centre, the spiralling maelstrom appeared to plunge down deep below them and out of sight. To what or where, they had no idea, yet it appeared as a tail that twisted tightly on itself, hanging like a snake, whipping around ready to strike.

Surely if you enter that, you will be crushed as well as drowned! Findol thought. *How can you pass through to the Portal?*

Flaytus was too busy gazing above the centre of the Vortex and admiring the Portal, hypnotised by its power and beauty.

'Now that is some piece of work so it is!'

Directly above the Vortex, the large golden ring of fire slowly rotated. Its light was so intense it appeared solid, with an almost smooth edge, yet somehow licked by orange flame. Blueish-white electrical traces intermittently arced across it, and the colours within it were in constant change.

Findol's mouth was agape. 'This really is the Portal, isn't it? ... It has to be!'

'I think we can make that a resounding yes, to be sure!' Flaytus looked at the young dolphin, bright, alert and so brave. He had already suffered far more than he should … yet still with so much to do! It tightened his own resolve to help him in any way he could, to assist the lad in achieving his goal.

The large ring of light was perhaps three metres across and its shape occasionally changed as it was pulled and buffeted from the bizarre forces contained in the Vortex. A rogue spark of electrical energy chased its own tail as it raced around the rim before dispersing into the water, which, incidentally, had a strange taste to it.

'But how do we enter the Portal without being sucked into the Vortex? How, Flaytus?'

'I don't know. I am not an authority on these things, but yeh must be trusting Cora's words. What did she say?' Findol was frantically running through the instructions she had passed on to him. She had said that you must enter the Portal without fear and it would allow through only those pure in heart and courage. She never said how to get across to it without being sucked into Oblivion. She had always spoken of "trusting in the Fates" and remembering things were not always quite what they seemed in the Big Blue!

'It's a real test of your faith, isn't it? Maybe the weak-minded are meant to think that they will perish!' he suggested. Looking down into the Vortex was terrifying enough and Flaytus couldn't disagree with that thought!

Time was running out and Findol knew it. There was little point trying to rationalise everything, with so many things buzzing around in his head.

Flaytus was still staring at the Portal, mesmerised. 'Sweet mother of mine, I've never seen anything quite like it, not even in the Elven King's Caves of Treasure!' he whispered to himself.

There was another sound creeping up from behind them, despite the deafening thunder of the swirling waters. It was the sound of the horde. They whooped and cheered, delighted at their find. One by one, various creatures began to break through the kelp around the edge of the clearing.

Flaytus gulped nervously. 'Now might be a good time for some positive decisions, don't yeh think?'

'Yes, you're right. Oh no! … LOOK!'

Findol's stomach instantly knotted, as on the opposite side of the clearing he saw the unmistakable bulk of Grampus. He was pushing through the smaller creatures without care or grace, knocking aside a shark that was sent careering into the Vortex. It screamed as the maelstrom claimed it; whipping it violently around and around before finally it was sucked below and crushed into oblivion.

Grampus was a truly hideous sight, barely resembling the whale that he was. His skin was scarred and patchy, fins disfigured and ragged. His baleen plates looked more like stained and rotting teeth. There was an overwhelming feeling of disease about him. Of madness. Of obsessive, evil purpose.

And the dolphin was his goal.

He chillingly looked straight through Findol's eyes and into his heart. His voice jarred within the young dolphin's head, his words like barbs tugging painfully at his flesh.

'So, Findol Lantica … the "Young Pretender". The time has come … we finally meet. You have led me a dance … but now there are scores to settle … debts to be paid … '

He lifted a fin to reveal a large, ugly scar.

'This, from your father for one! I have waited and planned for this moment for such a long time. My blood is warmed and my spirit lifted at the mere thought of destroying you!'

An evil laugh resonated within his head as Findol tried hard to block out the intrusion into his mind, his thoughts racing, grasping for ideas of just what to do. There appeared to be no safe way forward and certainly no chance of ever retreating through the kelp.

Flaytus was positioned close to the side of him and Grampus was still full of his own threats, shouting them now, instead of playing mind games. Then he suddenly became silent, a hideous leer working across his face. Findol saw the subtlest of gestures from Grampus to whoever was close behind him, beckoning them to attack. It was all the excuse and prompting Findol needed to motivate and make his decision.

'This is the better option! Come on, Flaytus! We go!' He turned quickly and bit into the snout of an approaching shark as hard as he could, sinking his teeth in and tasting blood, gagging at the bitterness. Together with Flaytus, he leapt forward, just before the jaws of two large barracudas snapped at the empty space where their bodies had been a split-second earlier.

There was the briefest of moments when Findol and Flaytus both surged towards the Portal. It was only an instant, for the two of them were immediately taken by the current and violently whipped around in the whirlpool-like Vortex. Findol felt like his blood was draining from his body down into his tail. His face betrayed the horror as he realised that he would be heading around towards the side where Grampus was eagerly waiting. Time seemed to take on a new dimension of its own, as everything slowed down.

Grampus was getting closer on the right, barking orders as he sensed his moment.

'Leave … him … to … ME!'.

He was inching his way forward, ready to lunge at his prey, wary too of over-reaching and being drawn into the Vortex himself. He stared wildly at Findol, an utter madness in his bloodshot eyes, and yet fearful of the swirling waters in front and the fate that could befall him.

Findol and Flaytus exchanged glances, seemingly resigned to their possible fates. As Findol turned his head back to face Grampus, the Camposs that was being pulled ahead of him suddenly broke free. The kelp strap snapped from around his neck, and once free of restraint it speedily raced off ahead of him. The deafening sound of the Vortex was replaced by a weird silence, as they were carried around, closer and closer, until they were almost upon Grampus.

A sudden guttural howl resonated through the eerie silence that filled Findol's head. The Camposs had struck the evil whale square between the eyes with a brutal force that had sent him reeling backwards, more with the shock than anything else. The split-second respite that it gave them as Grampus flailed, confused and angry, was all that they needed. They sailed past in a rush of victory as the beast could only look on, gnashing his fetid baleen plates together in a desperate rage.

It was not all over, however, and now they were truly at the mercy of the Fates. They were moving progressively closer to the centre of the Vortex with each revolution. Every time they passed Grampus he was a little further away, cursing them, cajoling his minions to risk their lives and give chase. A few stupid blue sharks, full of hate and keen to win favour, hurled themselves into the Vortex, spitting venomous threats at Findol.

'Let's get the little worm-feast!'

'For you, oh Great One!'

They were immediately sucked, just like the first, down into its centre.

Findol strained to see what was happening as he heard their screams in the distance, cries disappearing into the deep. He could hear the sound of them being crushed, bones snapping as their life was squeezed out of them. He didn't really want to know any more.

Still others entered the Vortex in the belief that they were the ones to succeed. All were quickly drawn straight down below, to the same terrible doom, yet Findol and Flaytus seemed to stay safely above and getting ever closer to the centre. As they passed Grampus once more, Findol saw him mouth words that only he could hear …

'I will find a way. Trust me. You have not escaped for long. I will make you pay and you will beg for a speedy death!'

It was more chilling than anything else he had ever experienced. Still, they continued to circle, not as fast as they'd expected. In fact, it seemed as if they were actually slowing down.

Meanwhile the experience seemed to have taken the very breath from Flaytus who just rode around the Vortex in stunned silence, eyes wide and mind racing. They were becoming bathed in a blue light as they neared the axis of the whirling maelstrom, with the Portal at its centre. The Camposs was spinning around, just in front of them, and getting progressively larger.

'Look. Look at that. It's getting bigger! ... No ... Hold on! It's not the Camposs getting bigger. It's us, Flaytus ... we are shrinking!'

As they approached the centre of the Vortex, the Portal that had been above them now seemed to be in front of them. There was no longer a need to shout over the noise for the sound of the rushing Vortex had all but gone. The centre of the Portal could be seen as a dark, circular void that was getting larger as they approached it. The electrical traces that had raced around its edge had appeared to have stopped.

'Wow! Well this is it, Flaytus. We made it, didn't we?' Findol approached the darkness with his friend by his side. The void was so dark it appeared to have no definition or depth, indeed no form at all. Flaytus was still too shocked by the experience for words.

Findol started to speak, 'So what happens nowwww...'

He disappeared as he was sucked through the void and down into the nothingness beyond. Flaytus followed close behind, arms and claws crossed in front of him and eyes squeezed tightly shut.

Now just maybe this is all a big dream, that's what t'is. Old Neddy, gone and given me a draft of the dodgy Coleyflower Ale and this is just the old wind in me brain!

There was a scream and he opened his eyes in an instant. But then he realised he was the one who had made the noise and his nightmare had yet to finish. Spinning and tumbling, he clutched his mouth and turned a very unhealthy shade of green.

I'm thinking this all seems terribly familiar, it does!

Findol, meanwhile, seemed more intent on catching up with the Camposs.

Chapter 16
Where Worlds Meet

Without warning, Findol and Flaytus were suddenly drawn into and down the dark, tube-like tendril of the Portal, their faces clearly showing relief and delight at their escape. They quickly became disorientated as they were swept down its length, spinning around blindly in the semi-darkness.

For Findol, it felt like he was in the middle of one of his dreams, although it was something he could never have imagined. He had assumed that the passage through the Portal would be instantaneous. However, it was more like some sort of underwater slipstream ride, like he had experienced in freak ocean currents before. As he looked around, the tendril's blurred walls were becoming a little brighter and seemed to be peppered with tiny beads of light. They were passing by them so quickly, it was impossible to actually make out for sure what they were.

Flaytus was beside him, occasionally brushing up to Findol's back as his shell swung round and round. Apart from that, their passage along the tendril was barely noticeable. Somehow there was a protective force that held them safe and away from the moving tendril wall. Except for his one dramatic scream, Flaytus was uncharacteristically quiet. In fact, there seemed to be something bothering him. For a change, it wasn't just his delicate stomach.

After the close call at the Vortex, Findol felt wonderful. After the long effort to get there, it felt fantastic to be transported, for once, as they passed along cocooned in a dreamlike state of safety and sanctuary. He even began thinking he could hear some sort of distant music gently playing, but again he couldn't be sure.

Is it only in my head, for I really can't tell? he wondered, though he didn't really care. Over the last few days he hadn't been too sure just when he was hearing with his own ears and what was just his imagination. Life was becoming very complicated.

And I thought the rules of Finball were hard! he thought.

Then it suddenly dawned on him. Something, he realised, that was pretty amazing. He was no longer sure that they were still in water, and yet they were still both breathing okay — and *without* wattling beads.

The rules that governed life seemed to be turning upside down. There was a tiny bead of light just ahead that was twinkling tantalisingly, as if to gain his attention. It began to grow and become brighter as they neared it.

It looks like one of Man's "lighthouse" things, he thought, reflecting on the strange structures he had seen on his travels. Things were definitely getting very weird. Before long they were upon the light as it loomed right up in front. They could now make out its detail. It was a large, round wall of light that swirled in strange patterns, obscuring what lay beyond. They came to a halt, just in front and cautiously poked their way through it.

They emerged into what could only be described as an enormous white-walled cavern. Findol glanced back to check on Flaytus, who had ended up behind him. Wide eyed and smiling, he shot a reassuring wink back at Findol who turned to survey their location.

'Now *that* … was quite something!' It was the only thing Findol could think of saying. As he looked around, his limited experience had not prepared him for the sight as he gawped awestruck at the wondrous place. There was no water yet they were supported in some sort of invisible medium that shared its qualities, and yet allowed them to breathe.

'This is just so weird, Flaytus, isn't it?' he sniggered. 'I mean you just would never believe anything like this existed, would you?'

'Well … actually you'd be a tad wrong on that score young 'un, since I have actually been to this place before, I think.'

Findol turned and looked at him, eyes wide.

Flaytus shrugged. 'I've only just been realising as we was travelling here. T'is like me memory comes back in little acorn cups. Me thoughts of this place or something like it is returning faster than Neddy Conkins when I'se making me Ale. Talkin' of which, I must be giving yeh a taste one day. Anyway yeh see, this place … bejaybers! Yes, I does remember! … T'is where all the worlds meet. There are many different places to be existing if yeh can grasp the concept and this very place is the stopping-off place between them. T'is called "Lymbow" and it's where yeh chooses yer next port o'call, so to speak. Now … take a look up there!'

Flaytus was pointing above them with a claw. Findol looked up, tracing the huge round walls that towered far above him. Far above, right at the top, he could just make out a ceiling. It glowed and seemed to subtly change colour, bleeding from pure white into subtle shades of red, then orange and yellow, shimmering as it did so. Around its perimeter, some way just below the shimmering ceiling, there were what looked like large openings — heavily framed, huge Portal-holes, separated at regular intervals and spaced out around the entire circumference of the cavern. Each one blazed with a light that matched the colours of the ceiling, and each of the glowing, enclosing frames seemed unique in structure and appearance.

'What are they, Flaytus?'

'Now *they* are why *we* are here. What yeh sees up there are the very doors and entrances to all the blessed worlds that exist. You takes yer pick and your chances and yeh goes fer it. Up there you'll be finding the Portallic Gate fer each of the parallel worlds and universes that exist. There is far more than you need to be worrying yerself about, I don't wonder.'

Findol looked utterly perplexed. 'But Cora said something about not being allowed to pass into different ones didn't she?'

'Yes, yes, yes. But what I believe is that the enchanted entrances will NOT allow those that shouldn't mix, *to* mix, if yeh see? That is not to be saying it can't happen, mind. T'is complicated, I believe.'

Findol began to swim upwards: 'So what's that right at the very top then?' He was pointing at the ceiling with his right fin. He could now see that it actually dropped down a short way with a ledge all the way around and a clear surface, sunken into it, like a completely circular window.

'Aaaha. I don't think yeh be needing t'be knowing about that one right now T'is special I believes and I'm not too sure myself, any ways…'

'How do you know all this, Flaytus?'

'T'is quite simple really. If yeh look at the entrance to each doorway, there is a special retaining conch shell known as a "Lymbollic Mentor" attached beside it. Not only will it clear yeh for passage, but it will tell yeh everything yer needing t' know. It sort'a inputs the details into yer noggin!'

'It's all clever stuff, isn't it? I guess it's all down to the Guardians, Fates or whoever!'

Flaytus cast a glance up at the top and sighed. 'Fer sure. Fer they most certainly put all dis together!'

Findol resigned himself to his own ignorance on these matters and placed his immediate future plans firmly in Flaytus's claws. 'Okay. So what do we do now we're here? Can we get going?'

'Yes, to be sure. Yeh simply move up to the Portallic Gate until yeh seeing the one yer wanting. Connect wid the Lymbollic Mentor and then simply pass through the Gate. Trust me, you'll be knowing which is the right one. It's like yeh gets butterflies, or in yer case "shrimplings" in yer heart that tickle and gives yer a warm glow. You feels yeh jus' has to be going in and catching the ride. It's just the same sort of trip as the one we took to be getting here!'

'But how do you know for certain that you have chosen the right doorway? Half the time, even I am not sure what I want. I seem to have spent most of the last few months with shrimplings flitting around inside! I have no idea where to start looking!'

'Now that's the clever thing with these Portals and the special powers that were put into them. The Lymbollic Mentor reads and knows what's in yer heart and understands where yeh be wanting to go. I don't think it will let yeh be going somewhere that yer not be wanting to visit. Besides t'is able to show yeh an image of where it will take yeh!'

Findol listened to all this, utterly amazed. 'Flaytus, there is something that has only just occurred to me about all this that I find worrying. Cora told me how to get here, where to go and what to do. But ... she didn't explain how

I actually get back home again — to the Big Blue — when I've found my family!'

'Hmmm, now are yeh sure about that? I mean it's not something she would be likely to be forgetting now, surely!'

'Well, she did mention the Morphing Stone that my father had and I know it has the power to transport the wearer. Surely she cannot think that I can somehow try to find that too. It's hard enough just to be thinking about how to find my family, let alone anything else!'

'I think that Cora always knew what she was doing and that there is maybe a good reason that she didn't be explaining it all clearly to yeh. I think we have to be trusting that something will be turning up. Think of it as a challenge and a test of yer faith in her!'

Findol scoffed, 'That's easy for you to say, Flaytus, but it sounds a bit sketchy to me. What happens if I am able to find my family and release them from whatever, only to find that I am not able to return to the Big Blue? Can you imagine how I will feel? Separated yet again!'

'Now didn't Cora be telling yeh to be trusting in yerself? There is an inner resource inside yeh that I think yeh have barely tapped into. Just yeh try to be thinking about that a tad more. With me coming with you, don't yeh tink I'm a wee bit worried too? Do yeh not be forgetting I needs to be getting back to me own land too?'

'Yeah, sure. Sorry! I guess I am coming over all selfish and self-centred, I suppose. What's actually stopping you going through the very door to your land, right now? You must be so tempted … '

The crab suddenly snapped back at him. 'Now yeh can be stopping that right now!' Flaytus had never appeared so angry. 'There is something stopping me, if yeh must know, and that is me own word and one that's called "Loyalty". True, t'is something lacking these days, but I at least have these values to carry with me … lucky fer you too, I might add!'

'Sorry, Flaytus … Dear Flaytus … I didn't mean anything, please forgive me! It's just that I seem constantly to end up in a position that offers me no certainties. It still doesn't seem more than a blink of the eye that I was able to go to mum for advice if things got difficult!'

'Yes I knows that! But don't yeh see that all this is about you, yeh young scallywag? Cora would have told yeh the same I bet yeh, but these tests are yer "Rites o' Passage", I am sure. Yer gonna be coming through them, I has no doubt and yeh will be a better dolphin for it. I just knows it! Now come on, cuz I think we should be going. Before I changes me mind! Loyalty … t'is only a word!'

He flashed a big friendly wink and smile at Findol. The dolphin beamed back at him.

They swam upwards towards the multicoloured ceiling and approached the intricate doorways of the Portals, each one a magnificent frame of light. As they got closer, Findol could now marvel at just how big each was. He was almost level with them and looked directly into the nearest one.

'I can't see anything, Flaytus!'

'Yeh have to be getting closer … go nearer the Lymbollic Mentor, that's it, towards the light.'

Findol swam cautiously towards the opening until he was bathed in the delicate lightbeams. He felt gentle fingers searching into his very soul and as they did so he was presented with images, wildly beyond his imagination. There were huge white swollen clouds that hung motionless behind a massive island that was floating in the sky. He could see microscopic movement around and within the island.

'I thinks we needs to be pressing on,' Flaytus said.

They passed from one doorway to the next, pausing briefly to be scanned and to mentally view its contents.

'Sweet Mudder, look … '

Flaytus was pointing excitedly with a claw that punctuated every gasp of his emotions. The image was of an enormous patchwork of green, like an emerald sea patterned with huge lines and dark patches.

'That there is the green, green grass of me blessed homeland. Belcha's Wood with old Baragwanath and Neddy Conkins in their treetop dens, I bets! If yeh looks beyond the Forest o' Grime yeh can just be seeing the Mountains o' Mawn where the Elven and Goblin Kings live! Do yeh have any idea how difficult it is to be seeing this and knowing I cannot be returning yet. To be so close yet so far!'

'Yes I can imagine, Flatus. But at least you have your friends and family to return to. How is it you can see exactly where you come from anyway?'

'Now I think that is because you are shown the place that yeh belong to or need t'be going ter. If it's a land that you've not been to before then yeh do not be seeing anywhere specific! Does that make sense?'

But Findol wasn't listening. He was at the next doorway, looking clearly upset. It was showing him his home in Lantica Deep, and there were his family and friends playing around near the entrance. His mother was just coming out, probably to call them in for tea.

'Remember these are sometimes only memories of the place from yer heart. They're not real right now!'

'How did you get here in the first place, Flaytus? I mean why did you end up in the Blue?'

'T'is a bit of a story, since me blessed memory seems to be rushing back at a rate of nuts. For now though, let's just be saying that it involved a bit of an accident with some stolen magic! Maybe I'll be letting yeh know more sometime but fer now we has an appointment down there!'

They were both positioned directly in front of a doorway that seemed very well used compared to all the others. Its sides were visibly worn down from the casual brushing past of countless bodies over many years. Although the material that made the glowing frame was unidentifiable, it was obviously not impervious to wear from regular use. Before them, they looked on at images of a land filled with cities, and manmade creations. Objects with men inside flew across the sky and moved across the dry earth.

Findol stared mouth open, eyes flicking around, trying to find anything he could recognise or identify with. He was trying to grasp the concept of himself actually living there. They were bathed in the searching Lymbollic light and the image blurred before stabilising. It displayed a small town on the edge of the Blue.

Flaytus was getting impatient and itching for adventure. 'Now's as good a time as any I think! I will have to be travelling on yer back fer we cannot afford the risk of getting separated. Now don't yeh be getting scared on me … ' He was looking at poor Findol's anguished face, as he breathed heavily and nervously.

'We can be doing this … especially you. Take yer courage and go with yer heart and think about the adventure to come!'

Findol heard another voice, whispering. It felt so close, like it was somehow nearby:

(God's speed, my child ... God's speed. I will always be with you!)

Just then a distant tinkling made Findol look down, far below at the spot where they had arrived. He fairly squealed with delight. There was a round object settling on the floor, light catching its smooth surface and flickering up at him, drawing his gaze. He frantically glanced back at Flaytus.

'Wait! We can't go yet. I nearly forgot the Camposs!'

He raced down in a flash and picked it up in his mouth, before returning to the doorway as quickly as he had left. He smiled at Flaytus because he really felt good. Yet again, fortune had favoured him and he now felt Cora so close.

'Okay, let's do it!' he mumbled.

They moved forward through the shimmering, light-filled gate, briefly leaving ghostly silhouettes. Findol had a last fleeting thought of the time he had seen Cora's face smiling at him through the rock in Lantica Deep. He wondered if she was smiling on him now.

Then suddenly he was whisked away once again along a new tendril with Flaytus riding on his back. Somehow, he felt his life was about to change forever as they raced along on their journey to the Land of Man and all the terrible uncertainty it posed.

About The Author

I am David Satchell, married, living in the South Hams and proud father of 4 boys and 3 grandchildren.

I was born in Birmingham in 1957 and moved to Plymouth when I was 12. The books of Gerald Durrell, Gavin Maxwell and George Adamson fuelled a passion for wildlife and suddenly I wanted to become a Game Warden. It never happened and so I spent 37 years in Pathology analysing blood.

I have always loved Fantasy and Science Fiction. The Lord Of The Rings being the most frequently read of all my books. Something happened in the late 80's … I saw a film called The Big Blue and it sowed the seed of an idea that would grow into FINDOL.

I wanted to create a hero and story that would capture everything I hold dear; the things that scare and delight me. The classic battle between good and evil. The family values that bind us to each other, but also something akin to an original 'road movie' with an epic feel to it.

More importantly, it was to begin a franchise that involved exciting stories grounded in todays climate of ecological disasters and Man's arrogant use of the earths resources.

I sincerely hope you enjoy/enjoyed the ride!
David G. Satchell — July 2012

Find out more at www.ghostlypublishing.co.uk

And connect with me on Facebook at: www.facebook.com/GhostlyPublishing

Lightning Source UK Ltd.
Milton Keynes UK
UKOW041342151112

202217UK00001B/5/P